ME & YOU

ME & YOU

A NOVEL

MARGARET DIEHL

SOHO

Copyright © 1990 by Margaret Diehl
All rights reserved under International, Berne and Pan-American
Copyright Conventions. Published in the United States by
Soho Press, Inc.
1 Union Square
New York, NY 10003

Library of Congress Cataloging-in-Publication Data
Diehl, Margaret, 1955—
Me and you: a novel/Margaret Diehl.
p.   cm.
ISBN 0-939149-31-1
I. Title.
PS3554.I343M38   1990
813'.54—dc20   89-21958
CIP

Manufactured in the United States
10 9 8 7 6 5 4 3 2

Book design and composition by
The Sarabande Press

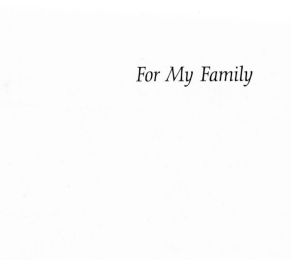

For My Family

ME & YOU

1

"The man I marry," I announced at the age of seven, "will be a gypsy horsethief, secretly a prince."

"As long as he's a gentleman," said my mother, vaguely. (The concept had grown baggy during her married life.)

"As long as he's a man," retorted my father, by which he meant not a Southerner. Not a relative of my mother's. Not too smooth, too suave, too courtly. My small-boned and elegant father cherished his rougher edges.

"Oh, really," said my mother. "Do you think she has a choice?"

A year before my sister's wedding, I was living in a cedar-shingled house in Berkeley, California. I spent my days reading Stephen King novels and watching *Sesame Street*.

My ambition to be a great artist had vanished sometime previously, I wasn't quite sure when. As I told anyone who asked, California was another time zone. It was my birthday and my boyfriend Lenny was coming to take me out to dinner. Of course he took me to dinner every night (neither of us was capable of cooking) but we pretended it would be special. Otherwise he would have had to buy me a present, and as he said, "You can't please women. I know."

It was late afternoon, the twilight time of the fading hangover when all the cells are at work, silently replenishing. The headache is smoothed away, the stomach calmed, the skin regains its youthful vigor: a lovely woman emerges.

Twenty-nine, I thought. One last chance to redeem my youth. I drank a glass of soda water and opened my presents. From my mother a silk sweater and a jade ring. From Lucy a mess of books. I didn't bother to look at them. I could only read horror novels, though they gave me nightmares. Somehow the nightmares comforted me. Such nice big monstery monsters.

The door banged and in came Lenny. "Hello," I said. We shared a moment of silence. It used to bother me, this silence. I thought he was girding himself to say something like, Do you know what you did last night? Christ, don't you remember? But it was only Lenny's way of making sure my attention was fully removed from whatever I was doing or thinking before he came in.

"Aaah," he said finally. "Shit. Sheeit."

He stood there, not looking at me, as the disgust of the day rolled out into my kitchen. His hands began to move restlessly, carving the air. Though he always described himself as a nice Jewish boy, he had such big hands, he was such a Cro-Magnon hulk. It was the way he stood, bent forward from the shoulder with his arms hanging loose; it was his big jaw and his little yellowish teeth—though he did have nice eyes, brown and mournful, which he used to great effect. There's nothing like being wrapped in the embrace of a muscular man, a man of moods and furies, while he tells you how vulnerable he is, how easily you could hurt him, his eyes bulging and soft, his tone faintly menacing.

"Okay," he said, bringing his hands together in a soundless clap. "Lemme take a shower, babe, put on a clean shirt, we'll go someplace fancy."

The shower roared, Lenny sang. I slowly put on makeup. My face looked so clean and fresh, like that of a trusting child. I felt regret for what I was about to do, but my regret was no match for my anticipation. The alcohol was waiting for me all over the city in its rounded bottles, dark or pale, sweet or bitter, alive with mysterious change. Waiting out there, the glass of wine, of whiskey, of brandy, the strong spirits. I put on my lipstick, combed my hair. It's not a compulsion to drink, I said to the mirror. It's more in the nature of a passionate attachment.

We went to Giovanni's where we always went. Steak and booze, we liked to keep it simple. The waiters there were used to us and took away my food without comment. Lenny ate all his steak, then put a cigarette out in the fat. He always did this, I couldn't stop him. The waiter grimaced, Lenny didn't notice. He was telling me how rich he would be at some time in the future. I wasn't exactly listening, but his eager voice filled the space between my presence at the table and the restless thing inside. I wanted the wine, I drank the wine. I wanted it again. I drank more. I wanted it *again.*

lways the same wanting without the satisfaction, although my drunkenness increased. Monotonously the same sequence of hand rising, lips moving, throat swallowing—agitation and pleasure raised another degree. For pleasure was there in the taste of that blood-red liquid. That blood-like liquid, that rich nutrient stew. Pleasure was there but growing dimmer, even as the agitation did. At a certain level there was nothing you could call feeling, and certainly not thought, yet I was conscious and knew myself, though you couldn't call it knowledge either.

And Lenny's voice went on, boasting and plotting. He wanted to go into business, he only needed a little financing. A hundred grand or so. I felt, listening, serenely superior.

I knew he was better off in his job than he'd ever be as a rich man. Rich, he'd realize that people still didn't take him seriously. Even if he had a thousand employees, there'd be somebody, several somebodies—his secretary, his wife—not taking him seriously. But now he was young, exuberant with crude hope and cunning. He was afraid it wouldn't work out, that's why he liked to monologue, and I was afraid nothing would work out, that's why I let him go on.

We had dessert, or Lenny did. He insisted on ordering cake for my birthday, then, when I didn't want it, ate my piece. I smoked several of his cigarettes. There was an unopened bottle of wine on the table—there was one on every table—which I regarded with annoyance. I didn't like this idea of using wine as decoration. The same bottle on the table, night after night! Of course I could ask to have it opened, but then they'd just bring another one in when they reset the table. It bothered me: the restaurant closed, dark, swept, and on every table a bottle of wine, forlorn.

While Lenny was settling the check privately with the waiter (he took him aside and pressed bills into his hand), I slipped the bottle under the waistband of my skirt. I got up slowly and waddled out, the wine nestling against my belly. It never occurred to me that I could be caught. I thought I was invisible whenever I chose.

In the car I showed it to Lenny, lifting my blouse for him to see how I had hidden it. He roared with laughter. He thought I was wonderful, daring, adorable. He opened it for me with his Swiss Army knife and we drove up into the hills, me swigging from the bottle, Lenny pawing between my thighs. I was fairly happy—I had reached the stage where the trees blowing in the wind, the masses of green, the massy dark, could hypnotize me—but Lenny kept talking about what he was doing in repetitious detail.

I told him I was bored with that particular subject.

"It never bores me," he said reverently. "Never."

"I feel that way about drinking." I held the cool lip of the bottle to mine. A tart, fruity Chianti: the power in it! To keep me drinking bottle after bottle. I liked being so addicted, I thought, it was magical. At least when I was drunk I thought that.

"What I always say—we're two of a kind."

"Doesn't it bother you that I find sex boring?"

"Why should it? You fuck me anyway."

Lenny stopped drinking when we left the restaurant and I went on alone, swimming through the boozy night while he was in his sex-world, driving me home, taking my clothes off, keeping my glass full, and going at it. I didn't mind; his mad passion, hands clamping my upper arms, was mildly distracting. All my organs had dissociated by then, my flesh was in chaos. When I was sober I didn't think about where I was in my body, but when I was drunk I had to. I was lost and didn't even know where I was supposed to be. Laboriously I tried to remember how muscles and blood worked, but I wasn't in the control room so, even if I did remember, it would be no use. There was nothing to be done, yet I had to do something—I got that message now and then. Like swords pricking my feet: Breathe! Think! Circulate your blood!

Lenny's body on mine helped me get my bearings; it was something I could focus on. The whole event was an imitation, but the imitation had its own power. It carried our histories and it was a sort of contract, although I had no idea what we were contracting for.

———

I was woken the next morning by the telephone. It kept ringing until I answered it. Once the receiver was in my hand, I considered hanging it up, but I felt lonely and cradled it under my chin. "Hello," I said gently as if it were the telephone calling, poor, black, squat, inanimate thing.

"Happy belated birthday," said my sister. "I tried to get you last night but you were out."

"Yeah."

"Did you have a nice birthday? Did you get the presents I sent you?"

"I guess so. The books, right? Thanks."

"So how are you? It's been ages since we've talked. You're

never there when I call. You ought to get an answering machine." But if I did that, Lucy, I wouldn't have the peculiar pleasure of sitting in my rocking chair, glass of wine at hand, listening to the phone ring and ring into silence. When you don't answer it, you can imagine anybody you like on the other end.

"I don't know how I am. I feel kind of weird but it's not painful. Have you ever had a hangover without pain? It's a great idea, they should patent it. Hold on a sec." I put the phone down and went to the bathroom. Lit a cigarette. Opened a beer. By the time I picked the phone up again she had decided to visit me. There was a distinct note of alarm in her voice I thought unwarranted. It had been my birthday after all. I made a few attempts to dissuade her, to no avail. I want to see you, she said. I want to meet Lenny. I had told her of the existence of Lenny simply because you have to say something when your sister asks for news.

She would come in a week, stay four days. She began talking about her life then, she'd just met a man named Malcolm, and I held the phone a few inches from my ear.

Lenny. Could I break up with him in a week? Or would he keep coming around, battering the door, breaking in? Waylaying us on the street more likely, shouting at me until I fell on the sidewalk screaming. We'd only had one real fight so far. It was then I called him a Neanderthal. He didn't actually hit me, but he shouted so loud I thought my eardrums could burst and then he collapsed in tears so I had to get up, all trembly and sick, and mother him back to manhood. He blubbered. He said he knew I didn't love him but couldn't I try, couldn't I pretend? I stroked his hair and murmured things, and inside I was saying, You sick, miserable shit. You worm. You baby. You stupid, stinking, sub-moronic greaseball, you plaguey rat. . . . And then I was smiling, giggling even, and I turned it into a smile of affection and I sat on his lap.

But what to do? I needed him. There was no one else left—no friends at all. I had used to have friends. The trouble was I didn't want anyone but my sewer rat. Lenny's normal emotional plane was akin to that of a drunk—maudlin and suspicious and infantile. We suited. Lucy would just have to see that and know the worst.

She arrived on Friday afternoon. I wouldn't pick her up at the airport because I didn't have a car anymore. Having forgotten where I parked it once too often, I simply forgot about it. I got a bill for towing which I ignored, and that was that. It hadn't been worth much anyway, and as Lenny said, "Baby, you'd be better off letting me drive."

Friday morning I cleaned the house, months of cobwebs and crumbs, of wine glasses in odd corners, each with its blackish dried wound. It surprised me that the house was so dirty; also, how nice it looked clean. I had bought a new silk shirt for the occasion, an amber brown to match my hair. It was actually a color that looked better on Lucy with her vivid darkness; maybe that's why I chose it. Maybe I thought if I looked like her, she wouldn't notice I was me.

She would be here any moment. I couldn't keep feeling excited. I sat at the kitchen table, set with my grandmother's silver, a vase of poppies in the center, drinking a glass of chardonnay. I hadn't had a good talk with anyone in so long. Not that I was capable of having good talks anymore. Still, I thought, it would be a pleasure to see her, the familiar dear face, sister of my childhood, of our wild adolescent nights . . . which of us would die first? I wondered. It was far more likely to be me, and how sorry she would be, but it could by some accident be her. I would never stop mourning. Even now her car could be crashing.

She was late. I poured more wine, checked the veal chops. The stove wasn't on, there wasn't any need to check them but I did. They lay calmly in the pan, side by side, getting in no trouble at all. What else? The lettuce was washed and dried, the cucumber sliced, the bread on the table. I could make a dinner if I really tried. Everything was ready. Wasn't she late? I had another bottle of wine in the refrigerator, a pint of Jim Beam hidden in the bathroom behind the Comet. Being forced to hide the booze had given me such a longing for Lenny—I'd been tempted to call him up and say, Yes I will marry you, I will live in your hideous condo.

Even so, I was glad she was coming. I hadn't had a good talk in so long—I heard a car stop at the curb and my heart turned over in panic.

She was wearing a neat pair of jeans, a white sweater, her hair in a French twist. She looked so pretty, so healthy, most of all so competent. I felt my brain begin to deliquesce. "Oh, Gwennie," she cried, "I love this place. So many flowers!" Yes, there were a lot of flowers. Sunshine, blossoms, green grass, a sort of country-club prison atmosphere. Very nice.

I ushered her inside, sat at the table and poured us wine. But there wasn't enough wine, that was the sorrow, there just wasn't enough anymore. Each dissolve of my tension was followed by a seize-up; the process was wearying, it was hard to pay attention. And I had to pay attention. Lucy knew I was drinking too much, but all the evidence wasn't in yet. We were about to begin, as I thought of it, my trial.

She asked me what I did all day. "You haven't had a job in a year. Are you painting?"

"Not really."

"Why not? You've got so much talent, and if you aren't doing anything else—"

I poured more wine, turned on the stove. "Actually, I did a painting recently. For Lenny's mother. A portrait of her dog, Elsinore."

"Did she pay you for it?"

"It was for her birthday."

"From you?"

"From Lenny. He hasn't told her about me. He doesn't think we'll like each other."

"Don't you find that insulting?" Her tone was much too sharp and I finished my wine. We don't talk that way in California, I wanted to say. We respect each other's space. I turned the chops over, poured wine in the pan, poured wine in my glass. Drank.

"It doesn't insult me. She only likes Jews, he says. It's not my fault I'm not a Jew. I'm just as glad anyway. Why would I want to meet his mother?"

"If you're serious about him. . . ."

"Not that serious. Not even remotely that serious."

"When do I meet him?"

"Tomorrow," I sighed. "He's taking us wine-tasting." He had insisted, he was very anxious to meet her. He liked a magazine called *Saucy Sisters* that featured naked twenty-year-olds with ponytails and lollipops.

Lucy told me about Malcolm. How wonderful he was, how she thought this was the real thing, etcetera. Her two glasses of wine had opened her up, her eyes got bigger and shinier. I noticed how white and even her teeth were, unlike mine. Of course I drank too much red wine, but they were always yellow, and I did have them straightened, but it didn't hold. I asked her questions, learned all about her editor, and thought of the young doctor I had gone to.

He said, "You have liver damage, you know. Not irreversible yet. But alcoholism in women happens much faster and does more damage. It attacks the reproductive organs." He flashed a brief smile, twiddled his pencil between his fingers. I don't know why I went for a checkup. He gave me some pamphlets to read: the ten signs of alcoholism. He said many people denied they were sick, then looked at me hopefully.

"I don't deny it," I said. "I've known since I was seventeen."

"Then why don't you stop?" he blurted, then blushed as if he knew. As if I might tell him. I smiled mysteriously and left his office. I felt evil as I waited at the desk to pay. My veins are full of slime, I thought, I have a witch's heart.

I served my sister dinner. We ate quickly, as always, and I remembered a night when Lucy and I double-dated in my mother's apartment, while my mother and stepfather were at a party. We gave the boys a meal and they ate so slowly they were still chewing when Lucy and I went into the kitchen to get dessert. Once there, on impulse, we snuck out the back door. They weren't quite as much fun as we thought they'd be. So we went dancing, leaving the boys, confused and well fed, to wait around haplessly, and then face our parents. Roy was furious at them, we found out later. He was worried about what we might be up to, out in the city alone.

I put on a tape of The Rolling Stones and poured brandy. She drank hers slowly and asked what was happening out here in the Reproductive Rights movement. I said I hadn't the faintest idea.

"Aren't you at all interested?"

"Well, you know, I believe the same things you do. I just can't get motivated to do anything about it."

"What do you use for birth control nowadays?"

"Why don't you look inside me and see?" Lucy had once persuaded me to look at my own cervix with a speculum. I was supposed to do it regularly but I didn't like seeing all that pink, helpless flesh.

"Does that mean you've got a cap? You couldn't be using an IUD. I use a diaphragm now with spermicide and a condom when I think I'm fertile."

Actually I didn't use anything. I hadn't had a period in nine months and I wasn't just about to give birth either. Maybe that was why I went to that young doctor, something like that.

"There's a feminist health clinic around here," I said. "You can check it out if you want to."

"I will. Why are you so hostile?" I reached for the bottle. "Gwennie, don't."

I ignored her, drank a long drink—more than I wanted—in fear she would take it away, and I asked inanely, "So what does Malcolm do?"

"I've just been telling you . . . you're going to be sick tomorrow."

"Don't worry about it."

"How can I help it? Gwennie, how can I help it?"

Lucy gets dramatic so suddenly, it always takes me by surprise. Her big, brown eyes swelled with tears, her warm hand clutched at my wrist. I shook it off and smoked my cigarette. I felt hideously drunk, far beyond any human connection. (And yet not drunk enough, not nearly drunk enough.) Pretty soon she started to cry, which I felt like I'd foreseen from the beginning.

"This," she said, "is what I was afraid of. And it's true, it's true."

"Okay, okay." I dumped the brandy down the sink. "See? Let's go to bed."

"It's not okay," she said. "What do you do when I'm not here? You don't pour it out then."

I thought that was a bit much. When anyone else tried to stop me, I got very nasty. Now I was sweet, and it was like a tightrope act. I hugged her and said, of course I drank too much sometimes, but it wasn't that bad. I just got carried away tonight.

I said, "I'm afraid you won't like Lenny. I really respect your opinion and I'm worried."

She calmed down and told me not to worry, she was sure she'd like him, and I said okay, and she said she wished Malcolm were here, which unnerved me. Then she said let's go to bed and we did. I drank some Jim Beam while I was brushing my teeth, but not very much.

———

Lenny arrived at eleven the next morning. He was dressed in a salmon-colored, button-down shirt and a pair of stretchy bro pants a little too tight across the ass. But he was handsome, I thought, looking at him critically. And he was big which seemed at that point to be a virtue. I remembered him hauling me up from the floor when I fell and, even my drunken and painless dissolve, I appreciated it. To tossed, light as a feather, on the bed again. Well, Lucy wouldn't understand the charm of that, would she? She had a thing about women moving under their own power.

"Pase ta meetcha," said Lenny, squeezing my sister's hand. She murmured something, her eyes wide with surprise. What was it, I wondered, the gold ring he wore? The cologne? Or simply all that black hair escaping from under his shirt, so dense and curly you expected to find little birds living there. "I'm gonna take you girls to a great place for lunch. Nobody knows about it but me and a coupla others. French food and California wine, what could be better?"

"Mexican food and French wine," said Lucy, who tends to turn contrary when someone refers to her as a girl.

"Are you kidding? C'mon, you can't eat that spic stuff. Nothing but grease, it'll kill ya."

"What do you think French food is made of? Butter and cream. Nothing but fat."

"Fat is not grease," he said authoritatively, and so it went all day. I sat in the front seat quietly looking out the window. Dark-green, rounded hills, with pale green moss hanging from the trees, a few puffy white sheep and a lot of grey boulders that looked like sheep.

"We ought to get up to the country more," I said, interrupting one of their monotonous arguments.

"Hey, we'll have a place up here someday, babe. Count on it."

Lucy shuddered and again I almost wanted to marry Lenny, make Lucy and her baby-editor boyfriend visit. Thanksgiving in our boozy stronghold. The men could wrestle in front of the fire after dinner.

We stopped at the first cluster of vineyards a few minutes later and took the tour. Lucy was still trying to be a good sport; she commented brightly on how interesting it all was. In rejoinder Lenny commandeered the vineyard owners, talking man to man. These guys are classic California types: either portly and rubicund, connoisseurs of goat cheese, or pencil-thin and shyly earnest, in love with their equipment. Lenny was good at talking to both kinds; he rested his elbows aggressively on the counters and kept them occupied while I drank the Gamay and the Pinot Noirs, the White Zinfandel and the Grey Reisling.

After a while my sister began to worry. I made no effort to reassure her; the tension between her and Lenny had the effect of making me feel unreal. They were so vivid and angry, I couldn't reach them. I didn't want to. I drank the wine as if I were made of wine, as if I were the ocean welcoming the rain.

"I think it's time we stopped for lunch," said Lucy. "We've been drinking so much wine."

We had already passed Lenny's restaurant, I knew, but he had decided not to take us there. He probably thought Lucy didn't deserve it.

"Are you hungry, Gwen?" he asked. "I'm not hungry. C'mon, food'll only make us sleepy. You don't want me to fall asleep at the wheel, do you?"

"I can drive," Lucy said.

"You're not driving my car. That's a rule."

"Nobody drives your car? Or no woman?"

"No woman who says she's been drinking too much wine."

"You've had more than I have."

"I can hold it."

"Just because I'm more sensible than you are—"

"Sensitive is the word I think you mean. You're sensitive to wine, like your sister. I have to take care of you both."

"I know what word I mean. I'm a writer."

"I know. You write about cunt diseases so women will think they know everything and not go to the doctor."

"I never recommended not going to the doctor. I'm sure you haven't read anything I've written anyway."

"I have. Gwen showed me one article. Do you have any idea how hard it was to turn medicine into a scientific practice? How many women used to die in childbirth? I'm not saying it's perfect now, but sending it back to the midwives and the witchdoctors ain't the answer, lady."

"Do you say 'ain't' deliberately to sound tough? I mean, I could give a shit about how you talk."

"Clearly."

"Clearly what?"

"Your own language is not the finest."

"Fuck you."

"We turn right at the next corner," I said. "They have champagne."

I'm a bit hazy about what happened after the champagne. I do remember Lucy saying they had to take me home.

"She's smiling," said Lenny, "she's happy."

"She's drunk, you fool."

I didn't want to wine-taste anymore. I wanted to lie down in a field somewhere and turn into a grey boulder—the peaceful life of a grey boulder. Finally Lenny turned the car around and we headed back. I said I was hot and he took my shirt off for me and Lucy started screaming that she wasn't going to have her sister showing off her tits to every passing motorist and, goddamn it, he'd better let her drive. Lenny was driving crazily on purpose and laughing and feeling me up. I remember Lucy threatening to kill him and the eagerness in his voice as he said, "Just try it, babe."

I woke up to Lucy wiping my face with a wet washcloth. "How do you feel?"

"Okay," I said warily.

"I doubt it," she replied. "I doubt it very much."

"Is everything alright?"

"I wouldn't say so. What specifically are you referring to?"

"Um, well, what's wrong?" I was beginning to remember the previous day but, before I worried about that, I wanted to make sure there wasn't something worse lurking in the gaps of my memory. When I first started having blackouts I used to keep a pad of paper on my bedside table so I could write down, before passing out, everything that had happened. Occasionally this worked, but usually I'd wake up to an illegible scrawl. A few words, a wine stain, cigarette ash—and those few words, worse than nothing. *Called*—

Called who? Said what?

I tried unplugging the phone before I went out at night

but my drunk self caught on to that trick. She plugged it back in and made her mystery calls. She started leaving me notes on the pad of paper. *It's worth it, Gwen, it's worth it,* underlined several times until the pencil broke.

"You're an alcoholic and your lover's a sicko creep," said Lucy.

"Oh."

"What are you going to do about it?"

"I have to go to the bathroom."

"The Jim Beam's gone, you know. You drank some of it, then you fell off the toilet and I poured the rest out." Her tone was matter-of-fact.

"I have to piss. Do you want me to do it in bed?"

"I'm sorry, Gwen. I love you. You know that. I love you. You're my only sister."

"Please," I said, and crawled to the bathroom. When I returned she had made the bed and she handed me a robe. I tied it around myself and went into the kitchen. I couldn't believe I'd be able to stay up, but it didn't seem to matter where I was. I could pass out on the kitchen floor or throw up in the hallway, what difference did it make. It was the end. They would come and lock me up. One of those very expensive East Coast places where I knew I would commit suicide. I can't stand being constrained. I can't stand it.

I was already working out in my head how I'd do it—the knife, the gun, the rope, like a children's game—when she said, "I think you should move back to New York and go to Alcoholics Anonymous."

"Oh. But what if it doesn't work?" I was interested to note that the scorn and terror I had once felt for that organization had gone. The one meeting I had been to, full of pathetic imbeciles, seemed in memory as soothing as kindergarten.

"It will. You're strong. You're such a great person, Gwennie! Will you try?"

"I guess."

"I think we should just leave. Pack up and go. Then you can recuperate in my apartment. You won't have to worry about anything, you can go to the meetings and you'll be okay. Okay?"

"Sure," I said recklessly. "Can I have a drink on the plane?"

"You can get bombed on the plane. But that's the last time."

"I have to see Lenny."

"No, you don't. He'll just rape you again."

"He doesn't rape me," I protested weakly. What had happened last night?

"What else do you call it when you're passed out? Consensual?"

"Well—I give my consent in advance."

"It's rape anyway. You could have been dead for all he cared. Tell him over the phone. From the airport. That's all he deserves."

I lay on the couch while she packed up stuff and arranged with a neighbor to have it shipped. How could Lenny fuck me if Lucy was here? Had she watched us? No, she must have tried to stop him and he locked her out of the room. I was surprised she hadn't called the cops, except that she would assume they'd be on his side.

I was intrigued by this notion of being dead. The cops would say, "You fucked a dead woman, Mac?" And Lenny would reply, "How was I supposed to know, she's always like that." Then they would drag him away.

We drove to the airport and took off. I didn't call Lenny. I never wrote to him either. I was looking forward to, and then experiencing, sobriety with such intense hunger that nothing else had any claim on me at all.

2

It was a beautiful day for a wedding. The first of May, billowing white clouds in the pale blue sky, and a breeze that smelled like peaches blowing down East Sixty-third Street. The French doors of my mother's apartment were open between living room and garden, and the whole sunny expanse was thronged with guests.

I stood by myself under one of the flowering dogwoods. Usually it's sparsely furnished out here with a wrought-iron table and chairs, and a few pots of geraniums that regularly die. But now it was transformed. The pretty new trees formed a line around the perimeter like a stage set for the *Cherry Orchard*, a play my mother persists in identifying with, although her ancestral home was sold at her parents' death not from necessity but for gross profit. There were Christmas lights in the trees that would be lit later on and a guitar player who sat rather disconsolately on a stool and played songs to which nobody listened. As far as I could tell they were all ballads of unhappy love. Against the wall was a bar manned by three old black bartenders—a nostalgic touch—and the first round of hors d'oeuvres was passed by my stepfather's niece's ballet class, dressed in pink and green tutus and glittering silver slippers.

The ceremony had made me feel peculiar and, in my tiredness and gladness that the whole thing was over, I thought of dark-haired Lucy as Snow White, about to vanish into the woods. But here we were, the party was just beginning. It was eight o'clock and still sunny, as if the day refused to leave. My little sister was standing in the middle of the crowd, being talked to and kissed, and I was remembering her at fourteen, making a toast at my mother's wedding: "Believing marriage to be nothing but the legal enslavement of women, an expression of archaic property rights in human flesh that will die out in the next generation, still we wish you happiness."

Of course her ideas had had to evolve somewhat. And I had nothing against marriage per se. I simply hadn't thought it would be Lucy who did it first. Yet lately I hadn't done anything, so of course she overtook me. Maybe I would never do anything while her life went on, jobs and children, while she betrayed everyday our miraculous power of being young.

I had nothing against Lucy's new husband. Malcolm was kind, he was smart, he had a good job editing a computer magazine. But there was a time when Lucy and I had thought each other enough. When at the age of seventeen I was expelled from my boarding school for drinking, Lucy had hitchhiked a hundred miles from her own school to join me, arriving not long before my mother and Roy. The parents didn't waste much time scolding me—my mother has always preferred the silent treatment—nor did they help me pack, which would have revealed Lucy in the closet. They left the car parked outside the dorm and walked down the hill to the administration building. My brilliant Lucy had an extra set of keys.

We nosed the Cadillac out the back way past the dairy barns and floored it into town, onto the highway, and off the next exit. We stopped for Cokes to relieve my hangover. Lucy said, "Are you sorry you're kicked out? How're things with Evan?"

"Shit no, I'm not sorry. Evan was kicked out last week, I wrote you a letter. It's a fucking war. They're trying to prove they're not a hippie school, good fucking luck." My English teacher was a witch named Wanda who wore purple miniskirts and talked to trees; my French teacher had us translating the Marquis de Sade. "Anyway, I've had enough of that place. They're all nuts."

Lucy and I spent a glorious day. It was the end of April, when Vermont is often thigh-deep in snow, but the snow was gone, the trees budding, and pools of rainwater stood in grassy meadows. Lucy, at the wheel of the enormous car, was confident, her round arms with their shading of dark brown hairs slung casually around it, while her booted foot pressed down, let up, pressed down again on the accelerator with a competent, vigorous joy.

We stayed off the highways, nervous of police, and drove through little towns, singing all the traveling songs we could think of, from "King of the Road" to "Route 66".

Lucy lit a joint, passed it over, and the countryside unveiled its fairy-tale charms. The streams were all winding and bubbling, the hills rolled, the gorges flashed sunlight off wet, sharp rocks. Vermont became New Hampshire and we believed we could detect the difference. "The sentries have changed," said Lucy in her stoned voice that I loved so much. The landscape anticipated us around every bend, stones and trees trembling with the tension of staying in place.

"My English teacher claims to come from a long line of witches," I said, forgiving her at that moment her immeasurable silliness.

"It passes down in the female line," said Lucy. Soon we were singing again. " 'I don't want a pickle/ just want to ride on my motorsickle/and I don't want to die/ just want to ride on my motorcy/cle,' "

I sang, " 'And she'll have fun, fun, fun/ till her daddy takes the T-bird away.' "

At Hampton Beach, we stopped for lobsters and beer. The place was called the Lobster Trap (or the Pirate's Den or the Captain's Cove) and the wood-paneled walls were covered with ropes and nets. The bored waitress was glad to serve us, though we were obviously underage, and by the time we finished eating she introduced us to her cousin. Walt was twenty-five, with a few teeth gone, blue jeans falling off his skinny hips and his cigarettes all broken, smoke drifting out the seams. He talked and smiled with somnolent ease, beer and girls relaxing him almost to sleep. He listened to my tales of boarding school with appreciation, understanding all the types, from the druggie-hippies to the veggie-hippies to the Jesus-freaks to the innocents. As

I drank, flirted, and reached new heights of lucid incoherence, he lifted his bent finger ("My dad smashed it once") to signal for more beer.

Finally Walt proffered an invitation and we agreed to go back to his trailer in the woods. We took the Caddie, since only Lucy was sober, and all sat in the front seat, me in the middle. Just a few hours ago, I thought in wonder, I was dry and hungover and wretched; then Lucy's rescue, our magical drive, an older man. I felt my love for the world well up, fill the car, and spill out the windows; I leaned into Walt's grip with a sensation of pure femininity.

When we reached his trailer, which rested on cement blocks and was decorated in orange carpeting and candy bars, Walt sat us on either side of him on the couch facing the TV and kissed us by turns. The kisses he gave Lucy were ninth-grade kisses, smacking loudly against her closed lips; then he stuck his long tongue down my throat. It tasted like months of cigarettes and beer, which was fine with me. After a while Walt and I went in the bedroom for a little more serious fondling, and Lucy made tea, let the cat in, and called our mother, assuring her we were neither strung out nor dead.

We spent the rest of the spring at home in New York, in disgrace. We were awakened at 8:00 A.M. by the roar of the vacuum cleaner under our beds and driven crazy at night by our stepfather's excited-millionaire business calls. Roy's capitalist ebullience offended us in a way our own family's low-key wealth didn't. Mom already had her money, for one thing . . . Roy didn't seem to notice the times he was living in. It was 1972 and he turned fields into shopping malls. Yet he was so easygoing, it didn't occur to him that we might not like him. He didn't mind our language or our dress. He referred to us, even after the car-theft expulsion caper, as "my wife's pretty little girls."

I was pretty. I wore gauzy shirts and eye makeup and an antique silver locket filled with hashish. But Lucy was something else. Her black hair fell in a braid down her back, she wore high black boots and carried a hunting knife. The round cheeks and rosy mouth of her childhood were still there, but were eclipsed by her jaw and her swagger. Her nose grew beaky and her bones firmed. She amazed me. So rough and tough, even if some of it was put-on. So rebellious, so smart.

Lucy was formulating her feminist position in those days and I'd sprawl on her bed listening, smoking, watching the strong planes of her face lit up by the high beam of her desk lamp. In a way it wasn't surprising. Feminism had given her what she'd always wanted: the knowledge with which to construct her independence. As a child she'd been at a disadvantage, but now she could think for herself, and it was a great relief to her. Lucy has a logical mind and she needed a structure, something self-evident and revolutionary, something to right her wrongs and provide direction to her intellect. She was lucky to be young just then. Nothing but feminism would have served so well, the feminism of the early seventies.

What caught me off guard, I think, was the sexuality of her transformation, the rough, tough girl with her boots and her knife. It's what I would have been, I thought, if I wasn't fatally drawn to the feminine role, if I didn't like to look at myself all prettied up in the mirror. I remember Lucy saying once that makeup was a symbol of women's bondage. I replied that I liked the feeling of rubbing a lipstick over my mouth. She grinned, unsheathed her knife, and drew the dull side across her lower lip. I was excited by that; I thought she'd bring home a motorcycle dude. But she didn't bring anybody home, she remained a virgin through high school. Once in the park we encountered a girl gang, real dyke bullies who were threatening to beat us up. Lucy talked them out of it with her feminist rhetoric, flattering and cajoling them with the way she said "Woman."

She flattered me that way too. "Look at you, Gwen, you're not submissive, you take what you want. You're proud, you're a Woman." Indeed. I took charge of my sexuality (fucked around), resisted indoctrination (never listened to my mother), and lived utterly the most famous slogan of the times: *Sisterhood is Powerful*. It was. She was. She still is, but she doesn't carry a knife anymore. She doesn't wear black boots. Of course she still thinks for herself. She writes about what she wants to write about— preventive medicine, gynecological services for poor women, reproductive rights for us all. She writes for the magazine *Women's Health* with a feminist slant, refusing all exercise-fashion and anti-aging cream assignments. She's also, in the last few years, womanned a rape-crisis hotline, donated time and money to a shelter for battered women, testified in a custody case for a lesbian acquaintance, and has spoken on the radio about abortion. (My mother called and asked me, "Why does she talk as if she's had a dozen abortions when she's never even had one?" "She's just embarrassed, Ma—she wants to be one of the club." "Oh, don't be so silly.") I'm proud of her, she makes me feel lazy and self-indulgent in the extreme, and I miss the old Lucy, that girl she was for a few years at most but whom I saw and chose and have never relinquished—my true sibling, my black-haired swaggering Loulou, my simple and explosive little sister.

My mother was glaring at me from across the garden. Norah has a way of doing this so that nobody notices: her round face smiling, her eyes wide and blue like Tenniel's Cheshire Cat. She bent her peachy bosom toward one guest and another—oh, my beautiful mother—but I saw the twitch at her temple, the brief narrowing of those wide eyes; I knew what it meant. I should be gliding with sweetly feminine grace through the crowd, pausing for a moment of chat, a kiss, introducing the strangers to the friendly, and distracting those who would talk to my sister too long.

But I'd been doing this for an hour, I didn't want to do it anymore. Every moment of this gaiety was acutely painful. Weddings are notorious of course. It's not that people necessarily drink too much but that we, who used to, remember what a perfect occasion it was, the festivity for once in tune with our desire. Alcoholics are big on festivity. Even for the merest after-work drink, we crave it, and cause no end of trouble with our unnatural celebrations.

I'd been sober almost a year, I didn't cause trouble anymore. I was polite to my sister's friends, the feminist yuppies in their pearls, to Malcolm's friends in their lawyers-doctors-bankers' clothes. I was polite to my mother's friends, whose favorite question was when was I getting married, asked in a sly and joking tone, as if Lucy had pulled off a coup. I joked back as their boozy kisses lingered on my lips. I said I'd been married secretly but my husband was a freak and wouldn't come out in public.

"And how old are you now, dear?"

"Twenty-nine," I replied, and endured their jokes about turning thirty. I stood there and smiled and felt more and more uneasy. Thirty, thirty-one, thirty-five. Thirty-nine, forty. Couldn't it happen like that? The decade falling on me like a pack of cards, King, Queen, Knave, like the Berlin street scenes of Kirchner. I had quit drinking to save my life, yet my horror at a past I could barely remember was nothing to my fear of what lay on the horizon. What was even now gathering in. Sobriety. It sounds so rational. It sounds like a Unitarian minister taking a walk in the church woods. It sounds safe but it isn't, of course not. Why ever would I have drunk if it were?

Then Lucy was beside me. "Come, O honorable maid! You have to be in the pictures."

She pulled me across the garden to where the long-haired photographer waited. He gave us a stoned smile, this favorite of my mother's crowd, whose mellow hippie attire contrasted strangely with his obsequious patter. He recalled to the aging matrons their children's youth, that frightening spontaneous insolence they now tell stories about, as veterans of an interesting war. Nobody here lost a child to drugs—or not yet—to jail or ritual murder, or to permanent estrangement. Everybody's back, mostly in Manhattan, the women are becoming pregnant and call their mothers endlessly. Or so Lucy tells me; she keeps up with these slightly older children of my mother's friends, the ones we strove to emulate, whom Lucy now uses as contacts. "Jean French is working at the *Times*," she'll tell me and I see the gleam in her eyes; she has a new source. Even unlikely postings please her. "I'm a reporter," she says, "I have to know everything."

"Nice," said the photographer, letting our hair run slowly through his fingers as he tilted our heads to the angle he wanted. Lucy's hair is almost black, mine ginger. Her eyes are brown, mine blue. Her nose is longer, her jaw squarer, yet we look alike when we smile: a certain willfulness is betrayed, the spark of our parents' attraction.

The photographer posed us again with Malcolm between us, arms around our waists. It wouldn't occur to Malcolm that he's stealing my sister. Having no siblings of his own, he comes to Lucy with a yearning for family. They regale me at dinner with the names of their future children. "Don't have so many," I plead when they get past the eldest daughter, the eldest son, the twins.

"Why not?" asked Malcolm; this is his favorite daydream.

"Don't worry," said Lucy. I don't worry, exactly. I merely feel uneasy. Aunt Gwendolyn, I think. That's a little bit close.

What happened to Aunt Gwendolyn? the children will ask. You have her picture on the mantel, tell us please, do.

She vanished on our wedding night and never was seen again. Some think she drowned, some think she burnt—

And some think she fell in the cake, the children will shout, and was eaten by mistake.

I took a breather. Strolled away from the happy pair, back under the dogwood tree. When my thoughts reach a certain level of negativity, I realize I don't have to think. Nobody is requiring it of me. I closed my eyes for a minute. Then, when I opened them, I looked at the reception as if it were a painting. It's easy to do this. Lock your eyes in a gaze, breathe deeply and slowly, and even a lively crowd will appear still, all the motion as it were averaged out. If I become very attentive I can predict each gesture before it happens and so in a sense it doesn't happen as life but as art: the final or perfect form of the scene is always before me, in my mind's eye.

This is the way to live, I think, this floating detachment is so sensuous really. It makes the world tender. I see the patterns weaving in and out, the children and the summer dresses, I see it all and it doesn't matter what my relation to it is. To see is enough. If only I could stay like this.

A waiter paused before me with his tray of champagne, held just so for the lady to make her decision. The glasses gleamed like circles of light on the sea, casting drops into the air, carried to my nose and lips. I knew what a taste of champagne would do. Within moments I would bask in a beauty so utter it would seem almost weightless; I almost wouldn't notice how its weight increased. No longer content to watch, I would act as if the world were my imagining, my symbolic stuff thrown out to landscape the wilderness. Each man and woman my man, my woman: my self and her offspring, who step away only to tease. Nobody is in such danger as the one who thinks that, who sees only herself and so wanders blind. Which did I miss more—the power to discover beauty or the power to destroy it?

Concentrating on the champagne, I hadn't noticed I was no longer alone. I heard a voice just behind me—Jack Price, Malcolm's father—a light baritone, self-consciously funny, and as familiar as if we'd known each other for years. "I feel like a dog lapping out of these glasses. Why don't they serve this stuff in beer mugs?"

"You want me to get you a beer mug?"

"No thank you, Gwendolyn." I turned and bumped into him. He put out a hand to steady me, a little wine sloshed on my arm. "Sorry," he said. I felt the cool burn of the alcohol on my skin; the waiter moved away. Champagne doesn't really burn, but it does me.

"You shouldn't sneak up on people."

"I thought this was a social occasion. Am I wrong?"

I didn't bother to answer. I looked at the glass in his hand, my gaze traveling up his arms, his bright amused face, down his body. He had delicate wrists, rounded shoulders, a barrel chest. A bit of a belly. Thick, curly black hair. The curls somewhat awry, very soft watchful eyes.

"Enjoying yourself?" I asked. We had both been in the wedding party. Jack was best man. I, maid of honor. Jack had kept looking at me out of the corner of his eyes as the minister spoke; I thought I'd burst out laughing. Nobody else can see it, I thought, what is so clearly on his face.

He sighed. "Yesterday morning I was in Mexico. They're making a movie down there of one of my books and they kindly said I could hang around. Somewhere in their dim brains they know their script makes no sense and they want me to fix it. Not that they'd say so. Not yet; not until there's about ten minutes before shooting. So there I was, lolling on the beach, drinking margaritas, and I had to come back for this."

"Nobody put a gun to your head," I remarked. Jack Price wrote science fiction. His heroes came to bad ends, lighting their cigarettes from the charred ruins of the last city or locked in a desolate way station in the Andromeda galaxy, but he had a lovely way with a description, the spray of stars outside the window, the breathing of the coals beneath the stench of burning bodies.

He laughed. His mouth, which did not appear unusual in repose, its healthy pinkness fading out at the corners, revealed itself in his smile as prodigiously wide and supple.

"No, of course I wanted to come, are you kidding? My only son, why I've known him since he was a babe . . ." His voice was soft, even wistful, I felt drawn in. "I used to have a routine with him when he wouldn't eat his vegetables. I told him that when he was married, when I was an old man, he could feed me whatever he wanted. He liked that idea, let me tell you. 'Sour milk!' he'd shout. 'Dirty socks!'"

I couldn't imagine Malcolm as a child. I couldn't quite see Jack in the role of father either. Seen together, they were clearly related, yet their relatedness was odd, awkward, as if Jack had just returned from a journey far longer than his two-week Mexican trip. (It was a simple admission he offered me, I thought: I don't want to be here, I want to be here. Yet it was enough to make me feel maybe I could bear being here, maybe I could watch the drinking and the flirting without remembering too often how it used to be, how it never was, how it won't ever be. What wasn't so simple was my physical response to him. He was standing too close to me, it was making me dizzy. The smell, the bulk, the hair on his wrists and arms. This was a fact, not an alcoholic fancy. But I have no idea what to do with facts.)

"Do you think they'll be happy together?" I asked.

He looked at me sharply. "Why are you asking me? I'm sure you have your own ideas. Or is that just a polite question, are we all supposed to speculate on their happiness?" He was a little drunk, I thought. I didn't mind. A little drunk is okay.

"No, it wasn't just a polite question. I really don't know, it's all new to me. I like Malcolm, who wouldn't?"

He sighed. "He's so agreeable." It was as if he were in mourning.

"He's sweet, and Lucy is too, you know. She's faithful. But I'm not used to people getting married. Except my mother. None of my friends have. . . . Of course, I don't really have any friends anymore."

He looked at me, smiled, shook his head slightly. "You just moved back here, didn't you?"

"Ten months ago. I know all these people but I don't particularly want to."

"I know how that feels. Marriage. I don't know what these kids mean by it, frankly. Ten years ago I thought we'd done away with the institution of marriage. I thought nobody would ever get married again." He paused. " 'Should I get married? Should I be good? Astound the girl next door with my velvet suit and my Faustus hood?' "

I continued the quote: " 'Don't take her to movies but to cemeteries, tell all about werewolf bathtubs and forked clarinets,' "

"Amazing!" He beamed at me. "Astonishing."

"That's all I know," I warned him. *Marriage,* by Gregory Corso, read during my beatnik phase when I longed to have lived on MacDougal Street in the 50s and worn black ballet slippers and a blond Jean Seberg haircut.

"I used to be able to recite the whole thing. I declaimed it to my wife on our second anniversary, but she fell asleep before the end." His wife, Ruth, was Lucy's idol. A prominent feminist, she taught and had written important books.

"Maybe you should have read it to her before the wedding," I dared to say. He glanced at me, lowered his eyelids, and smiled. His consciousness of his charm looked new to him, as if he hadn't flirted in a dozen years. It felt like as long for me.

"It didn't come out until 1960. By then I was a father."

I didn't say anything, I must have been four when Malcolm was born. His spicy dark scent reminded me of sandalwood, of overripe plums, of a boyfriend I had when I was seven. We locked ourselves in the closet once and kissed. His mother called the fire department.

"Marriage. . . ." His voice was idling, he was keeping up his end of the conversation. People will do that, I've learned. Once you stop worrying about being silent yourself, you'll find the work is done for you. "In my day, you know, it was a gamble. That was the fun of it. You were taking on the support of a family—the man was, and the woman took the risk that the guy she had picked was up to it. You married a woman, you didn't worry, Can I love her?—but simply, Can I afford her?" He lifted another glass of champagne off a tray and drained it. The color rose in his cheeks.

"Now marriage is comforting," I said. "Now it's cozy."

"Cozy? I was scared shitless on my wedding day. I had sold exactly one book by then—*Mutants on the Moon*—" He glanced at me sidelong, his snaky eyebrows raised.

"Great title," I said.

He laughed. "Those were the days when any hint of good writing had to be hidden well inside. You had to hope nobody would notice it, which was kind of a trick in itself. I had some fun with that—anyway, I wasn't exactly raking it in. List price, first edition of my novel, was precisely one quarter. And Ruth was pregnant. I figured I'd have to write a book every thirty-eight days just to get by. I was standing up there calculating how many words per hour, per minute."

"You wish Malcolm were in that situation?" I asked ironically.

"Nah, I'm just running off at the mouth. A man's supposed to reminisce at a time like this. Oh, the good old days when I was young and poor and shaking diapers over the toilet. We still have the diapers, Ruth uses them to dust with. Why not? Disposable diapers may just be what sends this planet over the edge."

"What?"

"Never mind, never mind. I can see it's not a subject that interests you. Will they be happy? I worry about it, Gwendolyn, and that's not saying anything against your sister, but I do. You know, I suspected, when he shot up three inches taller than me, that he wasn't a little boy anymore, but . . . I go visit him in his office, he swivels around in his chair, the phones are all ringing—"

"I know," I said, "he's very much in charge there."

He looked at me shrewdly. "Whereas here, on the other hand—well, it's a wedding. Your mother's done a beautiful job." The waiters assailed us with caviar and shrimp, rounds of garlic toast spread with goat cheese and sun-dried tomatoes. "Quite a spread. Quite a place."

"Most of it's Roy's money," I murmured, not that he had asked. I feel ashamed of our wealth, even now in the mid-eighties. Of course most of it *is* Roy's money. My mother, Lucy, and I have only enough to keep slightly above the fray.

"So what crime did he commit?" he asked offhandedly; I knew I had invited the question.

"He's a developer."

"Jesus, Malcolm didn't tell me. What am I marrying into?"

"You," I said sharply, "are not marrying into anything." Yet I felt a pull of sorrow as I realized this wasn't true. Our families were bound; we were bound in that binding; I knew what I wanted and it wasn't an in-law. Oh why, oh why, oh why, I thought. Yet I didn't resist my attraction.

"You know what I mean. Still, the man seems civil enough." His tone was conceding, placatory; I laughed.

"We only marry nice men in this family," I said grandly. He raised an eyebrow. "So that's why you're still single." I was thrown into embarrassment as if down a well. Such a stupid little witticism yet I felt engulfed in it. I blushed; how could I stop blushing while he continued to look at me?

"You're alright," he said gently.

I did my best to sound sarcastic. "Thanks, I was really worried."

"Yeah, I know what that's like. You look in the mirror and you say to yourself, It looks like a human being. You lift an arm, sniff, say, It smells like a human being. But is it? Is it?" He went into a whole routine with this, he was very funny, peering forward as if into a mirror, and my shyness dissolved.

"You didn't look happy, Gwendolyn, standing over here by yourself. I thought I detected a kindred spirit. My parents used to take me to enormous parties when I was a kid.

For some reason I always imagined they were looking for another couple to adopt me. Introducing me here and there, 'And this is Jack . . .' I'd have to throw a tantrum or pee in my pants to discourage them."

"You know what I just did? The opposite. I went to a children's party. Roy's niece had a birthday. It was wonderful, eighteen little girls swarming over me, wanting to try on my lipstick."

"Can I go with you next time?"

"Seriously."

"I know what you mean. I had a kid."

"Oh, God, remember that part in your book when the guy takes cells from his dead son and clones him and when the boy reaches twelve he kills him and starts again, he can't bear for him to grow up?"

"He can't bear for the clone to grow up. So you've read my books? A sophisticated Manhattanite like yourself, not to mention female? Miracles never cease."

"I read them when I lived in Berkeley."

"That explains it. In Berkeley science fiction is literature. Hell, it's practically religion. I go out there, I'm lionized, invited everywhere to dinner, to speak on panels, and I think, Gee, I guess I am somebody. Then I come back here, as soon as I'm off the plane, I feel like lowlife again."

"So why do you come back?"

"Well, my wife happens to teach here. But I suppose I take some pride in being a lowlife. It's kind of funny, after supporting myself for thirty years, after sixteen books, to be considered not really a writer at all. It's a kick . . . when I start muttering to myself, I go read my fan mail."

"I wrote you a fan letter once," I said, "but I didn't mail

it." His books, which I had read mostly in the depths of hangover, had often succeeded in dispelling my guilt-ridden gloom. Some lightness in them had made me want to get out of bed, comb my hair, take a walk. That those walks often ended up with a glass of wine in a sunny café was hardly Jack's fault.

"What did the letter say? Why didn't you mail it; don't you know you're supposed to thank people who give you pleasure?"

His face was suddenly so close to mine. Pleasure. The pleasure of reading a book is such a private thing. His books tossed in my bed among half-eaten sandwiches, dirty underwear, *People* magazines, and candy wrappers.

"I can't remember what it said."

"Oh, come on."

"No, really I can't."

"Sure you can. Whisper it to me."

I laughed, looking at his ear bent toward me. Not a small ear, faintly orange, rubbery, clean, surrounded by wiry black curls. It seemed a safe place, Jack's ear. But even to imagine safety—safety was a warm room with a table set for two, a bottle of wheat-gold wine. So don't imagine, I said to myself, and stood frozen.

A moment passed as his ear waited. Hadn't I piled it high with the unspoken? He seemed to catch some of it, he shook his head slightly like a man coming out of the water, and changed the subject. "Besides not mailing letters, what do you do?"

"I paint dogs."

"I like the way you said that: 'I paint dogs.' Of course you do, I knew that right away. What kind of dogs?"

"Dogs whose mistresses will pay for a portrait. Pure breeds."

"I guess you have to be a pure breed to have your mistress commission your portrait," he said, and I was startled by an image of him standing naked in my studio. "Do you paint them in their living rooms or do you make up a landscape for them?"

"You mean, like a black dog running through the desert at dusk, the yellow-pink beam of a headlight, the car in the left corner almost invisible?" The image came as suddenly, a companion piece to the other.

He smiled at me for a moment. "Yeah." I felt dizzy with happiness.

"No," I said.

"Maybe you should."

"Maybe I should," I agreed.

The car door, open—the way car doors seem to hang off their hinges. Blue. I would start it tomorrow, give up on these stupid portraits. I would be an artist again, painting all night, strict imagination, unsullied by the marketplace. For a moment it bloomed, it was like watching a sunrise, my hope and my enthusiasm, all the brilliance of youth.

Then suddenly I was as sad as I had been happy; I was pierced by sorrow like a knife jabbed in from behind. Lucy's marriage, my solitude, an opera of contrast, of deprivation. I was raised up on my emotion; I felt as if my body would hang forever from that stake.

"So," he said.

"So?" I smiled faintly; it was dark now. Maybe I should go talk to someone else. Yet I knew I wouldn't leave his presence.

We stood in silence for a few minutes, watching the crowd, the men in their pale summer suits and coiffed hair, the thin shimmering women. What am I feeling, I wondered. It's nothing. Only a mood. It wasn't surprising I should experience desire; he was attractive, he was paying attention to me, I hadn't had sex in more than ten months. (Those empty nights gathered around me like hungry children. Feed us, Mama; feed us, Mama; feed us, Mama. Shut up.) Certainly I wasn't what he wanted, if he wanted anything at all other than a mild flirtation. He's had a few drinks, I reminded myself. His son's just gotten married.

Lucy and Malcolm were laughing, holding onto each other. She looked so healthy, so untroubled. How did she end up like that?

Jack said, "Malcolm introduced me to your Aunt Agatha. She's some character, isn't she? She was telling me about your father. He was in publishing, I gather, in children's books? He didn't sound much like a children's book kind of guy."

"My father believed children's books should be subversive. Provocative, extreme, even cruel. He was always urging his writers to make the stuff darker. You know the kind of stories where in the end you find out it's a dream, the kid's asleep in bed, Mommy's bringing breakfast? He hated those kind of endings. My mother was always saying to him, 'Ned, people read to their children at bedtime so they'll go to sleep,' and he'd blow up. He used to tell us about reading *Huck Finn* as a boy, then running away from home. He was nine."

I spoke calmly yet even saying his name was difficult. I thought it would jump off my lips and escape, a hot bright bundle of teeth and fur and claws. Once out there who knew what damage it would cause? I repressed this thought with an effort; my calmness deepened and acquired an eerie sheen. I kept my eyes fixed on Jack as I perfected my composure; he seemed both weirdly harmless and completely unattainable.

"He took off at nine? That's fairly impressive, though I can see why your mother didn't think so. I would have had a heart attack if Malcolm had done that."

"Oh, his parents caught glimpses of him from time to time. He'd sneak in the kitchen, steal food. His father was raring to catch him, give him a whipping, but he never did. My father came back of his own accord."

"And was he whipped?"

"I guess so. You'll have to ask Aunt Agatha."

My father's eldest sister had sat me down this afternoon when I refused the luncheon cocktails and told me stories of all the drunks in the family. The car crashes, the financial ruins, the marriages in shambles. I had found it oddly comforting. It's a disease, it's not my fault.

Jack said, "Agatha told me he died when you were kids. That must have been rough."

"I was sixteen, Lucy fifteen. I suppose we were kids." I hesitated, but it was easier to let it out than keep it in. "He fell down the stairs, he was drunk. He was living alone by then, they divorced when I was twelve."

When I say this I want to smile. I feel embarrassed. Certainly it didn't happen to me, something so dramatic; I think of all the layers of acceptance and refusal, of yearning and relief and memory and what I've done to it. Nothing like tears could express this complexity, I thought. Only a smile.

Yet Jack was looking at me so kindly, neither asking me questions nor changing the subject. Sympathy—what use is that? I knew its clumsy paw would not remove the splinter. But there was something else, something to do with grief, that I had not done. I had felt it like a chink in the wall for the last thirteen years. A place for the wind to blow in; I had stood stoutly against it.

"I'll tell you about it sometime," I said dreamily. I'd forgotten how we knew each other.

"Sometime?" The sound of his voice recalled me.

"Well, not now. This is a wedding. My sister hated my father, you know."

"I don't think she cares too much for me."

I looked at him, the way his old jacket conformed to his body, his bright blue sweater. He was the only man at the wedding not in a suit. I love the way a sweater looks on a man like Jack, solid by virtue of build and inclination. He was well packed into his clothes. Even his shoes I approved of.

"No, she doesn't."

"No question about it, huh? So what have I done?" His voice had thickened, I felt immediately contrite. I had forgotten that this might upset him.

"She tends not to like men over a certain age. She has a sort of father complex." That schoolgirl with her round cheeks and soft temples, watching in astonishment as I walked past her classroom on my way to the principal's office. Somehow I thought she'd always be littler than me. She's not. She's taller, she's stronger, she makes more money.

Jack smiled skeptically. "Somehow, Gwen, I think it's more personal than that. Come on, tell me, you've already started."

"Well, for one thing you stayed in Mexico too long. That offended her." (Not returning till the morning of, she had said. What an asshole. And look what he's wearing. Malcolm said, He's a writer. Yes, she retorted, and what do you think I am?)

"I know. I know," he nodded. "She's right. Shit." He sighed heavily. "There were a lot of things involved in that. My wife—"

Your wife also says things against you, I thought. Lucy had reported to me several of Ruth's acerbic comments.

"Listen," he said abruptly, "you want to get out of here?"

I was startled, then suddenly alive with desire. Jack Price with his snaky eyebrows and black curls, jingling the change in his pockets, suggesting we leave. Jack Price in his bright blue sweater, inviting me to abscond. As I imagined it, the night outside the reception seemed as vast and chaotic as the sea and, like the sea or chaos, formed of a secret pattern. Its melting roar so distant and familiar as if Jack were a shell I had pressed to my ear; as if I were the shell. How could we be confined here? I smiled at him tenderly, then with a breath of doubt. What had he to do with my explosive response? What had he even meant by that invitation—Out of here?

"Forget it, never mind, a stupid idea," he said.

No, I started to say, wait a minute, not stupid, when we heard his name being called from across the garden by his wife. Ruth was striding toward us, a tall woman with a clever face and narrow eyes, adorned in African jewelry and russet silk. Her collarbone protruded from yellowish wrinkled skin; her gaze, I knew from experience, would never quite rest on me.

She wanted him to meet someone. Some young sci-fi writer, a friend of Lucy's. He gripped my hand in farewell and went with her, walking more slowly than she, so she glanced back in exasperation. His eyelids were lowered, he looked both blank and mocking. He turned to the left—the lights in the trees caught the curls of his hair, his old jacket a good dozen years on his body.

I held my own hand where it smarted from his grip. I felt the mark of each finger, I concentrated on feeling those marks. I wanted that hand. I wanted to twist it off his wrist. Sleep with it under my pillow. By morning it would be climbing happily around my body.

I stayed at the reception another hour. I ate three pieces of wedding cake and danced with Malcolm and several of his friends. The party had moved inside and Jack was always somewhere else. I noticed him with my step-father once, being talked to man to man. He disappeared into the library with Mrs. Farnsworth. I didn't want to pursue him. I kept thinking he'd come back and talk to me. How could I bear it if he did, this ridiculous infatuation? A married man, my sister's father-in-law. Why torture myself? Why not, I replied, why not. I've got nothing better to do.

I left about eleven. I snuck out without saying good-bye to anyone; the hallway and foyer were miraculously empty. I felt tranquilized by the quiet and by the soft lavender carpeting, the flower prints in their heavy frames, the cherrywood table with its rosy glow, and wondered if I shouldn't stay. Sit down, eat more cake. The wedding cake had mocha frosting and twining green sugar leaves; it was served with raspberry and lemon sorbet. No, no, I thought, out of the witch's house. I shut the front door behind me. I don't need a wedding night. There's nothing here I need.

A brief exhilaration—then the voice inside, so swift, so knowing. Oh girl, it said, I've got you, I've got you on a long string. "Some calls it the disease," said a stentorian-voiced black man in an AA meeting the other day, "I just calls it the Devil."

3

On the third day after the wedding I was painting in my studio. It steadies me to use my skill, to pick up a brush and feel the soft bend of it against canvas, to spread the paint like stroking a body. Alizarin crimson, burnt sienna, indigo. Carefully, carefully. How can people use rollers? Or slosh the paint on? How can they not love this delicate, fingery touch? Let the beauty out slowly, like leading a child by the hand across the street. It doesn't matter that I'm doing it for a client. To do this for anyone is a treat.

I was working on Mrs. Fishbeck-Perry's Doberman. He's scarcely more than a pup, awkward and gangly, amazed to be here—you mean me, say his eyes, I'm alive, me?—but already a handsome animal. She could show him if she wanted to but she won't; she bought him to love. She's a tiny old lady with white hair and white hands and she had served me vanilla wafers and ginger ale. The dog lay with his head and forepaws on his lap, gazing at her like a child who knows he will soon be talking. The portrait was almost finished. Usually I mind that, but not today. Hope, adventure, luck—all were there in the peach and ivory antique sofa my subject was lying on, his young head poised like a wing in the air. I painted all day, more and more slowly, pausing for long moments with my brush upraised.

I feel lucky to have this work to do. It's such a change from the kind of jobs I used to take in galleries, museums, offices, bookstores, each stint of labor followed by long periods of unemployment when I traveled or painted, supported by checks from our family trust fund. Then the money would run out, and I'd get on the telephone, calling everyone I knew to ask about a job. I'll do anything, I said, I don't care. Three or four months the checks would pile up, and the routine of the job—which I always like at first, getting up early, joining the workaday world, the camaraderie of the bossed, the pleasure of lunch hour—would fade; I'd start reading the ads for cheap flights to Europe. Memories of foreign streets would assail me: hotel rooms with balconies, the foreign script on the package of cookies, the rapid Spanish in the squares of Madrid. French shoe stores, Italian landscapes, the amorous murmurings of a Greek boy who spoke no English. I stopped traveling after a while; I stayed home and drank. I cadged money from my mother. I let the bills pile up.

I can't live in New York now without working and it fills me with gratitude that I can support myself with my art.

Nothing has felt as satisfying as this, not even when I was painting on my own. I was always indecisive, I didn't know what to paint. There was too much to choose from, and too many of my canvases ended up inches thick. Coming home from a night of drinking, I'd look at the work in despair, I'd pick up my brush and improve it all to hell.

I don't have that problem anymore. I'm not a genius anymore. I'm a court painter, skilled, talented, I earn my keep. Once every couple of weeks I take tea with a lady—it's always a lady—who's heard of me from one of her friends. I show her my slides and meet the animal, we discuss price, and it's over, the hour of anxiety I think of as how I really earn my checks. The painting is a pleasure. A couple of times the client hasn't liked the work so I painted her another and kept the reject. I have a Labrador, an Akita, and a Newfoundland in my closet. I take them out to look at when I get lonely, several times a day. They have something in common. They're all old dogs and they're painted too dark, eyes swimming out of the murky background, the murky head. They have too much pathos in their eyes. I like them that way.

A city dog's life, what can it offer? They're captives, bought to serve the loneliness of others at the cost of their own more absolute loneliness. Those beautiful noses and ears are never let free in the wild except perhaps for a weekend or a summer that inspires in them a desperate passion, evolving, as they get older, into a desperate ner-vousness. I've seen them after they come back from the country, the hunger they lavish on their mistress, on her face, on her hands. She says, "He can't bear to be apart from me. He'd follow me anywhere." And the beast presses his body against her as if he could merge with her alien, too often absent, flesh.

My customers are impressed by my rapport with their animals. When a high-strung Afghan places her head in my lap, or a spoiled poodle watches me with his black eyes and does not interrupt, the owners think they're getting something special, a real artist, a magician. They want me to tell them about all the dogs I've had, so I invent a few. I don't say I could never own one because I don't have a house in the countryside with acres of woods and hills, nor days of domestic contentment or the belief that my life will stretch out like that forever. It's peace the animals want and security, and affection when their work is done. It's work they need, to be a part of things. Work and wildness both, because they're dogs, not wolves, not people.

At four the phone rang. I picked it up without waiting for the machine to answer. I shouldn't feel this, I thought, I shouldn't know this. If you know who's calling before your mouth has even said hello, if you're able to intuit exactly what will follow, doesn't it follow that you should know better? No.

Jack invited me to dinner. I accepted. Just like that.

I hung up and sat on my pink couch and looked out the window at the woman across the street, ironing. She always ironed in the evenings; it looked restful. I imagined myself washing and ironing a man's shirts for the privilege of taking them off him, all those buttons to undo so it takes a long time, and the honest sweat—

We were to meet at a place called the Astray Café. It was my suggestion, it's right around the corner. Jack had chuckled when I told him the name of the restaurant and then we both held onto our phones in silence. I was mulling the strange fact that I could feel his breath in my ear, when he said, "Okay, see you there," and hung up.

I thought about what to wear. My closet was full of beautiful dresses, but I felt somehow too indistinct to put one on. I looked out the window again, off to the left where there's a hole in the block, and I saw sky and lumpy rooftops and a few green branches. I felt as if my heart were unfolding like a Japanese fan. My whole chest emptied to make room for it: the painted flowers vibrated in the still air. How careful I must be. I took a bath, combed my hair, dressed down for my date, and held on to this exquisite mood. Quietly, quietly, I left the apartment, slid my key in my jeans. Nothing had happened yet. Not really. The early evening sunlight on the street reminded me of a thousand days in the past, there was nobody watching me. I was a woman almost thirty, able to decide her own affairs. To be in error is to be alive, I thought, and the word "error" seemed comforting, it was smaller than "terror."

Jack was already there. I was grateful for that eagerness, for the way he got up and stood beaming at me, for his checked shirt, open at the neck. Why should I be attracted, I thought, to a plump, frizzy-haired, fifty-year-old science-fiction writer . . . and let the question die away. His shirt was red, his hair was black. His hands were warm as I clasped them quickly and let them go. "So," he said, and I smiled, settling into my shyness as if it were a leafy nest. I felt soft all the way through, soft and alert. The table between us, the friendly tall waiter, bread and butter. And it was June, and Lucy was out of town, and a sober body fits so well; I had forgotten such a thing as health allied with desire.

I ordered Perrier and he ordered scotch. The waiter left and Jack said simply, "It's wonderful to see you again. You left the other night before I could properly say good-bye. I saw you hurrying down the steps as if you were thrilled to get away."

It always surprises me that people see me when I don't see them; I feel an absurd delight, as if I'd discovered that I have a twin, of whom I'd long heard rumors.

"I was. I'd heard enough nuptial jokes to last me the rest of the century." How wise he had been, I thought, not to have come talked to me later. What a better idea this was.

"You're so pretty," he said.

"So are you."

"I'm not trying to embarrass you, I'm just so glad you came out with me. Surprised, I guess, an old married man like me."

"You don't have to tell me you're married, Jack, I already know," I said with exasperation. That little thread of guilt in his voice could worm its way too easily inside me. "So where's the wife tonight?"

"Ruth's in the Soviet Union." He smiled broadly. "Believe me, I had nothing to do with it, it was her choice." He laughed, looking at me sidelong to see if I appreciated the situation. I did.

"What's she doing there?"

"She's on a fact-finding tour."

"Found any yet?"

"I haven't heard. She only left yesterday."

"How long's she going to be away for?"

"Six weeks."

We spent a little time looking at the menu. I still have difficulty eating a formal meal. Dinner not as an excuse for wine, not as a preliminary to after-dinner drinks, but as something done for itself, to nourish and please. The people I dined with were always drinkers, too, and the meal would appear on the table like an unwelcome guest. How awkward it was to cut and bite and chew when our mouths and throats were in love with the easy swallow. Even now it tires me to eat three courses at once. I find it hard to recognize when I'm hungry; that empty feeling in my gut reminds me too much of sorrow.

The waiter brought our drinks and I sipped at my Perrier. It occurred to me that if I kissed Jack, I would be able to taste the scotch on his tongue. Would that constitute a slip? Nobody in AA had mentioned this as a problem. I wanted to kiss him—his bare forearms, the curve of his flesh, the curly hair over his wrists and knuckles, the square tips of his fingers—but I could wait.

"Shall I order a bottle of wine?" he asked. I hesitated. As if I could answer a different way and be a different woman. Gwendolyn who's never had a problem with alcohol. It seemed to me that woman was so close, she was practically here. Like those nights in childhood when I'd wake up to feel a ghost in the room standing right by my bed. If I only opened my eyes—but I wouldn't, I'd shut them more tightly and repeat the words to a Beatles song, whichever one came to mind.

"I don't drink," I said.

"Oh?"

"It got to that point, you know. I had to give it up."

"No wonder you felt uncomfortable the other night."

"Yeah, that kind of thing really stirs it up. But that's life. The idea, you know, is to redirect the longing." A longing which is boundless. Formless. A hole in my life I'm drawn to as if to a promise but there never was a promise; it's a dumb void and only when I'm pressed up against it do I realize I should have tried to get away.

"How do you do that?" he said. "Redirect the longing?"

Good question. I hadn't redirected mine so much as planned that I was going to. Kept it in confinement, roaming unappeased, while rumors of delight floated down from the AA heights.

"God is a popular substitute," I said. "Alcoholics like to lose control and God demands surrender. They like to reveal themselves and he sees all. They like having someone to talk to in the middle of the night."

"Yeah, so do I, but I like it better when she talks back."

He smirked; I blushed. That was, of course, the other possibility. That was, of course, what I was doing here.

"Sorry," he said. "Go on. I'm listening." I shrugged. "Of course," he continued, when he realized I wasn't going to speak, "it's true that you have to find a substitute of some kind. You can't simply turn into another sort of person."

"Oh, why not?" I asked: someone hollow and cool, graceful, dark, almond-eyed, speaking a foreign language. I leaned forward, he took my hands in his, held them loosely.

"Why not? You know, Gwen, all I have to do is see a guy walking ahead of me on the street and I'm gone, I'm in his life. Some scrawny guy with a limp or one of those terrifyingly tall bald fellows. A Puerto Rican doorman off-shift, smoking a cigarette. Anybody. Although usually, to tell the truth, it's somebody neutral, somebody I couldn't explain at all why he caught my eye . . . for a half an hour I'm in his life, I've imagined it down to the last detail, named his cat—"

"No," I said. "That's just you being a writer. I mean, *not* imagining it, just *being* something completely other."

"You imagine," he insisted. "You have to."

"Ye-es. But just a hint of it, just the vaguest intuition."

He smiled at me for a long moment. What could I possibly have done right, I wondered.

"So, is that what you mean by God?" he asked. "You can admit it to me, I'm quite a spiritual guy in my own way."

"Which way's that?"

"Oh. Let's say I feel a sense of apology for the human race. That implies someone to apologize to, doesn't it? The Great Spirit, that character who looks down every now and then and mutters, 'What the hell are you schmucks doing now?' The way I look at it, it all got out of hand a few billion years ago."

"Suppose that it didn't? What if this is the way it's supposed to be?"

"You mean the beggars on the streets, the babies born with AIDS, just keep it local, is that what you mean?"

"Yes," I said. "That's what I mean. What if?"

He shook his head. "I can't accept that. I know, I know, pain and suffering are part of the flow of things, it's our vision that's screwy. That's fine when you're lying in bed on a summer afternoon reading Lao-tsu. And maybe a few saints and sages in the history of the world could think it was fine whatever happened, but what about the rest of us?" He made a helpless gesture with his hands. "Religion is a remarkable tool. It can enable people to withstand misery, even torture, not to mention all the civilization and works of art that have been shaped by it. Something that powerful obviously has meaning, it's not simply a sham. But to take it at face value—God is great, God is good—I can't do that."

"You find it easier to see God as a screw-up?"

"Absolutely," he said.

"So what's this sense of apology about?"

"Don't you apologize to the other screw-ups in your life?" he asked with a crooked smile. I felt a rush of emotion that frightened me, as if I were on a level plain with everyone, we were jostling one another, I was concerned for them all.

"No," I said. "Actually, yes, of course, but people are different. And anyway, what about those moments when the world does seem just as it should be?"

"Then you're happy. Then you enjoy it."

I was silent for a moment. I was thinking of what he had said: religion as a tool. To what end? "Is it really a question of happiness? Isn't there something else?"

"I'm too old, Gwendolyn, to be looking for anything but happiness."

This remark made me shy. I glanced away, the waiter came to take our order. Duck for Jack, fish for me. Something smooth to slide down my throat. Jack's fingers were holding mine, or rather playing with them—rubbing them, bending them—it was almost erotic and almost funny. Happiness, I thought. The idea stood before me like a mountain I had to scale; even God seemed easier than that. Of course my vision was screwy. It always had been. I remembered how I used to love the sublime—what a distraction it was.

"Sometimes in AA meetings," I said, "I feel like half the people there have an invisible familiar perched on their shoulders, their own little god-thing they pray to with the simpleminded devotion one imagines in the medieval peasantry. I mean their techniques are like those of children beseeching their parents to please let them stay up late, please buy them a bicycle—" I broke off. Nobody was asking me to believe in such a creature. I couldn't help wanting one though. Some foxlike, catlike beast with green hypnotic eyes.

"Well, what do you expect? The medieval peasantry probably had a more sophisticated concept of God than most of us. This is America. We're used to Santa Claus and Ronald Reagan."

"It's not that I couldn't get into the whole trip. I could. But my tendencies have always been toward magic and propitiation. Would I end up enlightened or like that poor murderer who was getting his marching orders from a dog?"

"Yes, you'll have to be careful, especially in your line of work. Don't take any lip from German shepherds." He grinned, I made a face. But I didn't mind his mockery, it was even comforting.

"In AA they say, 'God as you understand him.' But what if you don't have the faintest idea? You need some kind of image to focus on, some direction . . . I mean, we're probably too sophisticated in that sense. There's too much to choose from." Christian guilt, for example. Hindu laissez-faire. Pagan self-indulgence.

"I think the idea is it chooses you."

He was smiling at me warmly, but he let go of my fingers to butter a slice of bread. Too old, he had said. I was too young. I felt about fifteen. That's something nobody on the outside understands, how a thirty-year-old who grew up on booze, who learned everything while drinking, reverts inevitably, swiftly, to her adolescence. As if a spell had been lifted, she wakes up in a daze. The glamour and the tricks dissolve, "experience" is annulled. There must be some advantage to this, I thought. Doesn't everybody wish they could go back and do it right?

Some of the big AA meetings, the ones where all the black-jacketed young artists go, are just like high school. The tough guys against the wall with their shades, the bossy girls involved in everything, the breakdowns and love affairs, the gossip and routine. Except that we choose to be there and teach each other. Except that there are none of those incomprehensible straight types.

I brushed aside a strand of hair. "I guess I don't trust it to choose me. I mean, I've always abandoned myself to fate and where has it gotten me? I can't afford to make any more mistakes, I've wasted so much time, my whole life—" I sighed, knowing I was again mistaken. As if I had a choice. But I was so twisted up with anxiety. The sight of Jack's glass on the table did it to me, the sight of his curious eyes. I would be naked in bed with him later.

I was frozen before these images of pleasure, before the whole idea of pleasure, even as I smiled, moved so my plate could be put in front of me, began to eat, and watched him eat. I felt cut off. Doubtful that I was alive, in the strict sense. Certainly unable to trust in any soaring intuition, any hope of the flow of things. (It's wine that flows. Pours at the next table, leaping into the glass, there to shimmer and excite—me, itself, the whole thirsty world.)

" 'My whole life,' " Jack mimicked, shaking his head. "God, I love it when babies not even thirty talk about how they've wasted their 'whole life.' It makes me feel like, hey, why should I be jealous? They've got their youth and it's shit to them. Why should I worry that maybe they're having more fun? Maybe they'll accomplish more." He was looking at me slyly while forking food into his mouth, his eyes glowing.

I felt wounded for a moment, then suddenly not so. Not anxious either. Not anxious at all. He was fifty; he expected me to be young.

I began to laugh. "You're so full of shit," I said tenderly.

"Me? What do you mean?"

"You are. And you've got duck feathers all over you."

"Honey, they plucked this duck. That much I know." He wiped his mouth. "What do you mean, duck feathers?"

His bewilderment made me laugh harder. I put my head down on the table and giggled. What I meant was that it all seemed so simple, so pure and uncomplicated. Eating his dinner like a wolf with a carcass, eating because he was hungry. I felt as if I were full of helium, all my insides dancing. Jack was shaking his head as I lay my cheek on the white cloth and trembled.

"I can see why you don't drink. You don't need to. Would you like to explain? I guess there's some sort of esoteric significance I missed . . . duck feathers? Gwen?"

"It's nothing," I gasped. "I can't explain . . . you were eating that duck. . . ." I started giggling again, then I straightened up and said, "I like a man who can make me laugh."

"Glad to be of service, miss." He picked up his fork and took a bite. "Is that what you like? God, you're easy to please. Talk about a cheap date. You can come over and watch me eat breakfast every morning. I'm great with fried eggs. Pork and beans, that's another good one. Hotdogs—"

"Stop," I said; I was trying to eat too.

But he kept on. "Is this what you call an alcoholic flashback? Or is it maybe that 'something else' you mentioned earlier? When do you start talking in tongues?" His voice was nudging me, buffeting me this way and that, each sentence like a soft blow, the imprint left on my flesh. Like wrestling at the playground, I used to do that with boys, hot, sweaty ten-year-olds pinning my arms behind my back. They weren't any stronger than I was then; I could leap up and roll them over.

Jack's eyes were on mine, shining, he would not look away. Simpler? I thought. I don't know the half of it.

"I'm not hungry anymore," I said, "Could we go home?"

Now it was his turn to laugh. I watched him contentedly; any slight offense he had taken at my giggles had passed.

"You're certainly jumping from topic to topic," he said after a moment. "You're wasting your life, you're crazy about the way I eat, and you want to go to bed." He let his eyes drop down from mine, slowly past my mouth and neck and breasts. I felt my nipples stiffen. "Well, it makes a certain amount of sense."

He paused. I ate an olive. I didn't want to go to bed exactly; I wanted to cavort with him in treetops. How constrained we are in this life.

"I'll ask for the check."

I nodded, and leaned into the corner of the booth, he continued eating. My mind was drifting, I was afraid I'd get too giddy. I was pierced by a memory that was gone before I knew what it was. I felt separate suddenly. I looked at Jack.

His plate was clean. He was smiling at me continuously like one of those statues of the Buddha at the Met. I shaped my mouth into a kiss. He looked as if he were about to grab me across the table. I felt like sliding beneath it and going to work between his legs.

The waiter loomed above us, friendly and bearded. Such a cozy place, the Astray Café. "We don't want any dessert," I told him. "It's too bad, it's so nice here, but we have to go."

"You'll be back."

Jack paid the bill with a credit card. It seems so anomalous. Money, banks, the whole financial structure of his life that supported this giggling in restaurants. And how did he earn his money? Giggling at his typewriter, no doubt.

The waiter bid us good night as did the bartender and the owner and several of the bar customers. I wasn't surprised, I was sure we gave off a glow. The poor world, I thought, that couldn't be us. But what if we were all part of the same thing? One race, one organism, all separation mere illusion. Who was starving then, who was dying? I didn't want it to be me. I wanted all my privileges, every one. I shivered with dread.

Out on the street Jack took my arm. I nestled in close, the smell of his body made me happy, so happy I was sad. Sad because my moods change so fast. I know there's no center, no place where I could invite a man to sit down and stay. I used to think of my mind as an underground queendom, full of birds with breasts of fire and creeping dark-leaved ivy. It was I who moved, room to room, garden to chasm; but I don't see it like that anymore. I don't know what moves, but it's not me. On the other hand, I don't stay still.

We were walking down West Fourth Street, which was lit up like a movie set. Ever since they started filming again in Manhattan, the neighborhoods have grown more and more photogenic. "Where are we going?" Jack asked.

"To your place," I said.

"Why not to yours?"

"Can't we go to yours? My apartment's not that great."

He hesitated. I felt a leap of panic that we might have to discuss his wife. I had no interest. She wasn't there. Oh, Gwen, I said to myself, the woman exists. Has a name, a presence. A very strong presence. I could picture her but not in life. She was frozen in about six feet of clear plastic, soundlessly, scentlessly, arriving on wheels when summoned by that syllable "She."

"I guess I might as well take you home with me," he said. "What's the difference?"

We walked the several blocks without speaking. He lived right off Washington Square, near the park where Lucy and I used to idle in our youth, whole weekends spent getting away from our mother. The buildings are old, circa 1830, and were among the prettiest in the village. We shook off two black men offering "smoke," and they grinned at Jack and spread their hands, as if it were only a greeting after all.

"I can't help it, I like those guys," he said, unlocking his front door.

I followed him up the stairs of the four-story brownstone. The building was well kept, its pale grey carpet as clean and soft as the fur of a cat. No sound came from the closed doors as we passed, and the only smell in the halls was a faint one of chocolate.

He stopped at a door on the second floor and I was surprised by an urge to keep climbing. There's a story by Violette Leduc in which the lovers rent a car and make love, their one and only time, during a day-long trip. They have wine, food, a whole picnic, and the chauffeur does the driving. I love being in motion, I never used to get carsick, I loved getting home and pretending to be asleep so my father would carry me up from the car to the building.

Inside Jack's apartment I immediately felt panicky. He bolted the door, lifted his eyebrows a little. We're here. He looked his age, the flesh wrinkled, and I felt a touch of repulsion. I reached out a hand to stroke where his jaw met his neck. Those warm grooves of skin, with their faint stubble, reassured me; the blood coursed beneath. He seemed to grow warmer under my touch.

Jack put a hand on my back, propelling me forward. We went through a narrow hall lined with bookshelves, living room to the right, thin rugs on wooden floors. He hadn't turned the lights on, the apartment was all in shadow. I could see a kitchen at the end, and a small room next to it, the door ajar, the rounded low back of an office chair. He steered me left, into a bedroom.

A four-poster bed, neatly made up, a bureau, a chair. The room was barren of ornament and for a moment I felt victorious. What kind of marriage was this, such an empty room. Then I realized it was Malcolm's room, cleaned out when he left home. It gave me a strange feeling, as if we were in a hotel, yet the room was redolent of childhood. The sanctuary of your bedroom in your parents' house: the shut door, the fevered solitude.

Jack seemed uneasy too. Because it was Malcolm's room? He took my chin in his hand and kissed me, his lips and tongue active and pressing. He wanted to get this done. I sensed the energy of his resolution and I put my arms around him, feeling at that instant only helpful, but it was such a surprise—his whole body in my embrace.

My hands slid dreamily up and down his back. I drifted away from his kiss to sniff his hair and neck. He smelled like a wild animal, that clean gaminess, but also like soap and cotton; his hair was coarse and oily, it had a powerful, protective scent. He was like a stubborn fighting animal, a badger or a boar grown human and softer, more intelligent and more perplexed. I breathed him in like oxygen; I could feel the soft scurry of my nerves awakening. I opened my mouth, tasted his skin. Salty, sour, bitter, sweet. He reminded me of everything.

Jack's hands were in my hair, plunging through the heavy, wind-tangled mass of it; my skull contracted with pleasure and a touch of dread. Sometimes it frightens me to have my head touched. I kissed him on the mouth again, slid a hand inside his shirt. His belly sucked in, the quiver, the curly hair tickling my palm. "Does that bother you?" he asked, his voice muffled and distant.

"On the contrary."

"I'm too fat."

"I like it."

"Ruth tells me—"

"Shh," I said, running my tongue between his lips.

"Sorry." We stood there for a while, our bodies shifting,

nudging, moving together and apart. I was completely
happy, my hips moving in a drowsy circle, when suddenly I
felt like nothing was happening. Nothing would ever happen. It was all up to me.

I was alarmed. I said, "Enough already. My feet hurt."
Jack stepped away with a small, surprised smile—a formal
smile—and began to undress. I was embarrassed. I said,
"Let me."

My fingers were clumsy with his buttons. It was hard to
get his shirt off. He wasn't helping at all, he was watching
me, I felt more and more awkward. Finally he said, "I could
get used to this kind of treatment. Where have you been all
my life?"

"Don't talk like a B movie, this is our big moment." I
smiled up at him flirtatiously; it was an act; I was outside
myself, not sensual but craving it. I felt as if I were doing
something complicated that would take a long time.

"I'm afraid you'll notice how excited I am." His voice was
soft, its mocking inflection barely veiling the real emotion;
I felt dreamy again, pulled back into the flesh.

"It would be hard not to." Naked he was lordly and well
fleshed, like Rodin's Balzac—the only statue of a male nude
that remains triumphantly carnal.

"I have to get these clothes off you." he said.

I glanced away, holding my excitement, and stood still for
his defter ministrations.

"I once knew a guy," he continued conversationally, "my
old roommate in fact, he picked up a woman in a dive, they
went out to her car and guess what, she wasn't a woman at
all." He unclasped my bra, I loved the ripple of his fingers
on my spine.

"You're worried about that, are you?"

"Oh, I'm always worried." I knew what he meant.

I was worried too. Even as we joked, as his hands uncovered and fondled each part of my body, each caress making me greedy for the next more intimate one, I was nervous. I hadn't had sex in so long, and the last how many times I was drunk and thrashing in the labor of intoxicated fantasy. In drunkenness men were both rough flesh and abstract entities, the act producing the merest flicker of male-female contact, like a tea-dance in the brain. Unsatisfying but, in a perverse way, a pleasure. Sex, reduced to fragments, takes on the charm of art, of an artform whose practitioners are long gone in the past. Its impact is nostalgic, even in the midst of the tedious dangers. (My last nights with Lenny — weeks, months — I often got hurt in bed. He would ask me to move and I'd comply slowly, trying to keep my balance, always losing it. I could never tell when my head was going to slam against the wall or my body, trying to turn over, simply kept going until it hit the floor. Lenny thought he could prevent such accidents and sometimes he did, one arm holding me back from a fall, but I tended to dissolve in unexpected places.)

Jack leaned me back on the bed and I wanted to slide away. Off the other side, out the door. How do people stand all the newness at once? No ease-in, no daze, no drunken certainty that life is simple or, if not simple, at least pointless. Instead — this big warm creature, his penis against his thigh like a log submerged in the water. That slight swaying motion and the mossy tendrils.

I tried to hurry him inside me, as if before a storm. He refused to be hurried. I could hardly fault his attitude. We had come here for the purposes of pleasure, why not do it thoroughly? But I was afraid I would lose desire, would forget the trick of it, that, as he continued in his methodical, gloating devotions, I would fall into a mood where his body looked obscene or frightful. Yet I had no choice but to trust him, or trust what had led me to him; as he switched on the light by the bed (how I craved darkness) I uttered a prayer: Let me be here. If you ask for what you have, it's surprising what can happen.

I lay in a pool of light like a specimen on a table. All the guilt of my drinking days rushed up at me—not a specimen but a suspect, here for interrogation. Then he said, "That's too bright, isn't it," and turned off the light. The dark flowed over me like a tongue.

I scissored my legs around him, pushed down on his back with my hands. "My, you're impatient," he whispered. I pushed harder, he entered with a grunt. That sound and the clasp of him, as I tightened and arched up, swept aside all my defenses; I fell into sex, giddy and gone. After a while, in mockery of my twisting, my giggly rapture, he said, "You know, you should be the one on top, you're the young one."

"But you're the man. That's what my mother taught me. Men open doors, take your coat, and do all the hard physical work."

"Yeah? And what do women do?"

"Women say, 'Oh, you do it so well! You're so strong! Do it again!'"

He grinned and I laughed, we fucked harder and faster, my laughter not stopping until it was knocked out of my throat. O love, I thought, let me forget myself—just before we regained our solitary selves.

MARGARET DIEHL

I looked over at Jack. He had a faint smile on his face; his body was mottled with patches of red. Was it supposed to be so enjoyable? Where was the high drama of the past, the cruel, casual post-coital phrase, like a key locking in the tenderness? I felt playful and sprawling. I nudged him with my foot. He put his leg over mine. "So, what do you think?" he asked.

"Oh, I think we acquitted ourselves admirably."

"What a way to put it. Yeah." He got out of bed, walked over to where his pants lay in a heap on the floor, fished out a crumpled pack of Camels, and lit one. "I suppose there are grounds for acquittal. Your honor, let me bring into evidence her breasts. Her smile."

I was silent, I didn't know how to respond. I could imagine, almost as if he were transmitting the pictures, Jack and Ruth unhappy in bed. The horrible sounds of sex when you don't like your partner.

"Sorry," he said. "Can I get you anything? Something to drink? Ice cream?"

"Do you have chocolate?"

"Ben and Jerry's chocolate chocolate chunk."

"Perfect."

While he was getting the ice cream, I tried to explore my new happiness. I tried to inhabit all of it instead of merely skittering around the edges, but some wiser part of me would not allow this. I floated through it to the open window and was distracted—the sound of traffic outside, the lacy trees in the park, the pad of Jack's feet coming closer.

"Don't lean out the window like that, Gwen. It scares me."

"I'm not going to jump."

"Well, Christ, I didn't think you were. You better not."

He sat down beside me, I couldn't stop touching him. His arms were both muscular and soft, his shoulders broad and freckled. His belly was that solid oval men have, so different from the lower wavelike curl of a woman's stomach.

I'd never made love to a man his age. I was surprised at how tough the skin was, even in its softness, at how the balls drooped like breasts, sagging down toward the earth. "Your ice cream's going to melt," he said.

"You taste better."

After a pause he said, "You don't have to try so hard." I stopped what I was doing and lay down on my back, looking at the ceiling. "I mean, you've already won me over."

"I'm not trying," I said. "This is what I do for fun." He lay down beside me and threw an arm across my chest. I wanted to shrug it off.

"Tell me something," he said.

"What?"

"Anything."

"No, you tell me."

There was a silence. I thought of the length of his life, the complexity of his situation. The years lived, the books written, the wedding anniversaries celebrated. "What do you want to know?" he asked.

"Where you grew up."

"San Francisco."

"Really?"

"You like that? Yeah, I'm a Californian. Born and raised in North Beach above an Italian restaurant. There wasn't much furniture and the meals were sketchy but it always smelled fantastic."

"Why were the meals sketchy? Were you poor?"

"No, Gwendolyn, I wasn't poor," he replied as if I were accusing him of something. "My mother didn't like to cook. Neither of them liked to eat. They lived on cigarettes and coffee and things they grabbed off other people's plates. We went to a lot of low-rent parties," he added.

"What did they do?"

"They were DJs on competing radio stations," he said with a smirk. "Naturally I had to move away as soon as I could, I heard their voices every time I turned on the radio."

"There are certain nightmare possibilities in that."

"Absolutely. I always wanted to put it in a book but it seemed somewhat tame beside—"

"*Werewolves on Acid.*"

"You read that one?"

"I don't think it was your best." Nineteen sixty-nine. The werewolves make the scene and are feted for their monstrosity. The silly beasts think LSD might cure the split in their nature, but no one will give it to them, the freaks prefer them as they are.

After a pause he said, "Yeah, the happy days of childhood. My mother had a talk show. I used to sit at her feet, playing with my toys. Advice to the lovelorn, the impotent, the miserable. You know, today on those shows they always mention professional help. My mother would prescribe long periods of solitude. She was never alone herself but she loved to tell other people to get away from it all, into themselves, out in nature; she banished them. God help those who listened to her. Her name was Ida. 'Ida like cigarette,' she'd say and I'd run get it for her. 'I have a pet dwarf who lights my cigarettes for me,' she told her audience; she thought it was a cute thing to say . . . Anyway," he continued, his voice charged up with cheerfulness, "I left home when I was seventeen, hit the road—"

~~I put a hand on his thigh. "Am I allowed to touch you yet?~~ Or does that qualify as trying too hard?"

He clutched my shoulder fiercely and pulled me on top of him. I felt a brief dizziness at the speed of the embrace. "Promise me, Gwendolyn, you'll never pay attention when I talk like that."

"Somehow," I said between kisses, "I don't think I'll have to. I don't think you'll do it again."

We both found it difficult to sleep that night. Every time I dropped off I woke up almost immediately. A strange bed—where? Not, In what house? but, Where in the wide world? This bed with its high headboard and footboard was like a small planet, its warm sheets the fertile ground between tall forests, sequoias whose roots met and knotted beneath me. Then I'd suddenly remember: Jack! What to do?—as if there were an alligator in my bed. I'd listen to his breathing, sense the whole length of him. Strange, strange (I was so close to him already, he seemed stranger than anyone else).

"Gwendolyn, are you awake?" A voice in the darkness like a rope let down.

"I'm here."

"I can't sleep."

A fond and plaintive voice. There was a thrill in hearing that plaintiveness from him: There are no adults, only big people. As a child I had asked my mother, When I'm grown up, what clothes will I wear? She said, You'll wear the clothes you have. But I wouldn't have any at first. She didn't understand: I thought it would happen overnight, I would come down big to breakfast in a little tiny dress.

"What are you thinking about?" he asked.

"This bed is like a ship we could sail away."

"Let's." His hand clasped mine, I felt the warmth shoot back and forth between us. "Where shall we go?"

"Ireland."

"Why?"

"I've never been there for some reason. I've always wanted to go."

"Okay."

"We'll live in a castle, you can write books."

"And I won't have to pay any income tax," he said. "In Ireland, bless their hearts, they don't tax writers."

"That settles it," I said, and I almost thought it did. We were big people, we could do whatever we pleased.

I woke up again, it was not quite dawn. The same sequence of emotions: Where am I? Here. With whom? With him. I felt the weirdness of all my assumptions and desires about life, and knew that what I was, this mere slip of an I, was only barely and arbitrarily connected to them all. I was like a seed floating between these sheets, the kind of seed that can lie dormant thousands of years.

4

I woke up the next morning to find Jack at the typewriter, wearing the same shirt he'd had on the night before, his hair uncombed, smoking a Camel. I stood in the doorway, watching. What I would like to do today, I thought, is buy things for our bedroom. Go uptown to Bergdorf's, wander through their quiet, lovely housewares department, buy maroon and indigo pillows, an antique mirror, a carved wooden box for his cigarettes and matches. New sheets and a satin quilt the color of oyster shells. I would paint a full-length portrait of him, naked, a three-quarters view, standing against a backdrop of billowing drapes. I could look at the painting while he was working. And sketches of his feet and hands — and low upholstered stools — and a new carpet, of course, twined with birds and beasts and flowers, and symbols of the Orient.

But of course this was not my apartment. That was the charm of it, I wanted entrée into his life. If only she were dead, I thought, embalmed in a case. "Ruth," he would say, "my deceased wife." And I would look at that clever wrinkled yellowish face and feel a distant pity, curiosity, interest. If she were dead, how young I would feel.

I watched Jack type. I love your back, I thought. Broad, slumped, clothed in a dingy red, like a wall I could climb on top of, like a brick wall baked in the sun. But so much warmer than a wall. I took his shirt off in memory. I had counted his freckles last night, running my fingers over the soft pouches of fat where he was most ticklish, the little hoardings of heat; I had even squeezed his blackheads, which embarrassed him so much he begged me to stop. I picked at him and groomed him until he was clean.

"Good morning," I said.

He rose from his chair immediately, came toward me smiling. I felt shy—had we really been to bed? What if I were dreaming this? I had never imagined what I wanted was goodness. For a moment the concept, the quality, the man, seemed almost uncanny. Jack put his hands on both sides of my face. "Hello," he said.

He kissed my lips, my cheeks, my forehead. "Do that again," I said. He outlined my face with kisses. The wet muscle of his tongue smoothed down my eyebrows. He held my nose between his teeth; I felt his breath in my eyes. Seriously, I thought, seriously, how can this be wrong?

You don't think I'm going to talk to you in this condition, do you? said the bored voice of my alleged conscience. What do you take me for, a fool? Hush, I said. Be nice to me.

Jack stepped back, smiling broadly, and I ducked my head. "You're working," I said. "I'll go home."

"You don't want some breakfast first? Eggs, pancakes, oatmeal?"

"No thanks." Guilt was working in me like yeast, I had to get out of here. And he hadn't contradicted me when I said he was working.

"You'll come over tonight."

"If I'm invited."

He looked at me as if I were a half-wit. "Of course you're invited. In fact, I insist. You must come." He put his hands on my shoulders, squeezing until it hurt; I slid an arm down his pants. His penis yawned and stretched, his eyes—which had retained a certain abstraction, even through our kisses, the faraway look of art—began to glow.

"Good-bye," I said, disentangling myself.

"Bitch," he replied, but turned away easily enough. I watched him walk like a purposeful beaver back into his room.

I ran down the stairs feeling excited and young. It's fun to be sober, I thought, I get to do everything all over again.

I went to a meeting, to a small room in the West Village, not a church or community center but what could have been a storefront, a room occupied by my kind most of the day. The neighbors complain about us, how we loiter on the sidewalks. Old alkies in cheap coats smoking their cigarettes down to the ends, tired girls in leather miniskirts, motherly women with bags of knitting, AIDS patients and truck drivers and bar-tending would-be actors. I took a seat in the back, speaking to no one.

The chairman turned out the lights, except for the one that shone from behind the speaker's chair. "I had my first drink at the age of nine, my Polish grandfather's homemade beer . . ."

Seek a spiritual awakening, Carl Jung once said to a friend of Bill Wilson's, setting in motion the chain of events that landed me here. I like to think of them, wise Carl and brave Bill, the mystical doctor and the dipsomaniac stockbroker, strolling side by side, discoursing in Heaven:

"That was a good suggestion you made, Carl."

"And you certainly ran with it, Bill. I'm impressed."

"Thanks, but the credit has to go to my higher power. You know I could do nothing on my own."

"Granted. Have you met the guy yet?"

"No, have you?"

I didn't know what a spiritual awakening was. When I was younger I felt spiritual—or magical as I would have put it. It wasn't a matter of faith or need. I had a gift in those days, in my late adolescence. Just a little trick of focusing my attention; whatever I looked at was beautiful, in the most inclusive sense of the word. The street, the subway, the bathroom linoleum, revealed the harmony of the universe with a willingness I found both flattering and disturbing. The mockery that all this harmony was outside! Leaves brilliantly alien against the sky, their pale new green faintly shadowed with soot.

I could escape into beauty if I chose. Wherever I was and even if I was most unhappy, I could do the trick with my eyes and exist for a minute or five minutes in a world utterly lovely. I could do it in school, or when I was being spoken to. When I did it in what I considered its proper place—in the country, alone, during my first year of college—the reality of another world became so vivid, and the feeling of knowing in such a way, beyond reason, became so consuming, that I often thought I was being offered a choice. This or the other. The world or the World.

It became unbearable because I couldn't choose. Because I couldn't speak of it. I certainly couldn't paint it, which I thought might be what I was supposed to do. My gorgeous cloudy canvases reflected an utter blankness. Finally I simply abandoned it, or it abandoned me. For a long time I didn't miss it; what was there to miss? There had been nobody there but me. You would expect, wouldn't you, in such harmony, company?

It had taken me months in AA to get past the clubbiness. Past the slogans and hand-holding, the hundred little customs. Now I scarcely noticed these things and when I did I admired how they worked. Threatening on one level, they reassured on another: nothing was too intellectual here, nothing required sophistication of heart or mind. And as much as I loved it when such sophistication arose, I could see it had to be the exception, not the rule. This was the place where we came to find the healing of like with like. We needed nothing above us that was not also below us, nothing that did not circulate in every drunkard's veins.

Where else can you go to hear the real story of people's lives? The honesty surpassed anything I had ever heard. Here were all the horrible parents, the child setting forth, the transformation into power; the battles and losses and periods in hiding; the weird twists of fate; the awful instant when the balance swings to life or death. Who imagines other people are so full of themselves?

"I wasn't going to drink that Christmas . . . There wasn't any booze in the house. At noon I bundled the children up and drove them to an Italian restaurant, pretending it would be a treat. They drank Cokes all afternoon, I kept urging them to get ice cream, until Andrew, my eldest, called his father from the pay phone. I didn't realize this until my ex-husband, his new wife in tow, came charging into the room. He started yelling at me. All the waiters were watching, I was taking quick gulps of my piña colada, I was afraid I wouldn't have time to finish it. The children were crying. Bill—my ex-husband—yanked me into his car and drove me home . . . took the kids. Later I swallowed all my sleeping pills. At the emergency room they told me, 'You come in here one more time, lady, we ain't doing a thing.'"

The woman speaking was radiant, tall and blond, in a white cashmere sweater. Gold clip earrings, a gold lion's head pendant. She and her daughter were in business together now; they had started a small cosmetics company that was just taking off.

"But that dramatic stuff wasn't the worst. The worst was the day by day loss of interest in life, in other people. The drift. I ascribed it to getting older, to losing my illusions. I thought I knew too much when in fact I was becoming more ignorant."

Yes, I thought. I know. If I had arrested my own drift it was because of these stories, these hypnotic tales repeating and suggesting each other like a contemporary *Thousand and One Nights*. It didn't matter who spoke, I always identified. I listened greedily, remembering myself at ten or twelve thinking there was a secret everyone knew but me. That English was not a language but a code. That I certainly wasn't normal, and possibly not human. That fear, never given up so much as built on top of, was dissolving now, was breaking up like concrete when the earth pushes through. The fragments were still there, great piles of rubble, but no longer continuous, no longer impermeable.

What I wanted to do now was speak. Raise my hand as the others did, pour out my quota of joy and woe. To say to the blond woman that I admired her strength, to say that I had been to a wedding recently and fiercely craved a drink. To say I was in love and didn't know what to do.

But as hungrily as I listened, I couldn't speak. It was simply beyond me, an impossible behavior. I imagined my mouth forming the words and the air became hard; it was like the white hull of a ship that would smack me underwater. I felt cold, empty inside, yet with a skin so abnormally sensitive, an envelope so vulnerable, one glance could pierce it. To know this wouldn't happen made no difference at all. I had to drop the possibility and drop the pain of that. If I focused on the pain I would become resentful, I would stay away from the rooms. That had happened in the beginning. I told myself: Speak or else. And the "or else" was no meetings for days, the desire to drink inevitably returning, looming and protean, altering the chemistry of my thought. What you want is what matters. What you want is what you need. Oh, my old friends, the lively bottles with their sentimental songs and salesmen's pitches.

Only here could I remember the taste of the genuine, a taste I was always in danger of forgetting. A taste I craved yet at the same time had to acquire. It was like nothing else I had ever done, it was unremittingly confusing, and I needed help. I knew that. But the thought of it. The contact, the response. The phone numbers, the suggestions. The insuck to a deeper, more transforming embrace. Like jumping down a well; I couldn't do it. I couldn't speak. Who would answer me, would anyone, what words would they say.

Jack called me at ten. "What are you doing over there, you're supposed to be here?"

"Okay."

"You were waiting for me to call. I didn't make myself clear enough this morning?" His voice startled me with its warmth and familiarity; already, in a dozen hours, I had sunk back into a solitude that was more physical than anything else. It felt as if my voice or spirit had to travel a long way out to the boundary of common discourse. A direction, as always, against the drift of my nature. Yet I was so excited to hear him! It was like finding the right color for a painting that had long been incomplete: that reddish brown, that earth afire, which was the color of no one of his features but which I associated with him, made all my blues and hidden green work; implied also, I thought, a violet pink somewhere . . . .

"So say something," he said.

"I'll be there as soon as I can. I have to get dressed."

"Oh, don't get dressed. Let me come over there. Five minutes."

"No."

"Why not?"

"I want to come to your place. I want to get dressed. You'll like it," I promised, suddenly heavy with lust. I wanted a dress made of pounds of coarse red lace, full skirted, dragging on the ground. I had nothing like that . . . .

"Yeah? Okay," he said, "but hurry. Christ, Gwen, I've been waiting since six with a hard-on."

"Tell me about it."

He paused. "No. I'll see you soon." He hung up.

I took my time getting dressed. First the perfume — *Paris* by Saint Laurent. *Paris* for the name and for its spicy sweaty scent. It smells like a perfume that's already been worn by a woman so beautiful you prefer her castoffs to something new. Then my Venezuelan pearls and my coral lipstick. My high-heeled sandals with their patent leather glow. I got carried away with the luxury of it all, I walked around, brushing my hair, feet angled high, until I felt entirely gorgeous.

The phone rang again. Jack. "What?" I said.

"I don't believe you're really coming. You're one of those snake-women who lure men with sex and then never return, leaving us to die of longing."

I laughed. "Don't worry, I'll revive you." What was the rush? Anticipation surrounded me, pierced me like a ghost breaking through into life, the air itself throbbing as if bent and twisted by kicking legs. I summoned it, called it forth, and my blood pressure rose. The painting on the easel trembled as if the animal sensed, as dogs do, the presence of spirit. It was only desire. Only desire!

Jack was complaining again. "Shut up, honey," I said, and put the phone down. I reached his apartment out of breath. He was standing in the doorway.

He put his hands on my shoulders. The space defined by his arms and chest was a jar I could crawl into, helped by his impatient fingers, closed by the lid of his jaw that sank with amorous murmurs into my hair.

Then he pushed me away and gave me a cool look. "Aren't you the babe from last night? I ordered a brunette this time, an Oriental."

I stuck my tongue out at him, he stuck his out at me. The two organs met and we stood like that for a moment, just the tips of our tongues touching. Then he sucked his back. "Weird. I haven't done that since third grade."

"Get a lot of work done today?" I asked.

"Who cares? That dress isn't bad but I was expecting something more extreme." I took it off. I had on some underwear Lenny had bought me. Jack started to laugh; he doubled over and staggered backward to the couch. "You must have gotten that in California," he gasped.

"Cute, isn't it? It's awfully hot though, do you mind if I take it off?"

"Please."

I stripped, threw the bra at his head and sat next to him, slinging my legs over his lap. As soon as we were in contact the jokey mood dissolved. I felt chilly in my nakedness and snuggled closer. He put his arms around me again and kissed me; we sat for a long time just kissing, then stumbled into Malcolm's bedroom.

We began, perhaps, like any new-made couple, urgency and invention within the realm of the ordinary, the tender-hot, sweet-sad dichotomy of sex. Imperceptibly we went deeper. It was all Jack's doing, I thought; he told me it was all mine. Certainly laughter was important—after a round of one of those jokes that get better the further you take them from the source, we both felt laid open, and the next caress or question, the next courteous peculiar request, unlocked more emotion than we knew we had. It rose like the tide and we built no dikes; in myself I was amazed at this lack of obstruction, in Jack that such feeling was there. His humor and ardor merged into a single quality that crackled through him like the blood shining brightly beneath his skin.

I felt like we'd been flung together into the half-lit windy dark of the underworld we were made of, as if our flesh were pleased into spirit, and our spirits manufacturing the raw material of lust. I'd never had an experience even remotely like it.

I told Jack how all my fears shade into desire, and he replied that you fear what you want and the wanting is the key. I lay inside my wanting as if in a spring flower bed, cool and shivery and lovely, the lighted house across the lawn. He had such a force, coming to get me. I wanted to hide and be found. He wanted to be adored.

But then it was over. Quite suddenly the mood changed. Each orgasm, each pause, had been leading into a deeper place; now we were outside again. It felt like a withdrawal of life.

Jack lay beside me, sweaty and worn; as I looked at him, I grew more and more anxious, as if I would die without delight. Why couldn't I have any more?

"Holy shit," he said, hauling himself into a sitting position and reaching for a cigarette, "I think we've just had what's called a religious experience." He sounded amused and curious; I could hear his brain click over. "Wouldn't you say so, Gwen? I think we've discovered the sexual route to salvation to which many are called, and few chosen." He chuckled, and told me a story or two about his old roommate; I thought he looked like a devil sitting there with his belly and his bushy black hair, smoke drifting up from his grin.

I didn't say anything. I couldn't tell if he was making fun or not. I didn't see how he could be, but in my anxiety nothing was sure. And as he continued in his expansive mode, talking about tantric yoga and sixties misadventures, I began to feel very much alone, and even humiliated. What I had let him do—and I knew it was wrong to put it that way, yet it felt righteous—was unnatural to me, it wounded my delicate equilibrium.

I rolled over to face the window. That act, which I intended as a sort of communication, a mild sulk demanding solace, sent me over the edge into panic; I didn't know where I was or who was behind me, I couldn't move. Terror held me fast, my heart rate lowered; this was eternity, the cold behind the veil.

Jack dropped a meaty hand on my hip and rolled me over. I followed his spin inertly. He said, "Okay, what's the matter?" I looked up at him imploringly. He still reminded me of a devil. It was only my craziness, of course, which I couldn't get away from. How could I possibly explain what the matter was to Jack?

"Okay, be a sphinx," he said. "Keep all your thoughts to yourself, see if I care. O mysterious lady with the auburn hair." He ran his fingers through that hair, probing my skull as if looking for the spot that would open the secret door. I grew agitated, unnerved by the pulsing electrical energy of those fingers.

"Don't," I said.

"Don't what?"

"Don't stick your fingers in my head."

He laughed. "He stuck in his thumb, and pulled out a plum, and said—"

"What an asshole am I."

Jack was silent. I'm a bitch, it's my nature, I can't help it. I listened to the echo of my words: a shivery shameful thrill. But everybody does this, I thought. He would be nasty now, I would reply. These kinds of conversations played themselves out like rope, then you climbed down. Of course there were aftereffects.

He remained silent, I felt panicky again. I glanced at him out of the corner of my eye. His face was immobile, his mouth as if carved shut, the eyes focused on the ceiling. I stared at his nose, thick and shapeless, his least interesting feature, it seemed less accusing than the rest. O Nose, I thought, O Nose. He turned his head solemnly and looked at me. I gazed back, suspended, and he sighed. "What's the matter?" he said.

I replied a little sulkily, a little haltingly. "I just can't stand that it's over. You know, the way we felt—"

"Oh, boy," he said, "you're depressed because it's over? I know you've been brought up with every privilege, fancy schools and silver spoons"—his voice was taut with suppressed violence—"but don't tell me the rich fuck like this every night. I swear I'll blow my brains out. This *is* a rare experience, isn't it? It doesn't happen every day? Don't tell me I'm wrong, please. I'm sitting here feeling on top of the world"—his voice was ragged now, I followed every thread of it—"I can't hardly believe it, and you're sad because it's over. It ain't over, honey. It's just begun." By the last three or four words he managed to sound as perhaps he meant to sound all along—simply amused; I was amazed, my anxiety had melted away to nothing. Because he got angry at me, I wondered, or because he was right. I felt blown clean by a strong wind.

"I love you more than anything on earth," I announced.

Jack was startled; his face changed several times, then settled into a subdued wariness. "Gwen, you shouldn't say things like that."

"Why not?"

"Somebody might believe you." His voice was light and uneasy.

"You think it's not true?"

"I didn't say that. I don't know whether it's true or not but it's dangerous."

"What's life without risk?"

He sighed theatrically. "Paradise."

"Which, as you may recall"—I was heavily sarcastic— "comes after death."

"Don't tell me you believe in that too," he lashed out from a safe distance; his head was angled away from me, yet our feet were still touching. His big foot lay heavily on mine; it looked, I thought, like an uprooted tree stump.

"I'm not sure whether I do or not. The idea that there's nothing afterward, a complete wipe-out, is just too attractive for me to trust, you know?"

"No, I don't know. Gwen, Gwen, what are we going to do with you?"

"You're pretty weird yourself, you aged pleasure-monger."

He began to laugh. "You're sad because our bliss is all too short, but you worry that death won't put an end to it. Do you think you make any sense?"

"So what do you think?"

"About what?"

"About everything." But it's over, I thought, our exquisite, remarkable, unreachable hour. I doubted we'd ever have one like it again.

"I have a little trick. I don't think about everything. I think about one thing at a time."

"Yes?"

"Right now what I'm thinking about is going to sleep."

I didn't want to go to sleep. I was afraid to go to sleep. Two nights had passed already; how many did we have? Three weeks, six weeks, a warm pocket of time. Did he have any idea how precious it was? Nobody around. As if nobody else even existed. I glanced at him as if he could stop it somehow. Prevent the night from advancing.

"Tell me," I said.

"What?"

"What your novel's about."

"Oh, right, you're one of my fans, aren't you?"

"I'm definitely one of your fans."

"I must know what that letter said."

"It said: Dear Mr. Price, I love your books, you look so cute in your pictures, can I come fuck you? Sincerely, etcetera."

"I've never put my picture on my books. The first dozen came out in paperback and then I thought, what the hell, who wants to look at this mug."

"You don't look pretty when you frown," I said.

He laughed a little, rolled over closer. "You embarrass me."

"You'll get used to it."

"Maybe. Maybe I will. So you want to know what my novel's about?"

"I asked."

"Sometimes women ask these things and then you see them politely covering a yawn."

"The eight million women you have in and out of this room?"

"No, the eight million women I meet at cocktail parties."

"Seriously," I said, "how often do you commit adultery?"

"Not often enough to be good at it."

"Which means?"

"Which means once before when I was drunk in Chicago. I don't even remember her name."

"What do you mean, remember. You probably never asked."

"Well, I believe I did. It seems likely."

"Was it fun?"

"I don't know. I guess so. Of course it was fun."

"Okay," I said. "Shoot."

Jack's novel was an ecological horror story. Everything we've been predicting for twenty years comes true: drought, famine, disease, the extinction of species. He was enthusiastic, describing with relish the way things went wrong, human error compounded by nature's chain reactions. It was a sort of a "for want of a nail" story, each mistake leading inevitably to the next. The hero, who seemed at the start an ordinary guy at the periphery of events, gradually becomes sucked in: his work, his family, his hometown, his old lovers, all involve him in some aspect of the disaster. This was a plot device but it was also thematic. And the story seemed to be, in the end, a curiously hopeful tale.

"So you think this is what's going to happen?" I asked. I don't read the newspapers anymore; everything frightens me. I've quit drinking, so the catastrophes will begin. I know it's silly yet I can't help feeling that the gods want my blood, one way or another.

"Oh, sure. We're not going to get away with this shit. Only lunatics and dopes think we will. But I also believe we'll survive." He paused. "I even want to say it serves us fucking right, though of course the we who are most responsible won't be the ones who suffer."

"In any person guilty of a crime," I said, "there are many selves who had nothing to do with it."

He shot me a glance. "You mean humanity as a kind of super-individual? Yeah, although that seems a little dodgy."

"It's what your book's about."

"Maybe. Maybe. Yeah, you're probably right, that's where it leads, but—" He grinned. "That's probably why Ruth doesn't like it. I'd never really figured it out before. She says it's not dramatic enough. What she means is the villains aren't villainous enough. She thinks," he added ironically, "that science fiction is a wonderful medium of propaganda. It's my job, you see, to reach all those teenage boys who would never listen to her."

"How dull."

"Well, dull . . . I don't know. It's a pretty sharp position. I just don't happen to agree with it."

"I gather she doesn't see humanity as a super-individual?"

"I don't think I do. But Ruth? Are you kidding?"

I remembered the one occasion when I had heard her speak. She was exhorting her mostly youthful audience not to lose what she and her generation had fought for. Her speech was angry, almost hectoring, the sheen of ego so bright I could understand her attraction; it was almost mesmeric, that belief in herself. In social life, of course, she was more politic.

"So what about Ruth?" I asked. In the silence I was aware of how late it had grown. The streets outside were quiet. Even the drunks and the drug addicts were sleeping.

"What about her?" He pulled the sheet over his legs.

I waited. "Never mind," I said.

5

The year I was twelve, when my parents got divorced, my mother, Lucy, and I lived on Seventy-fourth Street while my father lived in Brooklyn. It was strange and claustrophobic not having him in the apartment. My mother was suddenly brisk. She picked us up at school and took us on shopping sprees.

I knew what I wanted to buy: a black turtleneck, a yellow vinyl miniskirt, shocking pink tights and boots. My mother dressed us in pleated wool skirts and penny loafers, in crisp white blouses with Peter Pan collars. This was no surprise, but I had never felt so physically the desire to wear beautiful clothing. My legs craved fishnets, I adored the smell of leather. Most of all I needed color. Purple was the hue of royalty and magicians, navy blue of sailors and repressive institutions. Black was sultry, white virginal, yellow thrilling, peach sticky. Pale blue was moronic, maroon ironic.

"You're such a pretty child, Gwen, you don't want to make yourself look ridiculous." I left the shopping bags in the bathroom of Lord and Taylor, refused to go back for them. Lucy had to go, and Lucy had to carry them; I could get away with that much because my mother didn't make scenes in public. In private she took away my ice-cream privileges. How I scorned that device.

"You think I want to get fat like you two?" I asked, as they sat on the couch after dinner with their sundaes. My mother would smile, she thought I was putting on a front. But I didn't care for sweets anymore, I considered them childish. I even skipped dinner sometimes, claiming to be sick, so I could feel that hollow in my stomach, could meditate on it. I stayed up late, with the radio by my pillow, growing lighter and lighter, my energy rising to my head. My brain was as warm with ideas and fantasies, oblique dramas I fleshed out, according to the songs played, and abandoned as soon as the story was clear. My head was alert and my body was dreaming. It dreamed not so simply of being thin—I know what they say about that, that we want to stay children—it dreamed of being malleable, of putting itself at my command. I, the head, would know what to do with it. Sculpt beauty. Find shape. Plumpness here and there, breasts possibly—but I wished to see the designs first, I wanted veto power.

My body got high on its deprivation. The hollowness spread out, pushed against the borders. I sometimes got the feeling I could slip outside. I just had to find the right movement to do it, as when I learned how to wiggle my ears. It wasn't a muscle, though, I knew that; it was more like a direction or a forgetting. I simply had to forget I was trapped, then I would rise up to the ceiling. Up there, in the tranquil folds of my spirit, I would look down at my helpless body and be able to forgive its ineptitude and disgrace.

Our father had visitation rights every other Saturday. Lucy and I would get up early, bathe, eat breakfast, and go down in the elevator, arriving in the lobby by a quarter to ten. We waited in the green leather chairs, smiling at people who smiled at us, and holding our fingers out to the dogs. My feet, in their new oxfords, felt heavy; I was tired from having stayed up so late. (Very late at night I imagined that the voices on the radio were really the voices of vampires, softening me up with their crazy chatter before asking me to open the window and let them in.)

In the lobby, waiting, I imagined the beach. We hadn't gone there this summer as we had every summer before, hadn't rented the house in East Hampton for the customary four weeks in August. I missed the ocean. That infinite palette of blues—indigo, azure, cerulean, ice—the ice-blue of very hot days when the water lies like silk and the waves break modestly on the sand, revealing their insides of scallop shells, periwinkles, and baby crabs. Blue and more distinct blue, the blue of faraway places, the blue of goodness, of saints robes by another, warmer sea.

After we had waited for an hour or so, Philip would send us upstairs. He kept his big, jowly face averted, mumbling how our father must have been held up. Lucy's face would be flushed and trembling, she couldn't believe it, not even when it happened again and again. She stood hunched in the middle of the elevator, walked mechanically back into the apartment. She wouldn't eat lunch, she wouldn't talk to our mother, she simply went to her room and lay on her bed, her face trembling in a weird, silent, tearless way.

I was more detached. I knew what had happened. Our father had woken up with a hangover. It was beyond his control. I felt angry mostly at our mother for the sneer on her lips, the concern with which she asked us what we wanted to do that day. I felt sorry for Lucy. She was just an innocent; it was cruel what could happen to her. Things ought to be arranged so that children were protected.

Our father did show up occasionally. "There's your father," Philip would mumble and Lucy and I would jump out of our chairs.

In the distance his loping walk, his stride so casual, yet his narrow shoulders moving as if parting a sea. Determined, rhythmical. The jacket old, the tie askew. It's Daddy . . . closing my eyes, opening them again. It's Daddy closer. Lucy beside me, not happy as she is supposed to be, takes my hand. I wave at him as if he were going past, as if he were a ship far out on the horizon.

"Well, Philip," he would say. "You can turn these girls over to me now. I'm taking them into custody."

"Good to see you again, sir."

"Oh, I turn up like a bad penny. Can't get rid of me, right, girls?"

We wouldn't answer. We would stare at that thin, wiry man who had winked at us, who was standing right there as if there had never been any doubt. Yes, that's when I was amazed, when I actually saw him. On his feet again, his red hair combed, his nervous knuckly hand held out for my own.

His hand was chilly and I only barely touched it. His face was pale, almost white, and his clothes were beginning to hang on him. Yet he still seemed so large to me, so warm, so over-real, like an actor when you're sitting too close to the stage. There was nothing extraordinary about his manner or his conversation. He talked about his troubles at work, now that he had found another job, of his tiredness, and how he missed seeing us. He made himself sound pathetic, put-upon, a man deprived of the comfort of his daughters, and we listened silently, flattered but not believing.

He apologized for previous Saturdays. "I was sick, girls. You know what I mean. I'm sorry."

"It's okay," we said, and he would relax, his charm resurfacing. He listed all the things we could do. Horseback riding in the park, the Museum of Natural History, the Botanical Gardens. But we practically always went to the zoo.

"What do you say, girls?" he would ask at the end of his list, and I would be ready to take over.

"The zoo, of course. At the Natural History they're all dead!"

"We could go shopping," Lucy suggested, and I was tempted. But I didn't want to buy clothes in front of my father.

"Your mother has all my money."

"She does not," said Lucy. (Our mother would hold up his irregular checks disdainfully. "Whenever he pleases. He expects me to be grateful.")

"We have to go to the zoo, Daddy. I crave snakes."

"Ah, a snake-craving, yes, I know what that means." He raised his eyebrows and laughed up his sleeve—the only gesture remaining from the hilarious afternoon when he acted out for us all the figures of speech we could think of.

"What?" I asked, laughing, holding my own arms close.

"Oh, it's mysterious, my little Gwendolyn, I won't tell you. A snake-craving, yes indeed . . . very hard to resist."

"It's just silly," said Lucy tentatively.

"What do you know?" I said.

"Oh yes, yes, we must go to the zoo," said my father. "*Les Bêtes!*" He drove us there in the VW he had recently bought. My father was a bad driver, which I thought was funny. I sat in the front and he let me shift for him, grinding the gears—"Buy 'em cheap and drive 'em into the ground, that's the ticket."

"I don't want to be driven into the ground," said my literal sister.

"Shut up," I said.

At the zoo, while Lucy looked at the antelope and ate her cotton candy, my father would explain to me how the animals lived in the wild. He was a master at making vivid the world of each individual beast. To sleep on the wing, to be cold-blooded, to lay your eggs in the sand—he let me see that all these things actually happened to creatures who could sense and feel. I loved the singleness and solitude that was yet communal. I felt nostalgic for my evolutionary past, for the woods at twilight with no house yet built, for the cool safety of a stone or the surrounding caress of water. All the shapes of life were mine, had been mine, had been taken away, and I was young enough to feel that what had been taken must be restored. Someday like a lion I would leap on my prey; someday I would bound away from the lion. My body was changing and I thought about that,, but I thought with more excitement about impossible changes. Girl into wolf or hawk or wildcat. I imagined each such transformation with a rush of longing and of hope, as if puberty were a hall from which led many doors.

My father's attitude toward the animals was more abstract. He saw them as symbol and metaphor, though I thought then that this was merely his way of talking. He made them real in his speech yet their reality only mattered in order to create contrast. Man was puny and hairless, man was corrupt, man was the cleverest of all. Zoos reminded him of his inclusion in the human race, which made him feel less trapped in his particular circumstances. Yet it was the animals he pretended to identify with. "That fox has a certain look of me, don't you think?" he would ask, and I would be disturbed and attracted by the question. Was he like a fox? He was red headed, small-boned. He didn't have fox eyes though, his eyes were brown and bulging. They reminded me in a curious way of fists. As if a man had rubbed his eyes with balled-up hands and then, removing the hands, left behind something, an aggressive and blind quality he went through life with and never knew.

A couple of times my father, sensing our attention had wandered, would scale the fence and stick an arm in the tiger's cage. He did it so quickly, rejoined us so fast, he was never caught by tiger or keeper. He would hold the hand out in front of us. "Almost lost it, girls. What do you say to that?" Lucy said nothing but stared openmouthed at our father.

"I want to do it," I said. I wanted to put my hand in the

tiger's cage, I wanted him to snarl at me, attack—then change his mind, lick my fingers, and roll over like a pussycat.

"Well you can't. It's against the rules."

"You did it."

"Rules, Gwendolyn. Rules, rules, rules."

"Le tigre m'aime."

"Le tigre aime tu manger."

"J'aime manger le tigre."

"Oh, you vicious girl, you're going to eat the tiger, are you? Do you know how many tigers are left in the world? Not very many; in twenty years they'll be none. Vanished. Extinct."

"Why?" asked Lucy.

"Because of us, my dear, because of civilization. Marching ever onward. We won't stop until they're all dead—all the animals."

"But what will we eat?" she asked worriedly.

"Christ, just like your sister. Wanting to eat the goddamn tiger."

"No—I meant—you said all the animals—"

"A cow is not an animal. A cow is a meat machine." The idea put him in a bad temper; he lit a cigarette and turned away from us. I pinched Lucy in revenge. She started to cry and my father got irritated. "I never see you kids, why can't you enjoy yourselves?" I was sorry. I didn't want him mad at Lucy, Lucy wasn't to blame. Lucy was my loyal sister who would wake up if I asked her to, when I grew tired of my insomnia, who would go downstairs and fetch me a glass of milk. I'm afraid of the dark, I told her.

If I was mad at Lucy it was only because she made me

nervous. Because she was so unhappy and never pretended otherwise. Because she asked questions like, "Are you really coming next time, Daddy? Are you sure?"

His gaze slid sideways, he stepped back and sighed. "I do my best. You know that. You think it's easy, coming all the way from Brooklyn just to see my own children? Remember how I used to tell you bedtime stories, girls? You liked them, didn't you? Made you laugh and put you right to sleep, right? Why don't you remind your mother of a few things like that?"

"Mom's a bore," I said.

"Your mother's a bore? What a crazy little girl I have. You don't say your mother's a bore." He winked. "But I know what you mean."

After a day with my father, dinner at home was unbearable. My mother asked no questions, she simply watched us, her arms folded over her middle while we chewed our steaks. The food was always perfect, those evenings, and she never ate any of it. For the rest of the night her face loomed, round as a cheese, her eyes intent. When I think of my father in that period I hear his voice—midregister, crackling, full of inflection and emotion—while my mother stays with me as a visual image: the fat spy, the blond bomb, light on her feet.

Did she miss my father? I never asked. She watched a lot of television—*Ben Casey, Dr. Kildare*—and she tried awkwardly to fill his place. She took me to museums which had always been my father's pleasure. We used to go to the Met while my mother took Lucy swimming at her health club.

I loved to look at paintings with my father. I would gaze at the Constables and Turners and imagine entering in.

Once inside you, you could reach all the rest, just as every country in Europe is accessible by car. And there you'd find other travelers like yourself whom you'd recognize by a certain incongruity, a certain restlessness and brilliance of eye. In a band of three or four you'd explore the paintings, crossing invisible bridges with inaudible steps, and feed not off apples or rabbits but light. My father told me stories about the artists. Their crazy outrageous lives, how they managed to get away with it. Even the ones who died young got away with something in his eyes. "They didn't like the world, so they changed it," he said. I imagined them with paintbrushes painting over the trees and sky. Painting the houses and streets and people.

My mother would stop in front of each painting for forty-five seconds, and comment. She always knew something relevant, but it was never aesthetically or imaginatively relevant. It closed the painting like a box, and what was seen, the colors and shapes still there, was only a picture of the real picture, an advertisement.

I began answering her comments with subtle sarcasm, with an overly "bright" and "interesting" remark; it gave me pleasure to know she was not picking up the tenor of my conversation. "What a nice time we had," she would say at day's end; I would smile and agree. It was curious how the paintings, flat and hidden as they were in my mother's presence, seemed also more likely to yawn open. And if they did, I thought, if this one miraculous time they did, of course she would hold me back; she wouldn't even know she was doing it.

I couldn't refuse to go with her. I looked at paintings all that autumn while Lucy played basketball. I went with her and we had a nice time and I asked her to buy me a Cezanne for Christmas. I asked and asked, though I knew she wouldn't. She bought me an expensive coffee-table book of reproductions and I left it on the crosstown bus.

As time passed, visits with our father grew scarcer. I didn't know if he was drinking more or simply had made other plans. He would tell us very little about his life. We never saw his apartment. One of his few friends had told someone who told my mother that he'd caused a fire there; he'd left a cigarette burning and had woken up just in time.

I dreamed about that fire. My father was in the middle of it, laughing. I was shouting at him to get out and he was saying, I'll see you Saturday, you know I always show up. I asked him to take us to his apartment. "It's a dump," he said, "you girls don't want to go there."

"But what's it like? What does it look like?"

"It's a dump."

I wondered if he had a mistress. I thought mistresses lay in bed all day reading magazines; there wouldn't be any place for us to sit down. We would have to stand around awkwardly in our coats while she sprawled in a peach-colored negligee, painting her nails and talking to our father in the sexual code I had heard the ninth graders use.

I had no reason to think he was seeing anyone. The only woman he talked about was my mother. He seemed to think, even after the divorce was final, that this was merely a temporary separation.

"Norah is punishing me, that's what she's doing. Well, I can take it. She doesn't know how much I can take. I can live like a rat in a hole for years if that's what she wants. But she's just hurting herself. She's losing her best time. A woman like that needs a husband and she's still my girl. I know some things about Norah would curl your hair. Little Miss Norah! If she wasn't your mother—" he said with a grin, lighting a cigarette, his eyelids half-shuttering his smeary eyes.

These remarks would reassure me on the subject of other women, but they also made me acutely nervous. As I turned thirteen, fourteen, I began to worry about his being hurt. My mother was starting to date Roy. I could hardly tell her not to—we never spoke about anything important anyway—but I was concerned. I saw him so seldom. I might not hear from him for months; anything could happen. Often on Saturday nights I would call and let the phone ring. Forty, fifty times. I knew that if he picked it up anytime after the tenth, I'd hang up, but still I'd let it ring on. He wouldn't answer.

"Maybe our dear old Pa doesn't live there anymore," said Lucy.

"Where else would he live?"

"Maybe he's moved to California. Maybe he's dead."

"My father," I said, "would send me a postcard if he moved to California."

"And if he's dead?"

"He'd ha'nt ya," I said, in a good imitation of one of his voices. "He'd come out of the closet—'Don't ya miss me, Lucy?'—and wipe the snot off your nose with his corpsey fingers."

"You're so incredibly gross."

"Mom would wake up and there he'd be, a skeleton in bed with her. 'Norah, Norah, don't ya love me? Oh, babe, you're getting so fat and look at me, nothing on my bones at all. Hee, hee, hee.'"

"There are no such things as ghosts," said didactic Lucy. "There is only the guilt of the living. And if Dad died, why should Mom feel guilty? He's brought everything on himself."

I couldn't answer. I didn't subscribe to her philosophy (I thought of her as brilliantly stupid), yet it terrified me to think of a person able to bring everything—everything?—on himself.

6

L ucy called when she returned from her honeymoon.
"It's me," said the voice winding cozily through my
ear.

"Welcome back," I said. "How was it?" They had gone to
Puerto Rico, a little three-room cottage on the beach.

"Okay. We both have sunburns and mosquito bites. Malcolm has some kind of rash."

"You should have spent more time in bed."

"We got our sunburns the first day and couldn't touch
each other for a week."

"I'm sorry."

"No big deal. We talked, we named the kids again. What
do you think—Althea, Eliot, and Jane?"

"Three's too many."

"How about Martin, Renata, and Chloe?"

"How about Daycare, Disease, and Tuition?"

"The voice of reason, I knew I could count on you. But you left my wedding early!"

"I was tired. I didn't want to watch everyone getting drunk." That wasn't kind but I suddenly felt a profound regret that I had not gotten drunk. All that champagne gone by forever.

"Oh, poor Gwennie. It got good later. Roy's cousin Jubie danced on the table."

"I bet Mom enjoyed that."

"Oh, she didn't care, she sailed by like the QE2 . . . It was Roy who was worried. He thought she might fall and hurt herself."

I remembered Jubie. Strawberry-blond ponytail falling into a strawberry-blond cleavage, cowboy boots. She reminded me of somebody I once wanted to be.

"It was a great wedding," I said.

"You don't sound very convincing."

"I enjoyed myself." I was feeling weirdly disoriented, as if I *were* drunk. As if this were one of those dreams in which I realize too late, after the booze is swallowed, that I don't do this anymore, that I have months of sobriety. "You looked gorgeous, everyone said so. Malcolm looked great, too. He seemed really happy."

There was a pause. "So what's been happening?"

"Nothing. Does anything ever happen?"

"I think quite a lot has happened to you. And if you'd get out of your apartment more, things would happen now."

The words rose up in my throat: I love him, I'm in love, Lucy, listen to me . . . "I've been working," I said hastily, overwhelmed by the temptation to tell her.

"Dog portraits?"

"That's what I do."

She sighed.

I don't think she likes dogs. But how could anyone not like dogs? They're so loyal, brave, and steady-hearted. Lucy is somewhat like a dog herself. She merely lacks that last essential quality of doing what she's told.

"We've talked about this before," she said.

"Yes."

"But it's true, Gwennie. What do you want to do that stuff for? You could work part-time and do your own stuff, you could probably even get a grant. All the people you're meeting are those rich, Waspy old ladies."

"There's been a Jew or two. As you might remember."

"You know what I mean. Those women who think their pets are worth a thousand-dollar portrait."

"Mrs. Fishbeck-Perry thinks that Alexi, her Doberman, is a reincarnation of her late husband." That was stretching it a bit—she had merely said that Dearborn had been just as handsome as a young man—but maybe it wasn't. Maybe she did think that. I should ask.

"So you think the wacko ones are amusing," Lucy said. "Okay, but is that enough? You're bored, aren't you?"

"Not really. Not anymore." It wasn't my dogs who bored me anyway, though there had been times when I had admitted to Lucy that I wouldn't mind a job where I met more people. The problem being that I didn't feel fit to meet people. Not the ones she meant, the media folk.

In Lucy's office, or in Malcolm's, I felt as if I were in a hive. Everyone seemed so close to everyone else, not inti-

mate but attached with sticky, invisible threads. The myr-
iad jobs got done, the relationships got done, the personal
hygiene got done, and everybody helped. It saved time for
all the women to be skinny and have short hair. The gossip
network hummed across afternoons on the telephone, com-
plementing the smooth grey work of their computers. All
you had to do was submit once and you were sucked in, or
the knowledge of you was: your credentials, your associa-
tions, your weird personal habits.

I was in a state of rampant dread. Instead of the knowledge of me sucked in it would be me myself, dragged and
mangled through that gleaming, wafer-thin world.

On the other hand, I could picture myself in a certain
style of forties-inspired business suit. Nipped waist, padded
shoulders, tight skirt, the whole thing in dark red with big
black buttons. Black heels with straps and a black cashmere
sweater. A watch, of course. I would have to start wearing a
watch . . .

"I don't understand."

That's what Lucy always says and she says it so reasonably, as if there's just one small thing I've neglected to tell
her. "What?"

"Why don't you want to do your own work?"

"Whose work am I doing?"

"Your clients'," she said promptly. Lucy knows what she
thinks, you can't intimidate her into regarding dog portraits
as art. I've tried invoking the age-old history of animal
painting, but she doesn't buy it. I don't think about my
relationship to other artists, she says, I don't pay attention
to society, I have no idea of my work; I see what I'm paid to

see. That's why I like it. It focuses me nicely. I fall into my subject like Alice falling into Wonderland: wet nose, chin hairs, perked ears, paws . . .

"Don't worry about it," I said.

"I want you to be happy is all. I don't want you to bury yourself."

"I'm not dead yet."

"That's what I'm saying."

"Sometimes it's enough just to be alive."

"That was fine for a while, Gwen, but are you going to spend the rest of your life recovering from alcoholism?"

"Most people do." Actually most people don't. A 12 percent long-term success rate was nothing to feel smug about.

Lucy said, "Yes, but they have jobs meanwhile, don't they? They have lives. You're lucky, we're rich, but there's danger in that. Look at Mom. She had kids but she could have done so much more."

"She could have painted dog portraits, except she didn't have any talent."

"Okay. Okay, I'll lay off. But someday you've got to listen . . ." Her voice was so exasperated and warm, like an engine running on high idle. Wasting energy. Why do I let her go on, why don't I end it with something really sarcastic? It wouldn't be difficult. Her work has gotten more uncertain lately, as she's moved on to psychological ground. Her last article, about sexual fantasy, ended, "The meaning of your fantasies is no more obvious than the meaning of your dreams. You can enjoy them as they are, but if they worry you, remember that they speak another language.

Your body does not insult you, your body does not wish you harm." Oh, yeah?

There was silence for quite a while on the phone before Lucy said, "Gwen, are you there?"

"I'm here."

"I wanted to ask you what you are doing this week?"

"Nothing." Nothing but fucking your father-in-law. That's how I spend every night, Lucy; I put on my high heels, my perfume and a dress, and he takes off the last-named item. I walk around in my shoes, then he fucks me, sometimes from in front, sometimes from behind, and it's exciting, but my mind wanders. I have sexual fantasies. I imagine being locked up in his bedroom forever. Naked and thoughtless, sleeping when he's absent, waking at his approach. An angel of pleasure, a nonhuman thing. I have a hundred fantasies, Lucy, I covet every unreality I can think of. And I do try to interpret them, but it seems so much easier, so much more natural, to let them interpret me.

"Mom wants to have dinner with Malcolm and me, and his father. We want you to come too."

"What for?" What do you want me for, Lucy, why don't you just pretend I don't exist? Listen to me, Lucy. Go away.

"I told her she should wait until Ruth gets back from Moscow, but she has this idea that men alone can't take care of themselves."

"She may be right," I said. "Look what happened to our father." Lucy was silent. She used to dispose of such conversational probings with dismissive remarks about "that fucking drunk," but she can't do that anymore so she says nothing. "So where's this affair going to be?"

"At Mom's," Lucy said.

"Why not at your place? Don't you want to use your new wedding presents? Your cut-crystal nut dish, your floating candles?" I had a vision of these things as they accumulated, somehow blunting Lucy's reach.

"I'm going to give that shit to the Women's Shelter."

"They'll really be able to use it there."

"Elegant little birthday parties for the kids, why not?"

"Baby bottles in the wine racks."

"Diapers in the napkin rings."

"Toddlers in the microwave."

"Right. So you'll come?"

"I guess so," I said weakly.

"Good, I want you there. I don't know about Jack."

"What do you mean?" Did I want to hear this? I couldn't help feeling a certain predatory thrill to be the one in the middle knowing everything. Except, of course, that I've always hated this position.

"Well, for one thing, those stupid books he writes."

"I doubt he'll make us listen to one over dinner."

"I know, I know, but it's sort of—embarrassing. Don't ever tell Malcolm I said this, he thinks his father's a great writer, but I mean, compared to Ruth's work—"

Should I say something about Ruth's work? Its shrillness, tendentiousness, lack of originality? I decided not to. "His books are actually pretty good. You just don't like science fiction."

"And you have a taste for trash. I must have found the collected works of Stephen King under your bed in Berkeley."

It wasn't, I reminded myself, her fault that she was insulting me mortally. She didn't know I was in love with him for the simple reason that I hadn't told her. That was easy enough to understand. But trash?

"You watch *Cagney and Lacey*," I said.

"Only when I'm very tired. No, of course that's not my real problem with Jack. What do I care what he writes? I just think he neglects Malcolm. Always has. And he's so flippant about it. That Mexico thing, for example."

"He had work to do down there, right?"

"He could have come back sooner. All those parties, that luncheon Aunt Agatha gave us—"

"I saw him talking to her at the wedding."

"That's not the point. It's disrespectful."

"You sound like Mom."

"Well, Mom isn't wrong about everything, you know."

I thought of what it had been like the last few months. Constant telephone calls to consult about the invitations, the flowers, the food, our mother taking the opportunity to teach us the finer points of etiquette, that we had skipped in our rebellious adolescence. Not wrong about everything, of course. The wedding had been beautiful. And yet—and yet that moment when Jack had said: You want to get out of here? His face intent, smiling. Oh, why didn't we just go?

Lucy said in a tone of outrage. "I don't think Jack thinks Malcolm should have married me,"

"Maybe it's nothing to do with you or Malcolm. Maybe he stayed in Mexico because he was having trouble with Ruth."

"Did he say that to you?"

"Well, of course not, he wouldn't say that to me. I hardly know the man. It's just an idea. Married people do have trouble with each other, you know."

"Well, strange as it seems, they appear to like each other. Maybe not mad passion, but they've been married a long time. Malcolm told me Jack proposed to Ruth after knowing her only a couple of months. They got married at the drive-in wedding chapel in Vegas, if you can believe it."

"I can believe it," I said. Ruth—no nonsense, let's get this over with; Jack—slightly desperate, jazzing up his mistake. Standing up beside the pregnant Ruth (didn't Malcolm know that?). Jack had told me straight off—calculating how he'd support her while trying to pretend he was doing something funny. A drive-in wedding chapel, for Christ's sake. I wasn't surprised he hadn't told me that bit.

"Well, anyway. He just gets on my nerves. Mom likes him, so that's okay. But then she likes anything in pants."

"Don't we all."

"I don't. And you must be a bit choosy yourself, miss, now that you're sober. I've never seen you go this long without a boyfriend."

It didn't seem to occur to her that it wasn't choosiness but terror. That perhaps a person in the midst of transforming her entire way of life was not best suited to the travails of a love affair. But I wasn't going to think about that.

"I'm into bestiality these days," I said.

"I wouldn't be surprised."

"I have threesomes with rich, Waspy old ladies."

"I'll call and let you know what day the dinner is."

"We present quite a tableau. Now, I could do paintings of

that. Sort of a cross between Eric Fischl and David Salle, what do you think?"

"I think I have to get back to work."

"Good-bye," I said, and hung up. I had an impulse to take a drink. Not a craving, not even a temptation, simply the idea of it, flying in out of nowhere: a big glass full of cold gin. My tongue would lower itself like a leg into a mountain lake, shuddering at that icy, exquisite contact.

7

I walked over to Jack's that evening, already nostalgic. For three weeks I'd been spending my days idly, barely working at all, anticipating night. I read *Vogue* and *Elle* all morning and drank iced coffee, then went to AA meetings in a spirit somewhere between that of the matinee- and church-goer: a woman alone in the afternoon who slips into a dark, familiar place to remind her of herself as her thoughts spiral and drift. Walking home after, details of another life threading through my own in the name of our common disease, the idea of a common disease, "spiritual" as they say, curiously buoyed me, so I was fueled by an underground hope, limpid and cool, as well as by my feverish, ever-conscious desire.

At six or seven I'd take a bath. Soaping my body, it was

hard not to feel his hands on me, not only as memory but as something occult. I remembered the baths of my early adolescence—solitude, privacy, my head sinking underwater; I imagined a man so vividly it was as if a window opened in the room. Now, at nearly thirty, I chose stockings from the tangle on the closet floor—what luxury it would have seemed once, a whole apartment to myself—dusted my shoes with an old sock. Put on one of the well-made silks I had bought with my first inheritance check, dresses that had carried me safely through so many nights of magical oblivion. Black, white, green, yellow were the softly draped sleeves, flared skirts; the tea-colored, wine-colored lacy edges of old stains, marks of my past pleasure-seeking, pleasure-needing.

The stretch of Manhattan I crossed on the way to Jack's apartment, a diagonal moving southeast, was like a broad river shimmering with light. On the sidewalks, great stalks of deep-throated lilies for sale; on the street, the on-rushing excitement of the cars. All the temptations of night presented themselves: the couple bent over a bottle of Spanish champagne, the solitary girl with her brandy, the man standing at the bar with a beer. I recognized their power and their beauty and let them go. I had something better. Wilder, fiercer, drunker I could be if I wanted, then cool and quiet the next moment, clocked by the regular marvelous pulse of health.

A week ago Jack had told me that he loved me. I'd thought for a half an hour that he would—known, yet not been sure. How could one trust such intuition? It gathered in the air between us, the way his arm lay across my breasts, the relaxed sprawl of his thigh. His skin was darker than mine, brown, with black springy curls hiding muscle and sinew and fat, leading to the soft, melting mercurial weight of his balls. It felt so freeing to love even the age on his body, the sag and droop and the few grey hairs. In fact he didn't seem to me middle-aged so much as ageless; as if a body that has stood up fifty years can stand up forever.

Our heads were close together. I was propped against pillows, my hair spilling over his cheek. The quiet settled and settled. "I love you," he said.

"Thank you."

He laughed. "My pleasure."

Later he let me draw on him with magic markers. I drew sea monsters and mermaids, snakes wreathing his arms, and a beautiful naked lady all down his front.

But now I was back in the city of childhood, the dirty, roaring place. Block upon block without greenery or vista, the stench of urine and exhaust fumes, the jostle of the threatening crowd. And it was also, in the quieter stretch, the city of my visits home, the dull familiar place constricted by the claims upon my time and the nagging questions. This was the New York I'd hated. Of course I'd been here for months before I met Jack—here but not really. My spirit had been numb. Now I was alive, in full possession of my senses, and back again between these walls, hurrying through these mazy streets.

———————

"Your sister called," he said. He had a cigarette in his mouth. The remains of a frozen chocolate cake were on the coffee table, disturbing the usual neatness of the room.

"So?"

"Well, you know I guess: this dinner party she has in mind. She asked me for any night I was free. What could I say?"

"What did you say?"

"I said Thursday."

Thursday. Three days ahead of us, like a long weekend. Jack sighed and padded into the kitchen. I followed and sat at the table while he made himself a baloney sandwich. I admired the solid sculpture of his forearm.

"Christ, Gwen, I can't go to this thing with you. I'll have to call and cancel."

"You can't do that, you accepted already."

"It's nutty. We'll both feel miserably uncomfortable, and what about—well, if and when they find out we're lovers, I'll look like a skunk." If and when. The "if" upset me, the "when" was frightening, too.

"Whatever happens," I said staunchly, "they never have to know we were lovers now."

"They'll suspect, if they don't suspect already."

"What do you mean, suspect already? Of course they don't."

"Why are they asking me? Why don't they wait until Ruth gets back? It sounds fishy."

"It's my mother's idea. She thinks you must be lonely. The poor man, abandoned by his wife. She's used to inviting summer bachelors; we would stay in the city longer than most of her friends. We'd be here in July and these guys would come for dinner while their wives were lolling on the beach with the kids. My mother got a kick out of it."

Jack sighed and didn't answer. I continued: "Anyway, Lucy wants to get to know you better. She thinks this is a good opportunity since when Ruth is present, she and your wife get so caught up in each other." Now why did I say that? I wondered. What could be more unlikely than Lucy and Jack becoming friends? He seemed to agree because he looked at me skeptically.

"Your sister said about three words to me at the wedding."

"Well, you did arrive late."

"Late? I wasn't late."

"I mean you missed all the parties beforehand."

"If you want to know, and why should you, it was Ruth's idea I stay in Mexico. She asked me to talk to a guy who was flying down, one of the producers of that piece of shit I'll be proud to have my name on, about a project *she* had in mind, a Joanna Russ novel. My wife the screenwriter."

"Which novel?"

"Oh, she doesn't know. She hasn't done anything about it. She gets these ideas . . . she just can't stand to let people get away that she might have some use for."

"So did you talk to the guy?" I was not interested except insofar as we were talking about Ruth. I needed more information.

"She didn't want me to talk to him specifically, you understand, just to pal around, get drunk together. Yeah, I did that, and yeah, we're about as palsy as me and that fire escape." He sighed. "I'll have to think up a good last-minute excuse for your sister."

"You can't." Lucy would never forgive him. "I'll do it. I'll call in sick, it's no problem. If they don't believe me, it makes no difference. They never believe me anyway."

He looked profoundly relieved. "Thank you. Yes, that's obviously the best idea . . . Jesus, Gwen, we've really got ourselves into a situation, haven't we?"

"Shit," I said, "I've been in situations before."

He grinned. "I know, I know, *The Perils of Pauline*." I'd been telling him tales of my drinking days, edited and embellished. I felt as if I were doling out the truth so artfully, there would never be a moment when he'd recoil in disgust. He even seemed cheered. I could understand this, though I by no means trusted it.

"Alright," he said, "let's hear one of your situations."

"You want comedy, romance, horror, science fiction . . ."

"Comedy. Tonight, definitely comedy." He sat down at the table with me; I took the last bite of his sandwich.

"Okay." I paused; I had nothing in mind. "Okay, I'm in Paris; Paris, France. I have this monumental hangover, I have to be out of the hotel by noon. They've booked the room. But each time I get out of bed I'm attacked by a wave of nausea and have to crawl back in. There's a window-washer, of course, out on the balcony doing my windows. He peers in through the gauzy curtains, seeming to find my behavior curious. Finally I manage to get up and dress in a corner. He pretends not to watch. I lie down for a while again. The desk calls to tell me it's noon. I stumble down-stairs. I have a little problem—I spent so much on wine the night before, and I seem to remember a taxi ride from a distant arrondissement—that I don't have enough for the bill. Three francs short. The woman bitches and moans; I stand there until she lets me leave.

"So I have to go to the bank now, change money before I can even buy a Perrier. I crawl, lugging my suitcase, to the bank. Long lines. I wait in line. Wrong line. I wait in another line. I'm feeling very ill indeed. Time passes, I'm getting sicker but there I am, almost to the head. Finally I am at the head. The cashier smiles so kindly, I'm sure she's a wonderful woman. Just as I hand over my passport, my mouth begins to work. I'm going to vomit. She sees the signs and points me frantically toward the back. I rush past everyone in line, all the healthy tourists with their big sneakers and their backpacks, through the door into the inner offices. All the secretaries jump up screeching. They're talking French, you know, but I catch their drift. I'm not allowed, go away, awful American—shooing me as if I were a chicken or a dog. I work my mouth at them a little. *Mon dieu, mon dieu!* They all agree I should puke in their toilet, not on their shoes. They pound on the bathroom door; a colleague is inside. She won't come out. Undoubtedly has her reasons. It's getting really suspenseful now. The young ladies are all in hysterics, they're rattling the doorknob, they're about to break it down. Finally she emerges, a heavy, glowering, disgruntled girl, straightening her skirt. I'm pushed inside. Not a moment too soon—I puke in the sink. '*Le lavabo, le lavabo,*' they whisper among themselves in tones of awe and dread; the door's ajar of course. I run a little water, wipe my mouth. An ounce of yellow bile causing all that trouble. They draw back to let me pass; I go up front and collect my money."

"Comedy?" he asked.

"I guess you had to be there."

"My poor darling, you should have puked on their

shoes." He grinned. "Actually, it is sort of funny . . . in a bank . . . in Paris . . ."

He was shaking with laughter and hugging me at the same time; to hell with my sister, I thought. To hell with them all.

8

I was always my father's daughter and Lucy was our
mother's. Lucy was placid in temper yet physically energetic; like my mother, she was good at games. My father on
the other hand used to get nosebleeds as a child when it
came time to play sports. He got a nosebleed, he told me,
every day for several years—and also blushed so badly
when he had to speak in front of the class that he would
faint; he would wake up in the nurse's office and spend the
rest of the day there, reading her book of tropical diseases.
"It comforted me, let me tell you, to know we didn't have
any of that stuff in Indiana."

We went out on walks together. After dinner, especially if
my parents had been fighting, the two of us would go while
Lucy sat on the footstool in front of my mother's chair. My
mother would be brushing her hair, that long dark mass that

always had tangles in it, that would take a half an hour of deft, patient work to unravel.

"Get your jacket," my father would whisper, as if our going was a secret. "I need some air."

Outside he would breathe deep. "Away we go." As we walked down Madison, past the drugstore, past Stark's Coffee Shop where the ice-cream sodas had doubled in price the last two years, enabling me to negotiate more allowance for Lucy and me, past Paraphernalia with its window full of bright vinyl, metal mesh, and soft, Italian-knit, crotch-length dresses, my father would talk. "What do you say, should we hop a bus and head out of town? That would scare 'em, wouldn't it? We could take one of those cross-country bus tours, six days on a Greyhound, I did that once. You sleep in your seat, wake up rolling into some little burg, go in for a beer, your teeth are green, you haven't brushed them in a week, and those waitresses with the flat eyes, they've seen everything . . ."

I listened, I listened so carefully. "You wake up, you're in the South. You can smell it, all that perfume, you think for a minute you're in a bunch of women, as if a bunch of women had crowded around you while you slept"—He chuckled softly—"but it's just the flowers outside the bus window. You're in Georgia or some damn place . . . You know what I'm talking about, don't you?"

"Yes," I said.

"Your mother doesn't understand, she never wants to leave New York. You could tell her she wasn't allowed above Eighty-sixth Street or below Fourteenth and she'd be happy. I had to beg her to get away in the summers, for Chrissake . . . you have kids, Norah, I said, you have daughters who need to swim in the ocean. She thinks swimming in a pool at the club is perfectly fine. What a woman, and she wasn't even brought up here. As for travel, forget it. What for? she says. Never catch her on a Greyhound ... You wake up when the bus stops, you get out to stretch your legs, it's dark, you have no idea where you are, what state even. Say there's no moon, you just stand there and have to try to smell it out, where you are ... you know?" he said.

"Yes," I replied, and I almost did know. I felt it even closer, the thrill of other places, dark, empty, desolate country places like the Indiana he'd grown up in, which I'd never seen, which had to do with wild Indians, and where it was always dusk or midnight.

"Sometimes I get crazy in that apartment, Gwen. I say things I don't mean."

"I know."

"She drives me to it, she's always right. One thing a man doesn't need is a woman who's always right. You think I'm okay, don't you?"

He only asked me this once; I didn't know what to say. The question opened vistas too strange to contemplate. And immediately he said it, the subject was changed. My father's eye was caught by a beggar; he had a profound fondness for beggars. We would always stop and talk to them, my father serious and thoughtful, tipping me a wink, touching his hat when we said good night to them. He even enjoyed letting wiseguys con him out of a quarter or so. He looked at me.

"My daddy was a con-man, you know. It's a noble profession."

"But you know they're doing it," I said, "you're letting them. And you're not poor."

"It's your mother who's not poor," he said. "I'm hanging on by the skin of my teeth."

———————

Those were our night walks. Our daytime walks were different. My father was restless on the weekends. He'd complain all day while my mother went serenely on with her chores, and even outside his mood remained sour. He'd take me into shops and buy me things.

He'd say, "I don't like those shoes you're wearing, do you? Of course you don't. Ugly, ugly. I don't know what Norah thinks, you're an English schoolboy? You're a New York girl and New York has the prettiest girls in the world. Did you know that? French girls are too short, English girls are too fat, California girls are brainless, it's New York girls for me. Let's go in here."

He bought me pink sandals. I had to have my foot measured, the man down on his knees while my father watched. "Is that average? Are her feet big or small? She's nine." I glanced down at my foot on the metal plate. Clad in a white sock, alone against the grey, it looked just right to me. I didn't want it bigger or smaller. I didn't want it thinner or fatter. I only wanted to go barefoot more often, to climb trees and rocks, to venture out along the unseen ocean bottom. But I was a New York girl and went barefoot only in bed.

"Well, I would say her feet are about average. They're a bit narrow but they have a nice high arch . . . very pretty feet to show off in sandals. . . . The little lady could even paint her toenails to match."

Pink toenails! Candy pink, watermelon pink, the dizzying smell of the polish. I'd smelled it once when we'd gone to our babysitter's house and spent all afternoon in her room. Sue Ollenburg—fifteen, dark and busty, with a warm, breathy voice and big, shiny eyes—showed us every bottle, every tube and compact that was lined up on her white-painted, lace-skirted dressing table.

"No, no," said my father in annoyance as the straps were tightened. "There's a fine line girls have to be careful of. Toenail polish, in my opinion, is sluttish." He stared at me with his brows knitted, as if he might find the teenage Gwen in my face. I looked back at him carefully.

"Maybe you're right," the man muttered, "maybe you're right," getting up off his knees to take my father's money. Salespeople always agreed with my father. They had no choice, I understood that. And in a way it reassured me, although I was hurt by the pavement slapping up through my thin soles as we walked the eight blocks home.

Of course Lucy wanted pink sandals too and never got them. Our parents fought about it. "Your absurd vanity!"

"I try to make her happy, buy her something she likes."

"I won't let you ruin Lucy's feet, you'll have to buy her something else."

"Buy it yourself, Mrs. Knowitall."

My father put me to bed at night, my mother put Lucy. Lucy had her blankets tucked in, her night light switched on, her water glass filled, while my father told me a story. Animals, he said, wild ones, tame ones, even stuffed ones, creep through houses in the middle of the night to look at people sleeping and read their minds. Sometimes they creep too close and the touch of a cat's whisker will wake a child. Then you can join in their secret adventures as long as you follow them faithfully, and don't make any noise. You can sneak away from Mommy and Daddy, outside where it's not the city at all but a wild forest or a rough plain, where there are ships, sailing ships that skim along the top of the grass. They make a sound like singing as they sail. Who pilots the ships? Not the owl and the pussycat. Seadogs, said my father, old seadogs who stand up on their hind legs and smoke pipes, their tails hanging over the deckrail. Mice could grab on and climb into the ships, I said.

Yes, and rats too. Rats always join a singing ship, said my father.

9

On Thursday night at six-thirty I was watching television. I have a position for this: the TV on one end of the couch, balanced precariously (that's part of the charm, that it may fall off on its back), my legs curled underneath me, and a pillow clutched to my middle like a bulletproof vest. Light and sound rayed out at me, my face turned up like a plant. Hours of this would add weight to my body, would both muffle and alarm my limping heart; even in my dreams I would hear those cheerful, unreal voices, and the banging and screaming from the street would be taken in like another channel.

TV was my methadone. It humiliated me to use it. In the beginning, of course, it was necessary; I had insomnia night after night. Each hour I put off having a drink, my body became more and more manic in its outrage. I was twining around myself like a cat twisting between human legs: I want, I need, I want, I need, I'm not going to stop until you listen to me. During the day I said: one day at a time. At night that no longer worked, there clearly were no days or nights, everything was continuous, no breaks between experience. Gone were the silky hidden hours when the family is asleep, the city partly asleep, when you abandon your bed or your house or your caution, when the dreams slotted for that period spill out instead into the world. There was only television. Naked gay boys in Nazi helmets, futuristic music videos, old vampire movies. The nude talk-show host, the huckster shopping channel, transvestite etiquette lessons.

I watched. I waited. Ten months went by.

And I called that sobriety. And I had imagined I was getting better.

And they would sit around the table, like tonight, and laugh and talk.

Sometimes when my mother drinks she reminisces about her childhood. She grew up near New Orleans with no siblings but a gang of cousins: she was the only girl of her generation. The boys taught her to shoot, to drive a car, to drink whiskey, and to take what she wanted. What she wanted was New York, nobody quite knows why, and for a while my father. It sounds ideal to me, but she likes to dwell on the lonely afternoons when all the boys were off at war, and talk about the ones who didn't come home: handsome Rafe, meek brilliant Aidan. Listening to her. I feel nostalgic for the world before I was born. It ought to have belonged to me. I want to drift backward, in spirit-shape. I want to settle over the streets and fields, watching them, every private moment and public gesture, the young limbs and the lost-to-history clothing.

My mother is animated by her melancholy; Lucy and I are silent when she talks. It's a rare combination of two and a half drinks, family peace for an interval, and who knows what in her psyche or the weather. She talks as if we were her friends or her cousins; her face is soft, her eyes shockingly direct. Her cousins didn't want her to come north. They didn't like my father. ("One of those bastards," he used to say when she suggested a visit—the only place she ever wanted to go—"would mistake me for a possum some afternoon around four o'clock."

"If they shot you," replied my mother proudly, "it would only be on purpose.")

I got up from the couch, went into the bathroom and stared at myself in the mirror. Oh, I was getting older, wasn't I, that face I had been carrying from twenty onward was definitely changing; I was starting to resemble my mother. I was starting to resemble myself. I put on lipstick: slasher-red. It looked peculiar above my bathrobe. I shrugged off the bathrobe, put on a dress. I did this some-times, dressed up for myself alone, dressed up for the gin bottle or the television, for the Billie Holiday record and the sound of the neighbors' fights.

I put on my shoes, then went back in the living room and sat down. It was seven o'clock. Jack was in love with me; he had said so. It ought to be enough. I sat still for a while. The night was heating up outside, it was five after seven. The traffic makes me so angry sometimes—all those people invading the city, cruising for excitement. The cars full of teenagers, radios blaring, you can never sleep. I was in love but it didn't feel right. I went in the bathroom and put on a bracelet, combed my hair. The wrongness was not quite in him nor in me; it floated; how to find it, fight it, live with it, what? If I was being pushed, should I let go in that direction, like turning into a skid? How to let go.

I went in the kitchen, opened the refrigerator. I knew there was nothing inside; I like to lean against the door, let my eyes drift over the Perrier and the dried up rice in its cardboard container, over the soft brown apple. Lucy had called to consult about the menu. She always does this since she knows I don't care; I eat takeout and Danish, Hershey bars and ice cream. "Something healthy," I suggested.

"I'd managed to get that far by myself. You're lucky you have me to feed you now and then. I'll have to think of something that contains all the nutrients you've been missing. What have you been living on, pizza?"

"Hope."

"Right. Like a political prisoner on a hunger strike. You know, Gwen —" She went on for a bit while I thought about her simile. Was I on a hunger strike? Should I then let myself eat? Long drowsy kisses all over his body, his rich, sweet flesh. If Jack were food, I thought, would he constitute a good dinner?

I was out the door, my apartment was killing me. I'd go to a movie, I decided, something summery and dumb. First I had to call them and tell them I wasn't coming. What disease should I invent? Food poisoning? Migraine? How about, "I just feel awful, I don't know what's wrong. Everything hurts, my head, my heart, my bones . . ."

When I was sick as a child my mother took such good

care of me. She had a tin tray painted with red tulips on which she used to arrange the hot soup, the cold drink, the napkin in a napkin ring. She took my temperature with a thermometer, being a modern mother, but not before laying her hand on my forehead, bathing me in her coolness, coaxing out the heat. She brought me iced tea with mint, ginger ale with a cherry, sometimes mineral water that I drank slowly, thinking it alchemical. Little crystals of rose quartz would grow in my veins. Then, half asleep, I would hear her come in for the tray. She would smooth the sheet over me with her cool, creamy hands. The door shutting slowly, her footsteps dying away . . . knowing I could summon her at any time . . . quiet except for the occasional ringing of a telephone . . .

I was on the doorstep. I'd call them from the corner. I'd say I was on my way, realized I couldn't make it. Lucy would say, Oh, come on, you made it out, it can't be too bad. I'd say: I had an epileptic fit. I'd say the ambulance is coming. I'd say I was mugged, the state I'm in you wouldn't believe —

There's a malaise in this country, as my favorite president once said. Poor old Jimmy, I believed in him. He was real. He really fucked up. All those hostages and what to do? Better do nothing, the innocent will suffer. The innocent always suffer, why does it have to be our fault?

I put my token in the slot, pushed through the turnstile. The uptown Number Six, what a coincidence. I wasn't going. I wasn't going. I wasn't going.

The train stopped for a long time at Fourteenth Street. I could get off now. I could spend the evening shopping for cut-rate pillowcases and Spanish petticoats. Prowl through the long stores with their bins of cheap combs and shampoo, the bolts of cloth up on the walls, the children's T-shirts on the sidewalk. So many levels of poverty in this city, so much energy spent getting out of it, why don't I give my money away and live in a cloister. Somewhere quiet, upstate, with nuns. In my Spanish petticoat.

Twenty-third Street; twenty-eighth. He would be so angry at me. He had reason to be. I was causing him nothing but trouble; the thought was as close as my heart. I should have left him alone entirely, been patient and chaste. Left alone that pleasure. Just left it: no thanks. What else had I been suffering after all but pleasure? There was something else I needed to get to. And how could this possibly be the way, this deception, this theft? Yet as I thought those words, "deception," "theft," there arose in me such an anger, climbing and bright, at those who would deny me. Deprive me. My last lover was Lenny, before him Peter, a heroin addict with tracks on his neck, on his thighs. I felt so ashamed of these pitiful men. What sort of woman can't do better than that? An alcoholic woman of course; they were all like me in the rooms. All the single twenty-eight to forty-two-year-olds with their sex histories like long bedraggled finery, "dragon dresses" as Lucy and I used to say when we were small: the kind that drag in the mud behind you.

And what would these women advise, should I be so bold as to ask. They would say: Abjure deception. They would say: No relationships in the first year.

Forget it. This was Jack we were talking about, not some abstract, intrusive male. Not some looming force of disintegration, some dark, sex-shaped thing. Not a drink or a new strain of craziness, bred in the laboratory of mid-eighties New York; this was Jack, my beloved, himself.

And suddenly I was remembering how I could never drink in my mother's presence. At eighteen or twenty, home from college, home and missing my Gallo Hearty Burgundy, my friends and my boyfriends, my solitude and my make-believe, I would regretfully eye her bottles of expensive French wine. Lined up in the pantry for the holiday dinner the Chateau-Neuf-du-Pape, the Nuits St. George, the Chambertin. They stood tall and dark, silent, fraternal, sealed. How I longed to seize one and carry it up to my room. Dust the top with a damp finger, sink the screw in the cork, pour out the first glass. Such clear crimson red. The smell rising, the glass almost full. Drinking it down to the bottom before pouring another. I always hated it when someone topped off my glass, that missed the whole point. Empty and then full. Again and again. Whenever you please.

But I didn't do this. I didn't get passionately drunk at six in the evening while the others dressed, or on the day before Christmas while the others wrapped presents. I left the bottles alone. I walked away, hugging my arms across my chest and offered to go out for ice and candles. I did all the chores I could think of and then at dinner drank one glass very slowly.

Later, after my mother and Roy went to sleep, Lucy and I would drink a little more. Or rather I would drink and she would smoke a joint, blowing the smoke out the kitchen window. She didn't worry about my drinking in those days. She thought I was celebrating. (As the sweet, buck-toothed matron at the London drunk tank said, "What were you celebrating then, love? What were you celebrating?" I searched in vain for an answer. Such a flower as Gwendolyn at twenty-six, in that squalor! She brought me a glass of water. She cautioned me not to sit too near the men, those ~~bloodshot unshaven creatures who scratched while they~~ waited for the judge.)

But of course I was celebrating. Lucy was not a fool to see the happiness alcohol lent me. The world all in ribbons of color, in a warm dissolve, as if we were fluid merely and could pass through each other. Or like painted figures sharing a riverside, neither one nor the other preferred by the artist, neither one nor the other painted singularly. The little dog in the distance, each leaf on the tree. Such warm light in alcohol; it warmed her too. She liked me better a little drunk, for the first few years. (One of the men followed me out of the courthouse, asked if I could spare fifty pence for the tube. I gave him a pound, invited him for a drink. He refused.)

Late at night we would talk about our lovers. Our *Sex and Early Sorrow* stories, I called them. Hers seemed to me very pure and clean in their outlines, like chapters from a masterpiece of female sentimental education. It's 1975. Slightly older, handsome, courtly and slim, her first lover is a black man, a law student with skin as soft as ice cream, with coffee-colored eyes and a wife and child. He seduces her under a willow tree by the river. She is painfully shy but happy—no one else has ever been so tender, no one has talked to her about Plato while stroking her naked breast. They meet every day for a month. He begins to be late. He scolds her for having a pimple on her chin. Finally he doesn't show up for a week and it's then she sees his wife—tall, striding, in a yellow dashiki, her son held high on one shoulder. Eric, beside this Amazon, looks like nothing at all.

Her next boyfriend is Bob, crazy and passionate and eager to be loved; he takes her camping every weekend, he stays up all night on speed, he expounds on the rape of nature and the greatness of women. The problem with Bob is not that he leaves her but that he won't ever. He even wants to go to her consciousness raising group as an honorary woman.

The thing that impressed me was how Lucy learned from her experiences. She was naive, but she never made the same mistake twice. She didn't seem to be driven into the arms of anyone; when the next step on the developmental ladder didn't appear promptly, she'd wait. "Of course I get horny," she said, "of course I get lonely." But she didn't seem to need men. I couldn't understand this. I was in awe before the face of sex which seemed to encompass all the yearning of my previous twenty years. As long as I was unsatisfied, I could imagine a great and inclusive satisfaction, and as long as I imagined this to reside in the body of a man, men were the most necessary of beings.

Men like Monroe who showed up between girlfriends to drink with me and persuade me to more serious mischief; Tom, seriously sexy to the point of dementia; Eli, whose menace I never quite understood but which rose from his flesh like a perfume; and Henry and Alan and Doug. I told Lucy in detail about the last three, how straight and honest they were, until even she could tell something was wrong. "He doesn't sound interesting enough for you, Gwen."

"There's a lot I can't tell him," I agreed.

"Well, love is about intimacy, isn't it?"

Oh, yes, of course. Flat on our bellies in the weeds behind some house we'd attempted to break into (for no reason I can remember) while a man with a shotgun roamed nearby, Monroe and I were close. With Tom I pressed myself as close as a shadow, terrified on Forty-second Street where he had taken me to see some particularly low-down porno flick. And Eli—Eli had yellow eyes. Eli wanted to know every thought that passed through my mind.

I was afraid of them. So I moved on from one to the next with no gap at all in my college days, the gaps after college getting longer and longer. Time to recover, to digest. Time to drink in the afternoons, lazy and golden like my un-earned money, and to move to California for no reason but the change and perhaps the distance. It was a race. The alcohol won. Soon I could conjure up a demon lover, I could fashion for myself a homey sweetheart. They spoke to me, they lay beside me in this body we'd both been shut up in. Making the best of it.

The pale light of early morning, in my drunkard's glow, was as artful as the light of childhood which introduced me to beauty. The weirdness, the sentiment, and the pain of booze reminded me of adolescent anguish and glory. This was feeling. I didn't want it to mature or attach itself. It hung before me in the air like magic pictures, messages from the beyond there was no need to answer. I thought of myself as stranded in life but still remembered, still be-loved. I painted, I had relationships, as one might in prison.

And through all this my desire didn't diminish but rather

solidified. It stuck there in the foreground like a statue of the Virgin on the lawn. Something to go out and visit after a few drinks. Take the bottle with you, strike up a conversation—pretty soon you'll be swearing you saw the goddamn thing move.

10

I ran into Malcolm on Sixty-third Street. "Where are you coming from?" he asked. I'd been walking west from Second Avenue after circling the block twice.

"I was at a meeting," I said, "the Seventy-ninth Street Workshop, it's really convenient for this neighborhood." I'd never been there in my life. "Really great meeting, lots of amazing people, you wouldn't believe what some of them have been through, prison, rape, war, and now they're just incredibly serene."

"That's great," he said. "I guess before a dinner like this, it's a good idea."

Yes. It would have been a good idea.

"Does it bother you when we drink? I've asked Lucy. She says you have to get used to it, it's what people do, but if it does, you know, Gwen, we don't have to. I mean it doesn't matter to us whether we have a beer or not before dinner. Tonight I suppose your mother will have wine, but when you come to visit us . . ."

Such a sweet boy, and I'm fucking his father. So kind, so considerate, and I was destroying his happy family.

"No," I said, "it doesn't bother me at all."

Roy opened the door. "Gwen," he said. "Malcolm. I thought you were married to the other one, heh, heh." He wore an apricot cotton sweater and crisp white pants. He had a smear of something green on his cheek. He stood there for a moment, panting a little with hospitality. Roy doesn't shake hands unless he has to, and he doesn't kiss either. He doesn't believe people really like being touched. Occasionally he pats me on the shoulder; usually he just paws the air. "Lucy's made some eggplant thing," he said as the three of us walked inside.

"Baba Ganoush," I said.

"What?"

"The eggplant thing. It's called Baba Ganoush."

"Your father's eaten most of it."

"Good old Dad," said Malcolm.

Roy pushed the living-room door open, then stood back for me to enter. I walked in, enveloped immediately by the muted paisley and Oriental designs, the gleaming blond wood and the scent of dried lavender, the soft pale pink of the walls on which the old mirrors hung, the ones I had looked into as a child, looked and looked into that room even more remote and lovely.

Jack turned red when he saw me. Not all at once—it took a minute, creeping up from his neck. I watched with a dismal tenderness. I was not allowed to touch him. All the hours of our playfulness, our intimate talk, those late nights when, holding hands under the covers, the dense dark knit our words into itself, preserving them, joining us, when the bed underneath us was an ally, and the cool windows were too, and mostly the dark—all those hours, impossible to forget, impossible to replace, were not yet solid. Either one of us could throw them, with one gesture, over the side. Rise from the bed and not go back.

My mother was perched on the love seat, blond hair waving like the sea. Lucy was sitting beside her in a red-striped shirt and black jeans, clashing with the decor so purposefully it seemed to leave me nothing to do. I stood in front of them, blocking Jack.

My mother said, "Hello, darling, you look pretty, where did you get that bracelet?" She took my hand, slid a finger underneath the band to feel its weight.

"From an admirer." I'd woken up one morning, after a night I remembered nothing about, to find it in my handbag. Maybe it was from an admirer. (Am I that admirable?) Maybe I stole it.

My mother's hand lingered warmly on my own while she inspected my pale green dress, my gold sandals, my coppery hair. It used to bother me more, her relentless pleasure in my physical being, but now I don't really mind. I saw her so seldom, even though I lived here again, and when I did I felt a sensuous prickling on my skin as if I were swimming through fur. As if I were falling asleep. Why should she care what I think? She didn't create my thoughts, she didn't feed them or bathe them or tuck them in at night. But the body, ah, the body—she probably remembers every meal she ate in pregnancy and every one she fed me.

"You know Jack Price," said my mother.

I turned to face that disturbance at my back. He didn't belong here; I felt a sharp splinter of joy. "How are you?"

"Fine thanks, and yourself?" His tone was dangerously ironic. He looked ever-so-slightly out of control, eyes bright, hair awry, fingers gripping his glass of scotch tightly. I remembered the smell of those fingers. The taste. I wanted to coax them, one by one, into my body and keep them there, as the King of the Dead keeps his Kore under the earth.

"I felt ill on the train, I didn't think I was going to make it," I replied dreamily; the words snaked out of my mouth, across the space between us; I watched the twitch of his facial muscles.

"What was wrong with you?" he asked. My mother looked surprised, to have concern thus taken out of her hands.

"I was sick to my stomach."

"I hope you didn't have to throw up on the subway."

My mother wrinkled her nose, Lucy looked offended. Way to go, Jack, I thought, way to go. He settled back in his seat with a little smile, both his teeth and his dimples showing.

"I contained myself."

"Honey, do you want to go lie down?" asked my mother, leaning forward; I sauntered away, in motion through the thick soup of the room, as Roy also was. He was puttering by the bar, humming to himself. I twisted on my heel, looked at them in their soft chairs; I felt lean and cool and boyish.

"No, I'm fine now. It was just a feeling and it passed." As

this night will pass, and this life, and all of you: for a second I felt like Time or perhaps Death, charged with the passing.

"You shouldn't take the subway, no wonder you felt ill. All those smells—and those people who live on the tracks. It's appalling. I don't know why Mayor Koch doesn't do something about it."

"Because he doesn't give a shit," said Lucy. "He wants the poor people to live in the subways so his friends can co-op the city." Roy was humming more loudly. He had retired two years ago; this had nothing to do with him.

"Well, I don't know," said my mother.

"I know. All you have to do is listen to me and you'll be fine," said Lucy. They smiled at each other. My mother does listen to Lucy. Whenever she bothers to listen to anybody.

"Gwen?" said Roy. He handed me a drink—soda water with grenadine and a wheel of lime. It's what he gave me the night I told them I was no longer drinking, and it's what he always serves me. My mother had said, "But you don't drink too much, Gwen," then had fallen silent; Roy had padded to the bar in his blue leather bedroom slippers and spent a long five minutes inventing this for me.

"I hope you're not pregnant," he whispered to me now.

It took me a minute to catch his meaning. "Oh, no, Roy. I seriously doubt it. It's not morning anyway."

"Just kidding," he said. "It's your sister who'll be pregnant pretty soon."

"I guess so." I glanced over at Jack; he was talking to Malcolm, not looking at me. There was something ingratiating in his posture that annoyed me.

"You know, Gwen," said Roy, "I'm looking forward to your sister having children. Because, you see, they'll think of me as their grandfather. It won't matter to them that I'm not your real father. They won't have any memories of him."

"That's great, Roy," I said distractedly, looking at Jack's body twisted away from me, its dense vibrant abundance. "It'll be great for the kids to have a grandfather."

"Well, they will have a real one, too," he said delicately. "Malcolm's father will be their grandfather. But I don't think he'll mind sharing that task with me. Will you, Jack?"

"What?"

"You won't mind sharing your grandchildren with me?"

"What grandchildren?"

"When Lucy and Malcolm have them, I mean. I'll be their step-granddaddy; that sounds rather nicer than step-father, doesn't it?"

"You'll have to ask my wife," said Jack loudly. "I let my wife make all decisions in family matters."

"A wise idea," Roy murmured, "since she probably would anyway."

They laughed, two men together, Jack lounging with his legs apart, and Lucy gave a heavy sigh. Then my mother asked about Ruth and the company talked about the woman for quite a while. It was such an interesting thing she was doing off in the Soviet Union, wasn't it? Fascinating. And so important. I sat by myself on a hard chair and said nothing. I could be home in bed, I thought. I could be masturbating.

They talked politics and the environment. Five people grouped in my mother's conversational circle of soft green couches, cherrywood tables, low shaded china lamps. My mother put a cracker laden with cheese in my hands. As I bent forward to take it, I thought my body might spill away from me, out of this soul's grasp, stroll over to Jack and just lie on him with the innocence of flesh. . . . And still they talked, their discussion like a toy train grinding round and round the same track. What if we were stranded on a desert island? I thought. In the Andes after a plane wreck? My mother and Lucy were so stubborn; Roy, wily and tough; Malcolm, too good to kill. Jack and I were the ones, I decided, whose bodies would be eventually eaten.

He still wouldn't look at me. He spoke louder and faster: statistics, descriptions, how the world was leaking its riches, all vanishing in my lifetime, as if I had something to do with it. The web would come apart, the balance broken.

"Everybody wants their own country," said Roy, "with its own borders and its own laws."

"They don't much like us over there," remarked my mother vaguely, though they weren't talking, as far as I could tell, about any country in particular.

"Can you really blame them?" replied Lucy. "Can you really blame the peasants of Nicaragua for not liking us?"

"Well, you know, envy hurts you more than the other person," said my mother.

"We're not going to have a choice," Jack insisted. "Nature respects no borders and makes its own laws."

"The rain falls on the just and the unjust alike," I offered, smiling sweetly.

"But some people have umbrellas," retorted Lucy, thus completing the round.

Another drink, I thought, and we could do it again. We could do it all night, who would stop us? Rain, I thought, rain, how I would like to be out in it. Falling cool and grey and steadying, the wet drops sliding down my face, into my mouth, my hair. Out in the rain, under an open sky, Nebraska, Montana, some corn field where a bus could stop, where I could alight, take off my city shoes, and run—

"Dad's writing a book about this stuff," said Malcolm. The mood was instantly transformed; we all looked at Jack expectantly. Oh, rescue us, please, tell us a story. I could feel both his embarrassment and pleasure on my skin. I was such a sensitive instrument, wasn't I, so delicately attuned.

"A, er, fiction book, isn't it?" asked Roy politely.

"Yes, science fiction." That diffidence in his voice; what did he have to be ashamed of?

"Some of these fellows are making quite a lot of money with fiction books, aren't they? This man, what's his name . . ." We all waited but Roy could not think of his name. "Millions of copies sold. How do you do that?"

"Don't ask me," said Jack truculently. I wanted to explain to him that Roy was merely catching hold where he could, he meant no insult; but then I wasn't sure of that. Roy is so bland, one is never quite sure of anything.

"You know how they do it, Dad. They put out books to formula, which you never wanted to do."

"I'd 've died of boredom long before the bucks rolled in. You know, science fiction used to be the last place where you could get away with anything. I could enjoy myself, mess with this and that, all kinds of narrative tricks and dodges, and still tell a good story—the story could end up anywhere, it didn't matter, as long as it kept moving. Now they're trying to streamline it. You've got your star-trek adventure crap, your medievalist fantasy crap, your techno-wizard crap—"

"Your environmental catastrophe novel," said Lucy, stopping him dead for a full thirty seconds.

"Yeah, yeah, I know. I'm trying to do something different . . ." His voice trailed off, he rubbed one hand over his face.

I shot Lucy a cold glance, but she was headed for the kitchen and didn't see it. There was silence after she left. It made me feel I ought to do something. Go sit in Jack's lap, maybe. Put my arms around his neck, say, Never mind. Never mind, honey, we don't care what they think. How sweet, how sweet to kiss and comfort, and how easy to wish him a different sort of man. One who would lasso me over, plant a wet one on my mouth, announce, This here's my girl, folks, ain't she purty? We'll be leaving now, thank you kindly, the lady needs a bit of air.

Out into a pickup truck, a six-pack of beer. Make that two six-packs and a quart of gin. Destination a motel somewhere in Pennsylvania, a yellow dog named Sport wedged in the cab between us.

"Country pleasures," my father once said, in his cups, "are so refined. Do you know what I mean? No, of course you don't. You never will. I'd have raised you in the woods but your mother was against it." He fell asleep then, his soft pale hand curled in his lap, his shirt collar open, the clean white shirt of the New York professional.

How would my father have responded to Lucy? Oh, he had a thousand defenses. The sweet, crooked smile accompanying the barbed innuendo. The controlled explosion, my father admiring his own theatrics, strutting as he thought up wilder and stranger countercharges. The shaggy-dog digression, the hurt sigh, palms up, eyes glazed with moisture. My father could cry on cue, as he demonstrated to us one night. Lucy had been sobbing because our parents were fighting and my father told her sharply to stop that "blubbering."

"That's a disgusting word," said my mother, who was sensitive about her weight.

"That's what it looks like. Their faces get so swollen and ugly when they cry. They don't know how to do it right."

"And you do, I suppose?"

He stood there and grinned at her, two streams of tears jumping out of his eyes. Then he stopped. "I should have been an actor," he said. "Nobody appreciates me."

Of course I knew now that he hadn't really been brilliant. He was clever, he was smart, he was profoundly alcoholic. His alcoholism was an artform, he cultivated outrage. And yet . . . and yet. . . . I looked at Jack slumped in his chair. It was as if we were frozen here, forever in my mother's living room. What did it take but one stroke to set us free? To tell the truth for once, to go home cleanly. Instantly I felt hopeful, the miasma lifted. What could they say, after all? What could they do? I'd take him out of here—out into the warm, open, generous night. "You were right," he'd say in astonishment, tilting my face up for a kiss. "This was much the best way."

"I thought so," I'd reply modestly. "It just occurred to me that it was."

"My brilliant darling. Where to now? California? Ireland?"

"Anywhere. Anywhere with you."

Lucy snapped her fingers in front of my face. Everyone else was standing. "Dinner's served, Madame."

"Oh."

"You're certainly dreamy this evening," she remarked as we all filed into the other room. "If I didn't know better, I'd say you were in love."

"But I am in love."

Because we were only six, my mother had not put the leaf in the table. We were sitting close together, and as they all turned to look at me, I felt a panic so severe it was almost sweet. What does the artist care, after all, for suffering matter? The hormone producers release their jets of stuff and my limbs melt, my face pales, my eyelids quiver. A masterpiece of terror I could certainly appreciate. Perhaps I should remain like this, I thought, preserved in my sweat, both motionless and all atremble, face gleaming like a mirror, I would show them themselves . . .

"Well, Gwen?" asked Lucy. "The suspense is killing us."

Oh, what did I know about honesty anyway? Whenever I attempt it, it turns into cruelty. Even with myself. Maybe especially with myself.

"I've never spoken to him. He sits by himself in the corner at AA meetings and never raises his hand. Soon I'm going to get up the nerve to approach him."

As I invented this I could almost see the boy—slight, fair-haired, shy, full of his terrifying experiences. Not pickups and near rapes but barroom fights, not one night in jail but a dozen.

"Be careful," said my mother. "Those people."

"The cute ones in the corner rarely turn out to be as interesting as you thought they were," said Lucy.

Jack just stared at me with a heavy, outraged glare. I couldn't bring myself to mind; I smiled back at him defiantly. I felt so entirely separate. I wanted to be separate. Yet if I could speak now, from my wild isolation, if I could embody in one gesture my love and my shame—but this was the family dinner table, I must be well behaved. The only thing my parents ever agreed on: children should behave. Ask politely, accept refusal meekly, wait with the patience proper to the unformed. But I was never unformed, I wanted to tell them that. I was already finished and precious and swarming. My mother used to say, "When you have your own children, you can do whatever you please." She said this over and over. What difference did that make, I wanted to scream, I would not be that daughter so favored with my wisdom. But I knew what she meant; after a while I knew. Power is compensation. I didn't want it. I wanted liberty. I still wanted liberty—oh, more than ever—but all I had, I thought, watching Jack's eyes shift, watching Lucy spoon food onto my plate in abundance undesired, was power.

———

Jack left at ten. He gave me a dry peck on the cheek, the same one he gave to my mother and Lucy; he said good night to us all in a grave and muted tone.

I imagined arriving at his apartment and being met with

complete surprise. "My dear. What on earth can I do for you. Has something happened to Malcolm?"

I would not know, I would not be sure. I would turn away in confusion. He would gaze with lifted eyebrows and ironic smile at my departure, calling out perhaps when I was halfway down the stairs, "Watch your step."

11

The summer before the divorce, my father lay on the couch all day. He wore pale pink pajamas that had once belonged to my grandfather and drank gin from a glass kept on the windowsill. He woke at noon, took a drink, ate a bite, slept again. He slept all day and woke up at night. He'd been doing so for three months, since he lost his job. We didn't know if he'd ever get well.

When we asked him what the matter was, our father said, "My blood's tired, girls. There's a sort of paralysis on it. Have you ever thought how unlikely it is that your blood keeps circulating, hour after hour, day after day, that it never stops even when you're asleep?"

No, we had never thought about it. Our blood was fine.

Sometimes it was a headache. "My head," he told us, "is like a tower of dishes piled one on top of the other the way your mother tells you not to do when you clear the table, glasses, spoons, plates, piled higher and higher and the slightest wrong movement will send it all crashing. Like nitroglycerin. You know what that is?"

I knew what it was but I was still confused. It was true that he moved very slowly, that he winced at sudden noises and spoke without moving his head, but how could a person be like nitroglycerin? He had always gotten up before.

He had always drunk a lot. Gin and beer, scotch and brandy—the smell was the smell of my father, roughly following the seasons. But the smell was more acute now, the smell was dizzying—the sight of him even more so. He was thin, his skin had a greenish pallor, and his face was covered with a rusty stubble. That changed him more than anything, that fiery crust on his chin. It made him look like a beggar, whining and fierce; its bright aliveness scared me. What if it kept growing over nose and cheeks, over his tongue, up over his eyes. What if he were facing away from me, then turned around and his head was just the same, all covered with coppery glinting hair.

Our mother wouldn't talk to us about it except to say that he was drunk. Whatever questions we asked were answered thus, curtly. "No, your father's drunk." "I don't know why; he's drunk." "Don't ask me, I'm not drunk."

Our maid Reba said, "Your daddy's got a buddy in that bottle, child. No more to it than that."

"We're his buddies."

"No, you isn't."

"Why not?"

"Because you isn't."

"I don't understand," said Lucy.

"Don't nobody expect you to."

———————

One night in late June, Lucy crept into my room after we'd been put to bed. She wore a long, white cotton nightgown and her dark hair, unbraided, fell in a cloud around her shoulders. She climbed in beside me but her flesh was unnervingly hot so I indicated the foot of the bed where she could sit facing me and she rearranged herself. She was quiet for a moment and I waited, sprawled sideways across my pillows. I could hear my father moving around downstairs.

"Is Dad going to get better?"

"Of course."

"Is he going to get another job?"

"Sure. When he gets around to it."

"But most fathers have one all the time."

"Our father's different."

I felt a sort of pity for her that she didn't understand this. "Most fathers"—even to say that was a betrayal of her own stupidity. Our father, our family, were a law unto themselves; "different" was the bare beginning of that majestic inequality. And Lucy, poor Lucy, she didn't get it; my father was disappointed in her, I knew (and she knew).

"Is he going to die?"

I was shocked. Our father die? Actually the idea had occurred to me. "People don't die from drinking," I said. "They just lose jobs and stuff."

"If it's that bad for him he could die." She looked at me intently, as if I really knew. Her face was pale, her eyes so dark. She wasn't really as pretty as I was but she had her own prettiness that I couldn't touch.

"I know for a fact he won't die," I said. It was so easy to talk like that to Lucy, sometimes I even believed myself. "He'll go on like this for a while, then he'll get better. Of course," I added, "he'll die someday. So will Mom."

"When they're old!" she said passionately, her back arched like a bow. Her white face had turned rosy and was tilted to the ceiling. She believed me. It scared me, though I loved it. The thing was, we knew our mother lied to us. Lucy thought she had reasons to, mothers had to sometimes, but she never believed what our mother said without checking it out with me first. I did have a way of getting other adults to tell me things and I could figure out a lot, yet sometimes I wished she wouldn't trust me so utterly. It didn't console me that so far I had been generally right.

We could hear our father downstairs, the gentle shudder of his body moving through the rooms, the drift, the stumble, then a long, sure passage. He got up only at night. He roamed, he talked to himself; we could hear the sound of it but not the words.

Our father was a basket case. That's what Aileen called him and Aileen, who was clever and sarcastic and very rich, who was our mother's best friend and also a friend of Governor Rockefeller, spoke with the voice of the world. "Kiddos," she told us, "never marry a boozehound." The third or fourth time she said this, Lucy looked her in the eye disdainfully.

"But your husband's fat."

Aileen was startled, though it was the simple truth. He was also bald and spoke with a whine, he had damp fingers and a face like a pudding. Our father on the other hand was sexy. We knew it. "My dear child," said Aileen, "if you think that looks are what matter in a husband . . ." She raised an eyebrow. Lucy shrugged. Our mother said nothing.

Daddy had more than looks. It wasn't even his looks that counted, since he wasn't handsome in an obvious way. His face was too thin and his nose too beaky. It wasn't until you saw him with our mother that you knew he was sexy. He was always teasing her. Sometimes she liked it and sometimes she didn't; sometimes it was nice and sometimes it was nasty. He teased her about being rich, about always doing things the same way, about not liking to break rules. But he also stood close to her when she was cooking and tickled the back of her neck. When he was drunk he told us the story of how he picked her up on the Fifth Avenue bus after she had politely asked him what time it was. He had given her the time, asked her out to dinner. "The Algonquin or the Pierre?" He didn't have enough cash for the bill, but three months later they were married. "You wouldn't even exist," he told us, "if your mother hadn't forgotten her upbringing at that crucial moment."

It was easy to believe this story. We had seen our father in public. He always talked to strangers when he'd been drinking. He was sly about it, carefully choosing his moment and his audience. On line at the movies, buying ice cream, on the bus, our father surprised people with his wit and friendliness. They went away with a smile, with his opinions tucked into their thoughts; he'd look after them, his color high, victorious. "I can make friends anywhere," he said to us. "You see how that woman liked me? Tell your mother that, why don't you?"

We saw no reason to tell our mother. Of course Daddy

could make friends. But they weren't really friends, were they? If the stranger talked too long, responding to such unexpected warmth, our father would become impatient. He'd edge away, using us as his best excuse. "I have to get these children back, their mother wants them for dinner," he'd say, his hands tightly holding our own. Then he'd be silent on the way home. I felt sorry for the people who liked him but couldn't have him. With his hat tilted back, his red hair glinting, his raincoat flapping behind him, and his firm grip, he was the man nobody could do without. Yet they did; only we had him. Only we could keep him simply because we were his children, could see the parentheses on either side of his mouth as enclosing an aside meant only for us. "Don't ever tell anyone," he said. "But your father is a very unsatisfied man."

"Why does he get drunk all the time?" Lucy asked me. She had squirmed closer and her hot little feet rested on my thigh. It wasn't healthy, I had told her, to have such hot feet; people's feet, like dogs' noses, were meant to be cold. My feet were cold. My fingers were cold, even though it was summer. The sound of the traffic crashed on the building, those long waves of cars that never stopped, that kept my father awake and restless as he drank. Was he lonely? The idea was exquisite, it pierced my newest and most nearly adult soul. To pity my father!

"If I knew, I'd tell you," I said, though I wasn't sure. It might not be the kind of thing she'd understand. I felt like I could understand, if I only had time enough. There he was, right underneath us now. What was he doing? Faint crackling noises, then silence. Lucy listened with her head on one shoulder. She looked like an owl, suddenly too wise. I wanted her to go but I couldn't push her out, I could never do that. She crept in here for comfort and it was my pride to give it, to be unlike our mother who refused to get up anymore. Even Lucy had to put herself to bed nowadays. I asked if she wanted a backrub.

"Yes," she whispered, pulling up her nightgown. "Gwen, I'm scared. Mom's so angry."

"Don't worry about her." I rubbed her back the way Reba had taught me, pretending I was planting a garden. "Now I'm plowing the dirt, now I'm raking it smooth. I'm taking out all the stones, I'm making a wall with them. Now I make holes for the seeds and drop them in. Watermelons and pumpkins and green beans and peas . . ."

She sighed with pleasure as I kneaded her thin little back. What if there was a big wind, I thought, what if it blew away all the topsoil, all the bottomsoil, all the bedrock, down to the bone? Then no more Lucy. But I didn't want that, no; I only wanted to put the child to sleep.

When I had harvested the crops and fed them to the Indians, Lucy tottered out of my room and into her own. I stayed awake, for hours, and listened to my father. It seemed to me he was walking through a different house from our own. There were the crashes—or rather loud bumps—of walls surprising him, there was the way he paused suddenly, and then sound of his laughter and talk that weren't begun or ended but caught for a while in the middle, as if only now and then was I attuned to his other life. This idea fascinated me, especially as it grew later. My father was existing in another place, another dimension, a twilight zone. Not the one on television, my father didn't watch television. He read books, though not as much as he used to, and he listened to the radio. He said he preferred voices without the bodies attached, it left more to the imagination.

It wasn't just the gin. Other people drank. They talked too loud and waved their cigarettes around; they didn't sleep all day with their knees pulled up to their chests; they didn't wake at midnight and roam disturbingly, like ghosts surprised back into their bodies.

I wondered what it was like, down there in the dark. I had snuck down once, early Christmas morning, to see my parents arranging my toys under the tree, no Santa after all. I had snuck down when I had friends over to steal marsh-mallows and peanut butter. But it seemed I had never really seen it. Not in the way he did, not the way it was now. It was another dimension laid over the familiar rooms like a new watercolor over the old.

Sometimes when I painted I couldn't wait for a new sheet of paper, I saw the tree could easily become a woman and the sky be the wallpaper of the room where she was brush-ing her hair. But the brown branches bled into the mirror and the mirror poured out of its frame. Soon the whole room was dense with fog. If I was patient, I could still make a picture of it. Let the brown dry and cover it with yellow. So many of my watercolors had this golden glow. My father admired them, he said they were mystical. He said an artist always sees light in unexpected places and then shows it to the world.

"Am I a real artist?" I asked him.

"Nobody ever knows the answer to that question," he said, fixing me with his pop-eyed stare, his head tilted like a bird. He was smiling, he was wiser than I would ever be. "You can spend your whole life at it and never know."

12

I let myself into Jack's apartment cautiously. It was early, barely eleven. I had stayed only to help Lucy with the dishes, then my mother had given me ten dollars for a taxi home. I walked softly down the hall and into the living room where he stood looking down at the park. I knew he had heard me enter. That plump yet delicate body, that jokey cautious person, that man over fifty who wrote books with lurid covers read by pimply teenagers in study hall— how could he represent all delight, all desire? It seemed to me that my emotion, which I had been thinking of (I realized now) as an old one, streaming out since childhood, since birth—an intrinsic feeling turned in his direction because it had to go somewhere, because, as Lucy said, "Gwennie likes to be in love."—was in fact brand-new. I loved Jack and felt suddenly, disquietingly transparent.

"Hi," I said.

He turned around. Such kisses as I had lavished on his mouth, his eyes, were still there.

"Honey?" I said.

"Why did you come there, Gwen?" His voice plaintive and low. "Why? Did you want to make a fool of me in front of your family? Did you want to see me squirm?"

"Of course not."

"Well, I felt like one." His voice was so quiet. I remembered my father's joy in battle, how his eyes would heat up and his insults fly. He liked to call my mother by the names of insects. Carpet ant. Dung beetle. She would tell him how childish he was. I felt like I could play that scene, either part. But this one confused me. Jack's plaintiveness dug into me like a spoon scooping out my flesh. I felt poisonous and silly, stunted into adulthood. I slid one foot out of its shoe and flexed it against my ankle.

My silence roused him. "What the hell did you mean, saying you were in love? The whole table waiting, I was in agony. Agony! She's going to spill it out right now, and what the fuck will I say? Do you have any idea what that felt like? It was bad enough thirty years ago to be inspected by Ruth's family. Her useless father, the great dentist, mangling children's mouths, starting with his own daughter, treating me like a scumbag because I didn't go to college. Still, I was a young man and I had good intentions. But with you, what is it? Your lovely mother, your charming stepfather, I accept their hospitality at the wedding, then tonight, and I'm a rat, a married man secretly fucking their daughter."

"Is that what you're worried about? That my stepfather

won't respect you? I can assure you, Roy doesn't give a shit. Whatever family crisis you can imagine, Roy will totter over to the bar and make a drink for it. He'll pride himself on thinking up just what you'd want in such a peculiar situation."

"How *did* he get all that money anyway?"

"How he got his money is no concern of yours."

"Of course not. It never is." He smiled sarcastically and lit a cigarette. He paced the room, casting sharp glances at me from beneath drawn brows.

I stood my ground, righteously furious—Roy, for Christ's sake, he cared about Roy—yet the coolness and force of his regard began to unsettle me. What was he looking at? I didn't want him to look at me, my body writhing like a sack of worms. I was frightened, confronted with his justified anger. I also thought it wasn't justified at all, nothing could justify it, no one was allowed to make me feel this way, because—

Oh, I was sad, standing still in the doorway, wondering when I would collapse. When my bones would crumble, my nerves turn and bite. You wretch, I murmured, speaking to my self-pity that I could feel gasing through me. You bitch. But why wasn't he gentler? Why wasn't he smarter, why wasn't I stronger, why couldn't I escape? I thought of letting go as one lets go into sleep, falling down and down into the warm black of the mind. Then suddenly as I looked at Jack who was standing unhappily several feet away, something changed in my thinking. It took a sideways hop, un-premeditated. "You're right," I said. "I'm sorry."

His anger was gone. Just like that, which I wouldn't have anticipated. Once, in spite of my success, I would have felt humiliation, or at best a sour triumph. Now I seemed to be out in midair.

There was a pause while Jack savored my words. How does he know I mean them? I wondered. Yet it was clear that he did know. "So why did you do it?" he asked.

"I felt left out."

"But how could you have wanted to be there? I don't get it." He had come closer, I wanted to put my face right up to his. Yet I felt oddly shy, exultant and embarrassed.

"I didn't want to be there. I couldn't stand to be alone either. It's always like this with them," I said slowly, feeling how inadequate, how inexact the words were, yet lingering over them, tasting them. He would understand. There was time to say everything.

"Yeah, okay, I understand that feeling, I had parents . . . but, Gwen, this was such a sticky situation." He shook his head. "I just don't get it."

My disappointment was extravagant. I couldn't speak. I thought: You always expect too much. I was confused, ashamed of my feelings. Ashamed of which one? I didn't know. I smiled nervously. Jack was pacing again, though with less fervor. I had softened him but what did that signify? He was off on his own.

"If my father had ever done a thing like this, I would have been mortified. My old man going out with my girl's sister? I can't imagine anything worse. He used to make remarks sometimes, not about my girls—he knew better than that— but about my friend Bob's. He'd say, 'Hey, Bob, how can you go out with a flat-chested girl? What's the point? Don't tell me she lets you between her legs.' 'Okay,' says Bob, 'I won't tell you.'" Jack shook his head. "He was notorious.

Sometimes my friends would bait him. 'So what do you think of Jeanie, Mr. Price? Not bad, huh?' And whatever he said, they'd laugh, they were fascinated in a sick way. This man was on the radio, they all listened to his show."

"Well, it's hardly the same thing," I said, somehow holding my voice level. His father, his son. I felt divided and held at bay by their presences; why couldn't we be alone?

"Oh, I know, I know. I'm just trying to imagine how Malcolm will look at it."

"He wouldn't care about that. That wouldn't be the issue."

"Not the only one, certainly. He loves his mother. He's always been proud that we didn't divorce like so many of his friends' parents."

"Well, maybe you won't."

My voice was coming out steadily; it amazed me that I could control it. Why didn't the words break apart, why didn't the sound decompose? And this split between what I felt and what I was saying made me feel the more keenly the distance of Jack's thought, his memories excluding me; he was standing upright and aging in his flesh as if in armor, a little defensive smile playing about his lips.

"Oh, well, the kid never liked me much anyway."

"What do you mean? He adores you."

"He's always been Ruth's son. Three years old, I'd take him to the park to sail his boat on the pond, he'd be crying for her."

"He's always talking about you." Jack glanced at me, a naive, unguarded glance and I felt a sudden vertigo. I could reassure him. I could mend the breach. One thing I knew about Malcolm was that he wanted a family. As much of one as he could have. There was no way he would ever reject his father. "He loves you. You ought to see him more often. See him alone, call him up and invite him out to lunch." My voice was tender and coaxing, I was pleased with myself.

Jack sighed. "Not while this is going on."

I felt like I'd been punched. How had I managed to forget the salient fact of our situation? Of course he couldn't call him now, I'd make sure of that. You're crazy, I whispered to myself, you loco bitch.

"Listen, Gwen, I have to tell you something. This is how I feel. I'm not saying it's right. It has nothing to do with the fact that I love you. But I believe—I can't help it—that marriage is a promise one keeps. An odd idea in this day and age, I know . . . I'm not trying to sound like a good guy, I'm not sure I even believe in what I believe, if that makes any sense."

"Oh, that makes sense," I said wildly. "I know all about that."

"Well you see there have been times, many times over the years, when Ruth and I were not getting along, but I didn't want to leave her and I was afraid she'd leave me. I know what it feels like, you see. To think your marriage can suddenly fall apart, she can go off and take the child and there's nothing you can do—everything you've said to her and to nobody else over the years . . . Okay, things are different now, we never really talk anymore and Malcolm's grown. But still, unless I was sure—" He stopped. "I'm sorry. Why was I angry at you? I have no right to be angry at you. Of course you want this whole thing out in the open, resolved, and so you should."

I was paralyzed. Did I want it out in the open, or did I

want to take it deeper and deeper into the dark? To lead him away by a route he'd never suspect? I had an image of carrying his body, inert through the streets. And she would send her wolves after us, the white wolves of righteousness.

"I don't know what to do," he said.

Was he expecting an answer from me? I leaned my shoulders against the wall and looked at him. That head with its mass of coarse greying curls, those eyes. I could do nothing for him. Once I had the confidence, the joy. I believed that what welled up in me, this painful force, was love. Once I believed that.

"I don't know what to do," he repeated.

The phone rang. Who else could it be but Ruth, calling from the Soviet Union? Jack's voice immediately changed, took on a familiarity I couldn't hope to combat. He sounded almost conspiratorial as he asked her questions about conditions there, questions which she answered at length. His body was turned away from me, pulled up and nervous; he reminded me of a teenage boy on the phone with a girl.

I watched him for a while; absorbing the knowledge of my irrelevance. It felt almost bracing: O the cold truth, the cold truth. I left the room. I went into their bedroom. A more different one from Malcolm's could not be imagined. Where his was empty, this was cluttered: Mexican rugs on the floor, red curtains at the window, pictures and shelves of books. A big desk in one corner, photographs of Malcolm. Photographs of Jack!

I went over to examine them. So young, my sweetheart, so young. Twenty-three, holding a baby; thirty-five. I started crying when I saw how handsome he had been, such a fresh face, such eager charm. Well, was he so different now? Didn't he have something just as good? More concealed, perhaps. Anyway, not for me. Not really for me. She had his whole life tacked up on the wall. A picture, taken, I guessed, five years ago, of the two of them. Out in the country somewhere, his arm around her shoulders. She was smiling, dressed in a shapeless sweater. He had some sort of down vest on over a checked shirt. His face looked almost the same as it did now, but there was a smile on his face I had never seen, the smile of a paterfamilias.

I stood there for a long time, soaking up my pain like medicine. Perhaps I took more than I needed? I had always taken much more of everything than I needed. Finally the door opened and Jack came in. "Gwen, what're you doing in here, what're you doing?" He was speaking softly, gentling me as if I were a horse. I laughed at that, at the thought of being a horse; the tears were falling down my cheeks. He steered me out of her room, one arm around my shoulders, and into Malcolm's room. I fell down on the bed. He turned off the light and sat beside me. His weight on the mattress, his smell, so familiar, so strange, so impossible. I couldn't imagine being without him. I couldn't imagine being with anyone.

"Why didn't you tell me that you loved her?" I wanted to love her too. I wanted to love her or to erase her. He sighed and didn't say anything. I was sobbing and couldn't stop. "I wish to be unborn," I whispered into the pillow. Far away he shifted his weight, his hand lightly touched my shoulder.

I couldn't stop crying. It just kept on; why not, grief has

no natural end. It's as vast as the sea and would drown me when it chose to. How it rocks me, how it drags me. How it knows me, is me, takes me; who am I to struggle?

I didn't want to preserve myself. Let go, be anything else, even younger than I was, knowing absolutely nothing. Unborn, unbearable. All the others were so rich and full and grown-up, so human and alert. They knew about the world, they knew about each other. Maybe not much, but—shut up, I whispered. Fifteen years of assault by alcohol, you know less than nothing. Into the silence, deep and shining, but I kept making noise, "blubbering," as my father would put it. "The children's faces get so ugly." Go away. Go away. I curled my legs up under me.

"Gwen," said Jack, "I'm going to divorce Ruth. Hush, it's settled. It's my decision. I'll tell her as soon as she gets back. No, don't say anything, it's settled."

13

My father was combing his hair before the mirror in the hall. The spiky red tufts gave way to the spit-moistened comb and lay smooth; his narrow, beak-nosed face regarded itself. I watched him from the third or fourth stair. He was humming a tune from Mozart and sipping a small crystal wine glass full of gin.

He strolled into the living room and picked up a magazine from the coffee table. He sat on the couch and flipped through it. I walked into his sphere of vision. "Gwendolyn." I smiled timidly. "This is interesting. They've discovered a new drug that enables you to see God. What do you think of that?"

"I bet it doesn't work."

"Of course not. Of course not. But what if it did? What would you say then? Would you take it?"

"I don't know."

"Not me. Sounds dangerous. Who knows if God wants to see us? They never think of that, those scientists . . . He might get pretty angry. Might show them a thing or two."

"Do you believe in God?"

"If God believes in me, I'll believe in Him. He hasn't let me know yet. . . . Norah's Mama goes to church. I asked her, 'What for, Irene, you think you're going to Heaven? With all the nigras?'" He winked at me. "She said—can you beat it—'I don't expect anything. I go to church to show my thanks.' Well, natch, I said to myself, all that dough . . . Should we go to church, Gwendolyn, what do you think?"

"You sleep too late to go to church."

He laughed. "I do, don't I? I'd have to go to night church."

"There's no such thing."

"Oh, don't be so sure. There are many things you've never heard of. Many, many things." He waved his glass in the air and a few drops flew out, I couldn't see where they landed.

I knew there were many things. It seemed that was all I knew and the weight of my ignorance oppressed me. Why was it, I thought, that when you were young you had this huge weight to carry, while when you were older and stronger, your ignorance was so light you scarcely noticed it at all? Was that why they got drunk, that strange lightness on their shoulders? Why couldn't they just float easily through the world? I would when I grew up. Like a queen with a dress of roses, immensely tall, as they had once seemed.

My father began to walk around the room and I followed

him. He was restless, I understood that, roaming just to move, but what did he see, his gaze so loose and sliding? Eyes on me as if I were a lamp or a chair? As if I weren't there, yet he spoke to me.

"This is the night church where the animals come to pray, where the glass falls out of the windows and the music begins to play, and the wine turns into blood because they like it that way . . ." He smiled and repeated it.

I felt prey to what my mother called "figments of your imagination." Fig-men. There was a dream I often had of a white thing. My room full of moonlight, this thing on the floor. Like a sheet, white, rising, flapping, hanging in the air. Not very high in the air, only a few inches, hovering as if to protect what lay beneath. Yes, draping itself, contoured, that shining stuff! What? I would wake up in a sweat, the floor swept clean.

"Gwendolyn?" he said.

"Yes?" But he had already forgotten what he wanted, he stood still, his glass pressed to his lips. A ridiculous man — yes, I could see him that way. Let Eileen's, my mother's friend's eyes fit over mine. But then I would never know what he was trying to tell me. He was not an artist, willing to reveal it to the world.

Every night I crept downstairs; every night it was the same. My father awoke around midnight and looked at himself in the mirror. I couldn't tell how he felt, running a hand over his leaf-red stubble. He simply gazed for a while, then had a drink. He used the good glasses, selecting a different shape every night. Martini, champagne, brandy — I knew what most of them were for but in my father's hands they were all for gin, that oily, colorless elixir, and I could see how it pleased him to vary. His fingers slid up the flutes, cupped the balloons, held the red wine glasses loosely, like shaking another man's hand.

Sometimes we had music. He played it low and only for a moment. A snatch of jazz, a bit of Beethoven, then he would lift the arm, as if he had what he wanted. I imagined the music continuing in his head, the memory set going. The same music as was on the record? Or different altogether?

He caught sight of me when I insisted on it, when I walked in front of him, and always he seemed vaguely pleased. We held a short enigmatic conversation, which I could never remember in the morning, then his attention drifted away. He wouldn't answer my remarks. What I shared was his private life, and I felt forlorn in this privilege.

Such pain as that forlornness—held steady—can illumine. I became aware of the sensation of thought as it wound through me. What I thought didn't matter, but that thought had body. My own thought, my own body, the same coiling stuff.

I felt excited, as if I had discovered new land. Woods, glades, rivers, whatever was missing in this concrete city. Space, privacy. I saw how it gathered, solitude, like a protective army. I saw how pain was like pillars of wisdom holding the cosmos up, how I had to build them so carefully. As if I were dreaming awake, full of a busy awareness. Aware of every breath, of the peculiarity of vision—of the incoming tide of intelligence that was sweeping me up high.

I wanted to tell my father but hadn't the words. He roamed through doorways, lurched against walls, reared

back in graceful, prancing drunkenness. I trusted his peculiar navigation. I paused when he did by the window to look
out at the cars along the avenue, out at the sky swimming
with yellow light. My father took a drink, and another. I
knew he could die from it. But I also knew something else:
This was already his other life. This was the Underworld.

He sank down, he finished his drink and slithered to the
carpet. He sat with his head against the sofa and smiled
rhapsodically. His eyes were dimmer than ever but wide
awake, and his hands rose in the air, gesturing like flowers
in the wind.

When he no longer moved or spoke, I crept up to my
room. I felt lonelier the farther I got upstairs, but when I
was in bed I fell asleep instantly. I fell asleep on an inrush of
love and gratitude: my bed, my pillow, beloved bed and
pillow!

14

I woke up in the morning with the desire to buy Jack presents. Gift upon gift, a treasure heap to the horizon. I looked down at him, he was still sleeping. He was usually up at seven; I would hear him in his study typing for two hours before I got up. (And sometimes I would stay for breakfast, sometimes we would get back in bed.) But now he was dreaming of his new life, wasn't he. My precious love, my sweetling, my fig-man, my tawny tom. How innocent he was! Nothing he did wrong could ever be wrong, I would protect him even from myself.

I crept out of bed quietly and left the apartment. A Friday morning. When I was in school, Fridays were so much better than the actual weekend. Sitting all day in class daydreaming, mistranslating Latin, misquoting Shakespeare, moving around the terms of the equation just as I pleased. "I think she does it on purpose," they used to say to my mother, explaining certain anomalies.

"But you're so smart, Gwen," she would reproach me. Smart, perhaps, and also not so smart; my stupidity has always been legion. But able to enjoy myself, yes certainly that; in the midst of whatever unhappiness always able to find something.

I bought Jack a bright blue silk and cotton blend sweater. As blue as the sky, as smooth as ice cream. I tried it on. It was much too big, of course, it fell all over itself and covered me to the tips of my fingers. The salesman was attracted and began to flirt with me. I flirted back from my vast distance within Jack's sweater; I felt like only my head was at all visible, making its cheery remarks.

On the way home I bought croissants and a bunch of red tulips. I gave a dollar to a homeless man and paused receptively for his blessing. It was so easy to get a blessing in New York these days. All over the streets, for the price of a cup of coffee, the charity cases offer us relief from the weight of our greed. So convenient; they wait at the door. One of life's luxuries and nobody notices.

I gave away another dollar to a woman by the subway entrance, then, when I turned the corner, let a dollar fall from my hand. The wind picked it up and blew it ahead of me on the sidewalk. Blown like newspaper or a movie stub, like a candy wrapper, my little dollar. I watched it tenderly as it curled and scuttled along and caught itself on a bush, inside a black railing. Caught and fluttered; it might have been growing there. Okay, little dollar, I thought, there you stay. Someone will find you and think you're a lucky omen. If I can make luck happen, I thought, running the last half block, up the stairs, what need have I of art?

"Where'd you go?" asked Jack. He was standing right inside the door like a sentry, wearing nothing but his boxer shorts.

"To buy you a present, of course." I put my purchases down on the hall table, my joy held closer to my flesh. Clinging there. He didn't seem to hear me. His face was creased and puffy, as if he had slept too long.

"I woke up and missed you. I worried." His voice was growly and confused; I gave him a peck on the cheek and then another. He pushed me back against the wall. "Don't do that, don't go away." He lowered his head and began to kiss my neck and breasts. His mouth was rough, dragging at me through my thin T-shirt. It scared me, it excited me, and I couldn't tell the difference. His arm was between my legs, thick and powerful, his other arm around my waist as he half carried me to the bedroom, my feet sliding. I glanced over my shoulder at the bag on the table, the name of the store in violet script. My beautiful present. Why wouldn't he wait to try it on?

I was flat on my back, my shirt around my neck. He squeezed and pulled at my breasts, his hands twisting over and under them like the U-turns of sharks in a tank. On his face a fixed ecstasy, as if I weren't there. But then his face was next to mine, he was staring at me, he was saying, "I love you I love you I love you, do you love me?" on and on. I was battered by it as if by the wind and rain of a storm; something was happening everywhere without my consent. My body responded with a kind of spasm: it could be

couch and you just don't feel like getting up. Then you think about calling me later but you're just not in the mood. Right?"

"You're semicorrect. I can reach the phone from the couch though, that's not the problem. In fact I'm on the couch right now, and actually I wasn't in when you called. I've been going to a lot of meetings."

"You could've called back yesterday. I suppose I should be grateful to hear from you at all."

"Don't be grateful unless you want to be."

"Whatever that means. Listen, I called to invite you out for your birthday. Malcolm and I want to take you out for dinner."

"Oh, thanks, but I'm busy that night." I didn't know what I was doing but I was doing it with Jack.

"Doing what?" She sounded upset; I should have thought of this earlier. She likes to spend my birthdays with me when she can.

"I'm going out with some people from AA. I was thinking about birthdays past and it just seemed like a good idea."

"I thought you didn't talk to anybody there. You told me it helped to listen to the stories but you weren't into the whole group thing." Lucy believes in groups—CR groups, therapy groups, political coalitions. And even though she sent me there, AA gives her pause; she's leery of the God stuff. She had always been glad I got sober without becoming a religious freak. I felt a righteous anger until I remembered that I wasn't in fact going out with AA people. Then I felt frightened and, at the same time, wanted to laugh.

"Well, things change. There's a couple of intelligent peo-ple there, and they're, you know, *evolved,* as we used to say in California . . . Want to come along?"

"No thanks. If you come by my office in the afternoon, I'll give you your present."

"Okay, I'll do that. Sorry about the evening. It was really nice of you."

"Hey, shit, my sister turning thirty. Grown up at last. It's something I want to see."

"Me too," I sighed.

"Gwennie, I'm glad you're going out with those people. Truly."

"Thanks."

"I'll see you soon. Malcolm sends love."

"Ditto," I said, and hung up. I felt limp, my body reeked with sweat. Oh, well, I thought, getting up to take a shower. So a life of deception, so what else is new. So she doesn't understand, so neither do I, so who cares. What happens, happens. I just can't keep ahead of this shit.

15

Then it was September, the summer was over. We hadn't gone to East Hampton as we usually did. Your father's not capable, said my mother, and of course we couldn't leave him. The sandwich at noon, the dinner left on the coffee table—these offerings sustained him. We fed him and he remained here, not entirely in the other life.

He still talked on the telephone a few times a week. His friends called him and my mother brought the phone to couchside; she had hopes for those phone calls. She would ask what the caller had said. "Blah, blah, blah," he replied, waving his fingers at her derisively. Then he'd be sorry. "Tell your mother," he croaked to me once, "that I simply can't remember."

"Dad, you just finished talking."

"I couldn't tell you a word the guy said."

"Mr. Abrams."

"Whoever."

But I didn't tell her. I was afraid she'd put him in a hospital. Eileen had mentioned the idea and my mother had said she was thinking about it. She was worried about its being on his record though; besides, he was perfectly safe here, he never went out.

"That makes it worse," said Eileen, "don't you see? The man's crazy."

"Oh, I don't think so. He's just doing what he wants to do, he knows what he can get away with. He thinks I can't live without him, thinks he's embarrassing me to death . . . if *you* think he's crazy, what will the doctors think? I'm not putting him in one of those places where they never let you out."

"It might be the best thing you could do for him."

"Why should I do the best thing for him? No, seriously."

My mother took Lucy out to buy school clothes. I refused to go, saying I felt under the weather. She peered at me while I silently absolved myself of any lie. Under the weather was the kind of phrase that could mean any number of things. Didn't it depend on what kind of weather it was that you were under? In East Hampton sometimes I swam in the ocean when it rained. I wasn't supposed to, but when the rain fell hard, I liked to lie in the water just out from the beach and hold my breath as the waves rocked me. The rain poured down; it seemed less wet underwater; I began to think I could really — I had this power somewhere inside me to breathe water. I never tried yet I loved to play with the strange cool idea that yes, I had only to believe . . .

My mother didn't insist I come but left without me, after telling me to make my father a sandwich for lunch.

At noon I heard him stir. I had by now seen the difficulty he had in swallowing so I put orange juice and the milk and an egg in the blender. It came out tasting delicious—I tasted it again and again—and I carried it in to where he lay propped on his elbows, his face pale and sweaty. "I made you an Orange Julius," I said.

He grimaced. "How about a little gin in it?"

"Okay," I replied guiltily. He routinely drank gin with his sandwich, but somehow to put it in a lunch was worse.

"There's a bottle in the kitchen," he said. I knew where it was. I knew everything about what he did. I wondered if he knew that I knew, if he remembered in the morning my presence the night before.

I took his glass out to the kitchen, spiked it with gin, and brought it back. His hands were trembling as he grasped it. He positioned it at his mouth and drank. "Thank you, darlin'," he said.

"Mom and Lucy went out shopping," I told him. "To buy school clothes."

"School? In the middle of the summer?"

"Monday's Labor Day."

"The day of rest for the toiling masses. Poor shmucks. They should do what I did, marry a rich bitch."

"Daddy. . . ."

"She's a beautiful woman, Gwendolyn. A fine specimen." His tone was ambiguous. What I wanted to know was, What about me?

"She's not so beautiful," I said. "She dyes her hair."

My father laughed, a short, loud bark. "Not beautiful? What do you mean? Are you on my side, then? What a funny girl." He looked at me and he seemed to see something he had not seen before. I suddenly wanted to be smaller, thinner, as I had been last year, smooth and flat as a newly peeled twig. "You'll be more beautiful than Norah, sweetheart," he said. "You already are." For a moment it was like those dreams when you realize, sitting on the bus to school, that you're naked. Then he smiled with a peculiar vanity, inward and yet caressing. "Of course, you take after me."

I said, "Do you want another drink?"

"Well, I think I do. You're a good girl."

I took his glass in the kitchen and, trembling, made another. Without thinking, I made one for myself: orange juice and milk and a little bit of gin. Perhaps it's not correct to say that I didn't think, but it wasn't the kind of thinking I was used to. It was temptation but not as I knew it, as something to wrestle with. Instead there was a sweet, liquid hook in my brain connecting impulse to action in a strangely mechanical way. Liquid, alive as a river, yet precise and unbending; my hand reached out for the drink and I took a sip, then I carried the glasses back to the other room.

My father shut his eyes to drink. He smiled when he was done. "You make a great drink."

I sipped at my glass. The world began to loosen. The furniture lost its hardness, the air took on form. Everything mimicked my own body, warm and breathing and invulnerable. I sat there for some period of time while my father lightly snored. I was thinking about growing up, how easy it would be really. I would just do it. Tomorrow.

My father opened his eyes. "Gwen-do-lyn," he said, "would you bring in my bottle, please, Precious?"

I got up and started for the kitchen. First I knocked over my chair, then I bumped into the wall. Not very hard but it was startling—I couldn't tell where things were. I went very slow after that, walking in the middle of any passage like a ship making its way between rocks. I was frightened by this lack of control but I had an insight about fear: It wasn't me, it was a dog, a black dog; you only had to kick it now and then.

I brought the bottle back. It was almost full of this stuff, this magic that worked so quickly. I wasn't sure yet whether I liked it, but I was impressed. Even after watching my father for so long I hadn't really believed—how could I?—that my consciousness could actually change.

I poured straight gin into his glass and then some into mine. I drank half, tasting the cold spicy burn of the booze, its high-mountain herbal wildness. My head was flying.

"You're drinking gin," said my father, and his tone was no more than wondering. "Do you drink? So young?"

"Yes." The word was long, it was a like a tongue of a frog snapping out into the air. I felt it linger, still attached; everything I did lingered, every tiny movement.

"I should tell you," he began, taking a deep drink, "that it isn't worth it. It's pain and trouble, Sweetness. Pain and trouble. Is it worth it? I don't know. . . . Sometimes, I admit, I think it is. But you're too young, you bad girl."

He took the glass from my hand and drained it. I took it back and poured more gin. He took it from me and drank it,

I filled it, and we went on like that, my father drinking most but by no means all of the gin.

How kind he looked. His red hair was as homey as firelight. His brown eyes, pinked by the booze, were blurry and soft, swimming in a face that no longer twitched, was no longer pale.

We talked about everything. His fights with my mother, my feelings about boys, my desire to be an artist. I can't remember most of what we said. The fact that he answered me—or, as I thought of it, that I had learned what to ask him—was in itself so satisfying. I experienced for the first time that chummy agreement, that deep sense of alikeness that maturity brings.

Along with this was a heightened pride in my difference. I was Gwendolyn, made of the same stuff as he was, as everyone was, but with one original detail woven into the corner. I could linger there in my uniqueness or I could spread out into the common cloth, that gorgeous tapestry that alcohol makes of human life—all of which was here, by virtue of my anticipation, all of it mine.

My father fell silent but I felt no separation. He didn't need to talk to me. Beneath the surface of our lives, beneath all surfaces, was this connection that it was bliss to feel. I had felt bliss before, but this was the first time I had believed in its triumph.

———

The afternoon quietly vanished. When my mother and Lucy returned, I was slumped across the coffee table with an empty glass by my feet. Daddy was asleep. She screamed, of course, and woke him up, and shook me, and screamed some more. I don't know what he said, because her entrance precipitated an urgent need to vomit. I ran upstairs and threw up all over the bathroom. Lucy followed me, wide-eyed, and watched. "Go away," I said.

"What happened?"

"I got drunk, obviously. Go away."

"Why?" I didn't answer. "Did Daddy let you? How could you drink that stuff? Gwen?" Her voice was tearful and bewildered. I could hear my mother's slow tread on the stairs.

"Go away, go away, go away."

Lucy said, "You made a real mess. Aren't you going to clean it up?"

"She'll clean it up later," said my mother. "She's going to bed now. Lucy, go to your room." My sister obeyed—didn't she always?—and my mother stood there looking at me. My cheek was leaning against the toilet and I realized with surprise the relief it was, that sturdy coolness. I felt grateful to the toilet.

"Get up, Gwen," said my mother.

Aren't mothers supposed to take care of you when you're sick? "I don't feel so good," I whispered.

"I'm sure you don't. What did you expect?"

I threw up again, violently, and my body was shivering, or rather my stomach was; my stomach felt pale and cold while my face was flushed with a stabbing fever.

My mother stepped out of the bathroom. "Wash your face," came her distant voice, "and get in bed when you're finished."

"Mommy," I said, but she had already gone.

I washed my face, then started to cry, and the tears were

awful, they tasted like gin. They made me want to throw up again. I could smell the vomit in my hair, the flecks of orange and sour milk, and I tottered weakly into bed.

I lay still for some indeterminate time, astonished at the extent of pain, astonished at my own ability to endure it. I thought my heart, pounding with loud irregular thumps, would jump out of place like a train jumping the track. It would tangle itself in my ribs, snap its arteries, plummet; or simply stop, a sudden, weird—but I knew it now—entirely possible silence.

It was terrifying to be left alone. I heard footsteps up and down the stairs, doors were opened and shut. There were voices—my mother's, my father's, someone else's. A terrible thirst spread from my lips down the back of my throat. I made it to the bathroom, drank a glass of water, threw it up. She didn't know how much I had had to drink. I could die.

I tried to imagine that it wasn't my fault. I set up the argument: I couldn't have known. Yet hadn't I seen him lying on the couch day after day? What did I think he was feeling? "My head is like a pile of dishes . . ." Poor Daddy. Poor, poor Daddy.

By the time I went downstairs the next morning my father was gone. My mother said they were getting a divorce. Lucy was crying; Lucy didn't stop crying for several weeks. My mother explained to me that she had to protect me, it was her duty as a mother. My father had failed in his respon-sibilities, but she must live up to hers. I hadn't the faintest idea what she was talking about. It was all my fault, and how could she protect me from myself? She couldn't protect anyone; she couldn't even stop Lucy crying.

16

The night before my birthday, Jack insisted on coming to my apartment. He called me in the afternoon and proposed it; I was lying on the rug reading my fortune with the Tarot. I had laid out the cards: the Devil, the Ten of Swords, the Tower. I knew those particular cards like I knew my mirror image. "Why do you want to come here?" I asked.

"Do I need a reason? I want to see where you live. I'm lonely over here. What's the big secret, anyway? I want to sleep in your bed." He offered all this as if laying on colors of paint. I felt worked over by his plaintive, stubborn, sarcastic, warmth-inducing voice.

"It's a comedown from your place," I replied.

"My place won't be my place much longer."

"You're going to give it to her?"

"Of course."

"Why 'of course'? She makes as much as you do. You ought to sell it and divide the proceeds."

"No, Gwendolyn." His voice was heavy and patient, as if I ought to understand this.

"Really," I said. "What if your books stop selling? You have to protect yourself."

"Don't worry about me, I can make a living. I always have and I always will. I've supported one wife, I can support another."

"You won't have to." There was a pause.

"Fine, I'll see you at seven?"

"Okay."

I hung up the phone and swept up the cards. The dangers ahead of me would never go away. They were imbedded in the bone—a future never reached, never done with. It occurred to me that I'd known this for a long time now. The implacable nature of my self, her haul of shame and pity, the head I wished to open to the stars. I could see her—me— like a figure against the sky; drunk at eighteen, after reading the Tarot, I had seen her as I gazed at the embroidered flowers on my bedspread, the reds and yellows. I had known then that it was all right as long as there were reds and yellows.

But I was afraid. Jack would sense the evil under my bed, the weirdness radiating from the stove coils. All the nights I spent alone here the noise of the appliances grew louder and louder, as if in mockery of my lack of competing clamor. I'd remember California nights—the quiet, the flowery air, the local wine that tasted like pine and cedar, wild roses, sometimes like blood. I used to think of the Masai in Africa, drinking the blood of their cattle, as I emptied a bottle of cabernet, and when it was three-quarters gone, I felt the warrior stir within me. I felt his solitude and pride and oneness with nature as I walked around my yard in the cool blue night.

But I wasn't alone anymore; I never had to be again. (Until he died, that is. How long is the life expectancy of a fifty-year-old man? One who eats too much, who smokes, who is loved by me?) We would have an apartment of our own. A bedroom of our own. I had to talk to Jack about Malcolm. It seemed important to get to the bottom of that. How could he think Malcolm didn't like him? How did he think he had a choice?

When Jack arrived at seven I felt shy with him; I kissed him several times at the door to conceal it. But the kisses only made it worse. With each one I took in a charge of electricity and charged him too; when I was done, I felt giddy and dizzy, and he seemed possessed of powers not human: gravitational, occult. I felt under his influence, far more than he knew. But if he didn't know, I thought, how could it be his influence?

I showed him my three narrow rooms, the closet-sized kitchen, the security gates on the windows. His body, moving through my space, was something felt in my inner ear; it unbalanced me: I felt a dangerous confusion. If the present won't stay itself, if two people in a room can't remain distinct from each other, if everything rises up to be attended to at once — I was fighting this shimmer he gave off, this enchantment, and feared it was a fight I wished to lose.

He looked at my paintings for a long time in silence.

"Those are the rejects," I said.

"You're lucky. Now you get to keep them. God, I like this one." He stooped to peer at the old Newfoundland who stared mournfully back, his soft muzzle feathered with greying black curls.

"I know. He's my favorite, too. Sometimes I talk to him." Sometimes, I thought, he talked back. Even without booze I got quite fanciful late at night.

"They're like cave paintings." His voice was admiring, I felt despair. I couldn't believe him. To be an artist—you can spend your whole life at it and never know. Jack straightened up and smiled. "They're wonderful, congratulations. You know, I feel so incredibly good in this apartment. I feel fantastic."

He strode around, peering at everything, and I was guilty of my sorrow, how it kept us apart. It had been a mistake to let him come here, I thought. I'd forgotten myself, I'd been seduced by the idea of recovery. There was no such thing as recovery. Only more desperate fantasy, more elaborate illusion. To embark on such a thing as a love affair . . . as if I would be allowed that freedom.

I crept backward to the couch, sank into its cushions. How it enfolded me, night after night, the television glowing like a benevolent executioner. Smiling Dave and Johnny, *Midnight Blue*. A naked woman with her legs spread, the microphone held to her crotch. "So you can tell she really likes it." I'd lay awake and watch that, and imagined myself at ten watching that. How many ten-year-old girls in New York stay up late, have their own TVs in their bedrooms?

Jack sat beside me. He took off his shoes and swung his legs up on my lap. I pulled off his socks and looked at his feet, the yellow waxy skin on the bottoms, the tufts of hair at the base of his toes. His toes were long and thin and bent, his ankles delicate. It helped a little to look at his feet. "Why aren't you close to Malcolm?" I asked.

He didn't say anything for a while. "You really want to know?"

"Of course."

"Why?"

"You're offering me the position of stepmother."

He looked startled. "I guess I am. You poor thing. Well—"

He paused for a long time. I thought of all the drinking men I had ever known, pouring out their sad and violent pasts as I idly listened and cracked open another bottle. Just as I listened at the meetings. This was the same thing, wasn't it? No.

"I don't know where to start," he said.

"Start at the beginning."

I had to clear him of my debris. Gwen's the one with imagination, my mother used to say, and Lucy's got sense. I used to think I had the better side of that deal.

"Okay. In the beginning—in the beginning Ruth went through natural childbirth. Thirty hours of excruciating pain. 'Women can do anything,' the doctor told me, 'they're superb biological machines.' I liked that line, I must admit. I was more of a literary machine myself. I was sending out a story every two weeks, as well as putting in my time on a novel—really going nuts. Ruth used to get mad at me for not helping more with the baby. I tried to help. I can change a diaper, I can sing a lullaby. She told me I was doing it wrong. The kid would cry. All the time. After a while I figured you had to ignore it. What do babies want anyway? She'd get angry at me, say she couldn't trust me alone with him, I didn't pay close enough attention. I thought she smothered him. The kid needed more independence."

"What age are we talking about, three months?"

"Ah, you're a woman, aren't you?" he said. "Can't have those pretty breasts without the maternal instinct."

"Fuck you," I said. "I don't have any maternal instinct."

He laughed. "Sure you do." I didn't answer. I could hardly tell him that babies reminded me of large blood-swollen ticks; yet I didn't want to claim a longing—remote, surfacing only in dreams—that seemed to inspire such resentment in him. The problem was I understood that resentment. I could share it all too easily. The two of us against them, the women—but this was Jack's story, not mine.

"Go on," I said.

"This is ancient history, you know, we're talking over a quarter of a century ago." As he talked those days and nights—the first summer in the apartment in Murray Hill, no air-conditioning, no diaper service, the neighbors complaining about the crying—came to life and I could see the young, imperious Ruth, sweat darkening her upper lip, being given her first command, the tiny child. And Jack, worried about the bills in a way Ruth never was ("They won't evict us. We have a baby."), trying to be of help, doing the best he could, and being subtly excluded. Her pitying smile when she came back from her first solo excursion and found Jack trying to placate two-week-old Malcolm with a finger dipped in warm water. Her fury when she found him once stoned on pot, crawling with the baby and talking to him in French. "We were having a great time," he said wistfully, "the best time we ever had. I remembered what it was like to be a baby, I was down there with him, eyeball to eyeball . . . and I wasn't that stoned. Nothing would have happened."

Finally, her adamant refusal to negotiate the disagreements they began to have about child-rearing. She was both indulgent and perfectionistic; he wanted, he said, to give the boy a little breathing room. "Finally I backed off. I figured, she's the mother. Motherhood is sacred, right? Fuck it. Fuck it."

He lit a cigarette, I rubbed his feet. I remembered his story of the clone, the child who grows up exactly like the original, a boy dead in an accident, except that he never recognizes his father. Each time the man leaves the room the clone forgets. In desperation the man murders the boy; in desperation he clones him again. Over and over, and nobody questions these "accidents," and nobody seems to grow any older.

"But you loved her," I said.

"Yeah." He laughed shortly. "I think she hypnotized me."

I knew what he meant. There was something extra-human about Ruth, all her wants and needs beaming on and off like headlights coming toward you through a swirling fog. You couldn't help but pay attention.

"Can I confess something to you?" he said. I didn't answer but smiled, lifted his foot and kissed his toes. The more he spoke, the calmer I felt. "I guess that means yes," he said. "Our lady of the body language. Okay. I was relieved. It was so much easier just to do things her way. I had one of those great false revelations: I don't have to use my mind or my heart or my imagination, or whatever you call it, for anything but my work. There are some advantages to living in an autocratic state, you know. I would go into my study in the morning as if into a cave and write whatever crazy shit I wanted, then at the end I'd come out and do whatever she wanted. I didn't care. I felt like a sponge, absorbing things. Go with the flow. Let it happen. I was caught up in her dynamic and I thought being a writer made everything okay."

"I can't quite picture it," I said.

"What?"

"You being off in your own world like that. You're so sensitive to me."

"Am I? I'm completely obsessed with you, for one thing. I don't understand you."

I was unhappy and yet excited by this remark. It occurred to me he probably didn't know what he had been like. On the other hand, I knew little about marriage. The marriage of one's parents is always the perfect crime, while what Jack was describing seemed so much less ordained. He didn't have to have done it that way; it seemed almost as if it wasn't too late for him. And this not because of any rapprochement that could happen now, but because of something open in his character that tempted me. I loved him for being older. Yet at the same time he seemed to me young. We could start a life. It didn't matter that he'd already had one. "You wrote some wonderful books," I said.

"Well, I'm hardly Tolstoy to use that as an excuse."

"It doesn't matter. Every bit that's any good at all is unique and a great gift to somebody."

He smiled. I felt happy. Then he said, "Spoken like a true artist," and I was frightened and depressed. I wasn't talking about myself. I didn't want to talk about myself. "No," he said, "honey, I screwed up. It's as simple as that. I didn't know how to handle my life and I was too arrogant to find out."

"Or too scared."

"Yeah. You're really getting a prize, aren't you?"

His voice was ragged; I silenced him with kisses, tasting his lips, cheeks, and neck, the old soft tough flesh of the man, as close as I could get to the almost incorporeal particles of memory. He clutched at me fiercely; it was like the night after the dinner party, not repeated—that desperate possession of my body by his. Yet there was something different. He admitted as much. His breath hot in my ear, he told me everything Ruth would not do, which was practically everything. She liked her pleasure straight, in that style of timeless elegance that can drive the rest of us around the bend, my sweetheart no exception. He told me ridiculous things, heartbreaking things, the accumulation of denial and fond hope, of her power and his evasion into fantasy and masturbation. Why wasn't he more adulterous? "Because I'm a stubborn bastard," he said. "Because I'm a wimp. I don't know."

His body battered against me, my face pressed to the sofa cushion. I thought I had learned by now his hunger and his rage but this was new; I wasn't Gwendolyn, I was Ruth. And if a part of me was forlorn, another part rejoiced: this would bind us, this couldn't be returned from. I felt strangely calm and untouched. Safe. There was something elemental about absorbing his pain. It wasn't my pain, it couldn't hurt me.

Jack was spent and tired, his weight heavy on me, his

heart beating against my back. "You know the thing that kills me," he said, "is that after all of this, in 1970, 1971, when Malcolm and I had practically forgotten we're related, she becomes the raving feminist and motherhood is a dirty word. Not as dirty a word as penis, of course— Malcolm and I used to slink around like old dogs, go out for hamburgers when her CR group met in the kitchen. We'd have these awful conversations. I talked to him about nuclear war. What twelve-year-old wants to talk about nuclear war? The more I said, the guiltier I felt. My generation handing this shit down to him. Then I'd go home and argue with Ruth. Imagine, all your opinions discounted. It's just taken for granted you're wrong because you're male. Everything I said, she'd smile triumphantly and take it apart. I was trying to remind her I was a human being, and she'd be dragging out sociology, anthropology, whatever. And there was Malcolm, listening."

How often had my opinions been discounted because I was female? I wondered. How often had I discounted them myself? I had no idea. There was no way to begin to have any idea.

"So you were a male chauvinist pig?" I asked ironically.

He sighed. "No, I agreed, basically, with what she was trying to accomplish, was even excited by it—the kind of changes that were going on in society— It was what was going on in our family that gave me trouble." He paused. "I'm not so stupid I couldn't see that one led to the other. So there I was, my wife working her ass off with revolutionary fervor, and what do I do? I spend my days in my study not writing a word, staring out the window at the girls in the park. The little girls, the fifteen-year-olds."

"I was fifteen in 1971," I said. Hanging out in Washington Square, probably visible from his window. I wouldn't have been interested in him then. I thought older men were disgusting.

"Yeah." His voice was dispirited, he was not interested in this coincidence.

"Your fantasies were premonitions of me. You knew the love of your life was near."

"No, I was just horny and sick of women. Although even the fifteen-year-olds were women then."

"Not quite. We just thought we were."

Lucy using that word over and over—woman, woman— as if she were saying goddess, queen. What did we know? We'd never been women; we thought it might be something wonderful. Miraculous. And history was a force that would sweep away our mother. Her mistakes were not our problem, her solutions not our guide. Did I ever believe in it as Lucy did? I couldn't really, I was compromised. I once spent an hour panhandling, then gave away all the money to a gypsy-eyed boy. His hair was as black as a raven's wing, he lived in a tenement, his ribs showed through. I could still hear his soft, sexy thank you as he took the pile of coins.

Jack stirred. "I didn't know how to be a father in that situation. Now we act as if it never happened, all those days and nights of women talking murderously about the innate murderousness of men, talking about stuff like separatism, revenge. Ruth never took that position, how could she, and now she pretends she never was involved with those people. But we'd hear them talking, Malcolm and I, and he'd look at me and I didn't know what to say. I didn't want him to know how much I wanted to kill his mother . . . I made jokes. 'The oppressors have finished the laundry and request permission to go bowling.' I never asked him how he felt; I was afraid to. And I can't blame Ruth for that. I look at him now, he seems to be happy enough. Married to your sister . . ." His voice trailed off. "Do you think I'm an asshole?" he said.

"I think you're my best beloved."

17

I woke up to the sound of my sister's voice calling. "Happy birthday, happy birthday! I've brought you croissants, peaches, Devonshire cream from Balducci's."

She sang her catalogue of morning's treasures and I was smiling as my eyes opened. In my awakening I had grasped the whole meaning of my relation with Lucy. I understood the necessity of her kindness and the courtesy of my ability to receive. I knew that I loved her almost infinitely, yet only a portion of that love would ever be available. It rose up and stopped, brilliant as a fountain, trembling in the air, then was pulled down again by its own rushing underground weight.

About to speak, I raised my eyes and caught her frozen stare. There was a pain I didn't so much feel as recognize — yes, this was it, this burn along my body as if I were shrinking and expanding at once, as if each cluster of nerves had turned inside out and in that turning lost every sense of direction, indeed every direction. With a swing of her black hair and a clatter of footsteps, she was gone.

I listened to the apartment door slam; I heard the thump of peaches rolling off the table.

"Shit," said Jack.

"I knew it would happen."

"You knew it would happen? Why didn't you tell me?" I shrugged. Jack had pulled himself up, the sheet was clutched around his waist. "She looked at me like I was garbage, did you see that? Where does she get the right?"

"We lied." It was so simple. Nothing could affront her more, not even the love affair itself. That pure sisterly cry, Why didn't you tell me? echoes through our relationship, destroying my every fantasy of escape.

"It's none of her business." He climbed out of bed, began pacing clumsily around. My room wasn't big enough for the emotion he wanted to expend. I put a pillow over my face. "Are you all right?"

I didn't answer. What I felt was fate. I felt clutched so firmly in its claws there was no need to even think. Each breath left my lips only so the next could enter, there was no choice. We think we choose but we never do. Time was not a river but a stone.

Jack lifted the pillow off, looked at me and sighed. He sat down on the bed. "What the hell," he said finally, "what the hell."

"Will you make me some coffee?"

"Yeah, sure. Why don't you get up?" His tone was abrupt, his body radiating heat. It was too much.

"No. And bring me the peaches. The peaches Lucy brought me."

He carried it all in on a tray. I noticed how sweet he was being. Yet all I could really pay attention to was the fruit, piled up rosily. I sank my teeth into the first piece. The juice spurted, sweet and sticky on my lips. I was so hungry for that sweetness, for the flesh falling in hunks down my throat. It was like eating summer: June and July. We used to run through the meadow behind the house in East Hampton picking wildflowers until they overflowed our arms and fell to be trampled underfoot. Yellow petals and leaves would cling to our dresses and curl on the floor of our bedroom at night.

When I reached for the last peach, so round and golden, Jack laid his hand on my shoulder. "You'll make yourself sick." It was true, I didn't feel well. The sugar blared through my veins, a white wave, a froth, the peach pulp dissolved, the ripe fruit gone. Even summer turns chemical, especially summer. I sank my teeth into the peach.

Jack got off the bed, began roaming restlessly around again. "You were right, we should have stayed at my place. Did you know your sister was coming over? What did you mean, you knew it would happen?"

"I didn't know," I said. "She has a key, obviously. She's never barged in like this before."

"I should call Ruth. Should I? Malcolm won't call her. I suppose when she gets back is soon enough. I don't know, is this a relief or what? I feel—" He paused to light a cigarette. I was irritated at his chatter. It was like a goad, I felt stung and prodded, I didn't care how he felt. "I feel like a fucking clown."

I didn't say anything. He drew hard on his cigarette. I thought of Lucy's voice, so clear and happy, of days past when we would escape our parents, running off to hide and play in the park, arranging pretend feasts of acorns and leaf salad.

"So your sister is telling Malcolm now. She's saying, 'Guess who I found in bed with Gwen?'" He shook his head. "Absolutely caught in the act, naked as jaybirds."

"He's not a three-year-old," I said.

"No, he's old enough to know his father's an asshole."

"Oh, stop it. Everybody fucks around."

"Yes," he said ironically, "that's why you're taking it so calmly. Stuffing a bushel of peaches down your throat, slamming a pillow over your face. Everybody fucks around, why should anybody mind?" He sat down on the bed again. He lifted my hand and kissed it. Pressed his face, the hot agitated mass of it, into the cool small length of my arm.

I was sinking deep into my body, like an invalid. Into my heart, beyond. Jack's face was moist. Was it sweat, saliva, tears? I couldn't tell, I felt only the heat. He bent down farther, laid his head on my breast. The weight of it was almost insupportable. I tensed. He got up abruptly. "I have to get out. You want to come for a walk?"

"No."

"Oh, come with me."

"No."

He dressed and left and I immediately fell asleep.

I dreamt I was making love to him. We lay side by side, entwined, mouths and bodies clinging. Oh, sweetheart, can you nourish me? Our skin would fuse together. First our feet, then our knees, thighs, hips, his belly into mine, his chin, his tongue—and I was terrified, I struggled. How to get away? I fought the sticky, clinging flesh.

I dreamt I was inside Jack's head. I was looking for the womb of a man, that hidden, high-up backwoods spot where the children play happily, untroubled by birth. I couldn't find it. I kept walking and walking through fields of grass. The moon was in the sky, as bright as the sun, bathing the scene in an ambiguous enchantment. The grass grew thicker and softer. It wasn't grass, it was hair, it was Jack's hair, and I was outside, stumbling through the rich strands of it, to fall gasping on the beach of my pillow.

I opened my eyes and gazed into his face, hanging over it closely. Ridged nose, balled eyes, the tough sag of aging flesh like a dry fountain with stone statuary, a Roman copy of the Greek.

His eyes opened and he gave a start. "What? Oh, it's you."

"What did you think it was?"

"Nothing." He shut his eyes again. I kissed his mouth but he wouldn't wake up. Harder and harder I kissed but he refused to respond, his mouth smooth and impervious. I began to shake him and, as I shook him, his hand fell off his arm, his arm off his shoulder.

I woke up for real and the bed was empty. The apartment was empty, an hour had passed. I was seized by the most terrible loneliness. It didn't surprise me, I know it never stops. All the days and months you don't feel it, it's piling up behind your eyes like snow. You have to be more and more careful as you get older.

I was thirty. What had happened to all my years, twenty-two, twenty-five, twenty-seven? Oh, the lostness and squandering of twenty-seven, the drink in my Berkeley garden where the roses bloomed, the lemons weighted the branches of the lemon tree, and the crumbling wall with its gate was like something a child might come home to over and over. I used to put on my purple shoes and take walks, the wine murmuring its nonsense syllables inside me. Often I'd be joined by a dog or two. In Berkeley the dogs wander free, sedate and friendly; they rise up off their porches, trot across their yards, and stroll by the side of the drunk girl who lives alone, who likes to sweet-talk them and press their soft-eared heads against her knee.

I climbed out of bed and looked in the mirror. It took me half a minute to see myself and then I wished I hadn't. That pretty face with its little markings, as if the slow-fingered angels were just beginning to cross out the picture. Do other people imagine this, I wondered, that they age because they do not please? He looks down and says no, that's not it either, that's not what I meant at all.

When Jack came back I curled myself around him like a weed. Smelling on him the outdoors, his good sweat, I coaxed him into bed, although he was willing enough. Willing enough to begin with.

I couldn't feel anything. All my sensuality twisted inside my body, twisted and twisted and couldn't get out. My flesh was thick and white and numb. It felt nothing. I could smell him and hear him, and that was all. I sniffed like a dog at the back of his neck and cried.

"What's the matter?" he said. "What's the matter?"

18

"Well," said Jack, "if you won't call your sister, what about your mother?"

This question was merely his latest attempt to get my attention. He'd been home only once in the three days since my birthday; he'd come back showered and shaved, wearing the sweater I'd bought him.

"Silk," he'd remarked. "The last time I wore silk was when my cousins Albert and Arnold dressed me in their mother's nightie and made me be the princess. They tied me to the bedpost, I got away, the coast was clear, then I tripped on my what-do-you-call-it—train—and gashed my cheek open on the andiron."

I had smiled weakly at that, and now shrugged at his question. I was looking at my reflection in a soup spoon. Weird oblong Gwen.

"Once we do something, we'll feel less depressed." He didn't mean we, he meant me. I didn't feel depressed. I was lying on the couch wearing nothing but a T-shirt, rolling my neck so my hair flowed back and forth across my shoulders. Inside the same rhythm prevailed. I wasn't depressed, I was fire itself contained within the body of a woman. Not the kind of fire that burns witches or houses, the hypnotic fire on a winter afternoon that lures children into dreams of their preborn existences. I was the fire that burns by itself in the air.

"Talk to me, Gwen." His voice was pleading and coaxing, the better to worm inside me. It *had* wormed inside me, I was riddled with its holes.

"What's there to say," I said.

"What's there to say? What's there to say? Obviously you must have a lot to say. You blame me for this, don't you?" His pain was so hurtful to me, I didn't understand why he couldn't stop it.

"Why should I blame you? It was my sister who came over. You have more to lose than me."

Those three sentences exhausted me, as did the thought of his life, his wife, all of it. What was someone who could be married to Ruth, the virago who dared berate the Russians, doing with me?

"You don't seem to think so."

I was silent. I certainly did think so. Whatever I had to lose, I had already been losing it. I'd been losing it for a long time. It was not his fault.

"Are *you* having second thoughts about us?" he asked. Just like a man, I thought, always thinking about himself.

"Well," he said, "are you?"

"What?"

"Having second thoughts about us?" His voice was as tense as a wire.

"I'm not having any thoughts at all." It wasn't as if he'd ever be able to know, no matter how I explained, what exactly, what the texture was, of my thinking.

"Yeah, right, that's an uninhabited body there on the couch. Funny she can still move. Not that she likes to. No, she likes to imitate a corpse, but I've noticed her getting up to eat these past few days. She shits on schedule. I think she must be a woman, maybe even the very same one who told me she loved me more than anything on earth."

I winced. Such language embarrassed me. Such emotion made me feel ashamed. I was willing to grant that I had said it, meant it, and might conceivably mean it again, but not now. Now I wanted to rest my eyes on all the objects in the room, the books and dishes and ashtrays and pencils, to look at them steadily and feel the cool fluid fire of myself. But Jack kept at me.

"Yes, she's here, she can't deny it. My girl, my darling, whom I've fucked a good four dozen times, I know her well. She said she loved me when she was coming, and when she was not coming. She sobbed her heart out until I said I would leave my wife. And do I regret it? Not at all. Not one bit, but I think she owes me a little conversation. One or two kind words, don't you think so, Gwen? We're stuck here together, I'm not leaving. Talk."

"No," I said.

He laughed. "No? You can't just say no, my dear. It's not your style." He grinned at his little joke, but his eyes were dark with fatigue.

He was fighting with me, though I was not fighting back. If only he would lie down and sleep, I thought. It was three in the afternoon, a good time for a nap. His nervous energy, even when he was silent, clutched at me; his presence was electrical.

"Come on," he coaxed. "What're you thinking about? Let's start with the easy stuff. Are you thinking about me?"

I wanted to laugh but I was afraid of what it would sound like. He had no idea what I was feeling, of course, he was too coarse, he was too hot. I thought of all the calories it had taken to make up that body. Billions and billions, all those busy units of energy. If he was so energetic, why didn't he go somewhere?

"I understand that you're depressed," he said, reasonably. "Believe me, it will help to talk."

I didn't see how he could call me depressed. Depression was something gloomy and I felt content. I was aware of the colors of everything, the glow within them. I loved the give of the couch beneath me, even the monotonous turmoil of the traffic. Certainly the way the light caught the hair on his arm; if he would just stay still perhaps I could love him again. There are ways the slowness of shock resembles the slow of peace; perhaps I would make that transition in time. I knew I was shocked but I thought this was where I was supposed to be. This sideways pocket of mind, this self-sufficient place. The first impulse is always to remove the pain. You try to pry it out but it won't come. It's lodged like a meteorite in the permanent landscape. So you must balance the composition, draw the eye away. Build a haven out of new wood. Strew the floor with green leaves, plant honeysuckle under the window. Let the bees come. Become a bee. Suck on sweetness all day long.

I'd always taken care of myself. I was adept at self-delight. As a child, I remembered, I made friends, then I would go through periods of not having friends. I changed schools several times, nagging my mother until she sent out the transfer applications. Each time I made a big splash in the beginning, met everyone, talked compulsively, and couldn't sleep at night. I lay awake thinking about my friends and boyfriends with a deep and delicate pleasure. Then I would withdraw. What would trigger it? Some sense of ennui? All the gossip was the same, all the outings, all the kisses. In seventh grade we kissed until my lips hurt. It made me uneasy. So I lit a cigarette in Algebra and kept smoking it until the teacher snatched it out of my hands.

"Are you crazy, Gwen?" Well, perhaps.

When I was asked to explain myself in the principal's office, I told a detailed story about my unhappiness at home, analyzing the effects of my parents divorce on my behavior (not forgetting to mention puberty) until the old man was fascinated: the heart and mind of a twelve-year-old! Then I laughed maniacally and fell off my chair, at which point I was suspended for a week.

What I remember best is the time after those events, the long drifting periods when I would think about the stars. I would wonder about life after death. I read about ancient civilizations; I started this in seventh grade and continue to this day. The rituals of cannibals, the paintings at Altamira, what happened to Pompeii—this was more exciting than social life, this had scope.

My father and I used to talk on the phone a lot the first year after he left. He told me that one must learn to see humanity as a kind of virus on the earth, beautiful in its way (he referred me to textbook pictures of viruses) but not to be borne forever; the earth would recover from us. She would shrug us off. I could see the attraction in this idea. I liked to identify with the earth, flushed and drowsy in her fever dream. All the violence would pass, all the strange visions, and a spring empty of man return in a shower of blossoms. Then she would remember us with fond awe, as I seemed to remember Altamira. She would remember us as one race, indivisible. And weren't we? The same myths repeated for millions of years, the same wars, the same peace, the same desires, the same death. It was all in me: all of history, all of art, all of sex.

Especially all of sex. At fourteen, wearing a thin blouse, looking out the window at men walking down the sidewalk, I wanted to coax them up the side of the building. I wanted to lean out and call and have them stop, turn, their shiny black shoes sticking with ectoplasmic force to the stone, up past the first floor, past the second and the third. Up to my window where they would sway in their poisoned trance. Quick, inside. Then a shift, the room going black, the man sauntering in from the hall—Marlon Brando playing Stanley Kowalski.

Remembering this fantasy stirred something in me. It was so vivid, captor and captive chasing each other across the plains of my mind, changing places, changing roles, and I was inside one and then the other, or inside both, or inside neither. Man and woman? It hardly mattered. Man and beast. Girl and universe. Always two.

That was all right, I thought, that was all right; it was immutable. Woman and child, father and daughter, all chasing each other down the centuries, life after life. There was something else though, another perspective. One needs a lot of perspectives to get by these days. And one night, or several nights, the texture of experience with Jack was different, so different I could not hold on to it.

Jack was pacing the room again. I thought the walls would fall down. "I should be calling my son, I should be calling my wife, I should be finishing my fucking book, but what am I doing? I'm going crazy, you're driving me crazy. Do you hear me?"

I heard him. Suddenly I wanted to say something, he reminded me. "I came close to dying so many times when I was driving. Going through Nevada, I fell asleep. Just an instant of blackness, the car horn, swerving. I was driving on, saying to myself I almost died. Then having a drink at a roadside bar, told the bartender, he shook his head and topped off my drink. Sometimes I think there's a conspiracy of devils in the world. I got back in the car—"

"Please, Gwen," he said in a shuddery, harsh voice, "please stop that."

"What?" I was liking talking now, it felt easy. I remembered another story. "Once in Florence I got drunk and told a man I'd go on his yacht with him. We drove to another city where his boat was and went to bed. I don't remember that part. I woke up. I didn't want to be there, of course, so I crept out, I left my amber necklace behind, the one my mother gave me. I thought I was still in Florence. I didn't remember the part about driving. I was going to my hotel, I had a map, I would walk. I looked at the street name. It was on the map, there was no problem. So I walked, I looked at all the street names, but it was so strange—all the streets were on the map but not in the right order. Everything was all jumbled and whole blocks, whole sections of the city, were missing. It was so strange, and the city was empty. I couldn't find anyone to ask directions. My map was some kind of trick, you see, and I had a hangover. I was really hungover, I could hardly think."

Jack was silent. My voice got lower and sweeter, I loved the sound of it.

"Then I remembered. All of a sudden. I was in the wrong city, that was all. I walked to the highway, I found it easily once I knew, and hitchhiked home. To Florence, to my hotel." I was excited; what a good story! Safe at home in my hotel, all those years I was never, not even once, killed.

"Leaving only your amber necklace behind." His voice was bitter, I was flung into confusion. Hadn't I just told him? What had I said?

"That's not the point," I protested weakly.

"Isn't it? Isn't it really?" His words battered me—oh, his thick stupidity, his emotions crashing down on me like his body trying to have sex last night. He said he thought it might help. All I could feel was the tiny, twisting lust deep inside me, miles from where his body heaved and grunted and gave up.

"Shut up!" I shouted. "Leave me alone! Go away."

He was stunned. "You're kicking me out," he said. "I can't believe you're kicking me out."

I was silent. I wasn't kicking him out, I hadn't moved. I hadn't laid a finger on him.

"She says, 'Divorce your wife, I love you more than

anything, live with me forever, get the fuck out?' Does that cover it, Gwen? I mean, is that the story?"

Which story, I thought. You think there's only one. There's ten thousand and they all end up . . . I didn't know where they all ended up. I thought I'd had it but I'd gotten it wrong again. I shrugged.

I could feel him look at me, I didn't meet his eyes. I was suddenly terribly embarrassed, as if we didn't know each other. He looked at me for what seemed like an hour, then left. I listened to the door slam and it was a trembling negative ecstasy, an anti-orgasm. What an idea. What a day. I lay back, carefully, into the pink cushions.

And woke up three hours later as if my heart were bursting. As if all the feeling had risen up to that old-fashioned place, that soul-chamber, and found only a bloody pump. In rage it was seething, it was churning, this emotion I hadn't the guts for. It would kill me if I didn't make room. It would kill me.

19

I spent the next morning in Saks, buying silk underwear
from old ladies. Snap-crotch teddies, camisoles of flame-
red, black garter belts with long straps like the accoutre-
ments of a horse's bridle. After twenty minutes in the lin-
gerie section, I felt drugged; I had to go into the rest room
and sit down. Then back out again, hair combed, lipstick
freshened, to sift through the bras with their tiny pearls and
rosebuds, the panties cut high, fringed with gypsy lace.
Fifty-five, seventy-two, ninety. I handed the money over —
cash, that's how I like to shop — as if it were an evil to be got
rid of. It left a residue of dirt on my hands while the clothes
themselves were a pure gift, passed down from the old
women to me.

I went into the ladies' room again and changed. Bra,
panties, garter belt, sheer stockings with curls of white

frosting down the sides. I felt the stuff whisper against my
skin. Comfort. Warning. Girl talk.

I walked uptown to Bloomingdale's and had lunch.
Chocolate mousse cake and espresso in the little coffee bar
on the subterranean level. I wanted a lipstick. Crimson,
scarlet, unswiveling from its case. The colors I crave don't
suit me. My hair's too auburn. If I were as dark as Lucy, I
could wear the red I want. I love the way the tube of color
slides itself onto my mouth. Just like that—brilliance. I paid
the bill and went upstairs. They'd redecorated the first floor
again. Young men and women assailed me, hawking perfume and free gifts. They reminded me of the homeless. I
couldn't buy anything. The saleswomen clicked past, their
faces smooth and high. One after another, not seeing me,
until I felt dizzy; I staggered back and stepped onto the
escalator. Going up. Long columns of women gazing at
each other as if we might be for sale. I'll take that one. That
one. That one. Please.

I got off on the fourth floor and went to visit the chained-
up dresses. So beautifully designed, so carefully sewn
(though not as carefully as they used to be) and hobbled to
the rack. How could I free them without buying them? And
I couldn't buy them all. Yet I felt it, nascent, the desire to
empty my bank account. To hand the money over, over and
over. To buy dresses and lipsticks and bracelets and
combs—to buy the things which, heaped on a dressing
table, would evoke nothing so much as the cover of a cheap
novel, the kind you read in the bathtub and, at the last
embrace, drop into the water so the pages can swell to their
proper unreadable bloat.

I took a taxi home, pushing inside the cab ahead of the

woman who had hailed it. She screamed at me, the driver giggled and drove off. He was eating curry from a bowl in his lap and listening to sitar music. Stuck in traffic, he made little clucking noises and I amused myself imagining scenarios of random murder.

I left my shopping bags in the taxi. I told him to stop at Seventh Avenue, I got out and went to a meeting. I took the last seat in the back corner. I was proud of myself. I had come here, I could have thrown myself under a truck.

All around me the chattering, the laughter and gossip. I would have to speak. Raise my hand and say: help. I could do that. Help. I'd seen other people do it. They burst into tears, they sobbed and moaned how alone they felt, even here in the rooms. And like flies to honey, the comforters came. Arms around their shoulders, the weeping ones were led away. Help.

The voices went on, the lively talk was like a wall. Then the gavel calling for silence, the meeting began. A long, riveting story such as you'd only hear in New York. The sad and lonely and ugly boy, deviant sex carried to its furthest extreme. We listened without surprise. We knew the sad and lonely, the rest made no difference. The rest was easy to take in. The people in this room—artists and actors and bartenders, ex-thieves, ex-whores, ex-drug-dealers—were here for the honesty as well as the hope, for the shared wicked life remembered, turned this way and that in the curious light of sobriety. How could we know how to think about it? We were nostalgic. We craved experience. Loneliness was a word being shouted in our ears. Get the message, honey. Oh, I thought, so this is what it's for, the longing that burns. It's here to be transformed.

And before I even knew what I meant by this—transformed into what, compassion?—I was soaring on the beauty of the thought. Compassion, yes, the way certain mathematical shapes can flip over into radically different shapes without any discontinuity: a secret identity that makes the world cohere.

I can say this, I thought. Raise my hand, speak. How fine it will sound. How much more interesting than listening to one of those ten-minute rants, the kind of thing prefaced by, "I've got to dump this shit."

The boy closed his mouth, the basket went around the room. I would raise my hand, all it took was a single command, brain to nerves: go.

My arm would not move.

I didn't know how to compel myself. You can't start at the hand, lift it a little; it all happens at once, that single neuron firing. One action, one decision. Or does the decision start before? I felt my face crawl over my bones. My brain was smooth and closed, I could not command it. I could do nothing. Yet there was a weakness in that certainty, wasn't there? There was another way, off to the left.

Perhaps I would forget, in a swift chain reaction, how to use my brain at all. All the paths would shut down, the nerves long and dark and withered. Each organ on its own, then, in its bath of dirty blood, each muscle snapping uselessly. The images were distinct, the feeling thick and smothering. The feeling was an ooze in my flesh, a choking mud. A pinpoint of light, a wandering craziness was I, trying to pierce that ooze with my surrender. I won't try to speak. I won't try anything.

O lovely coolness, calm, clarity. The memory given to

put me back together, sitting alone all these months in back. My face, my ginger hair, the black coat I wore all winter. I looked somewhat like my mother, somewhat like my father. Silent, slouched, mysterious, pretty; what a pity, what a pity, to destroy that possibility, to break anonymity, to speak in my harsh caw.

I got up and made my way out, dropping ten dollars in the basket. Muscles, nerves, all functioning perfectly; I threaded my way through with deliberate grace. I had grace in solitude. I had solitude. What was I really supposed to do but paint? I could create such loveliness as none of these people even imagined. I felt my work in my mind as an exquisite present, white and whole as an egg; I would tap it open. Nobody saw the beauty in my painting yet, nobody saw the subtlety, the delicate, complicated, secret connectedness . . . I had to work harder. Work and work until it was visible. Every hour of every day, every day of every month, every month of the year, every year. What did it matter: social life, romance, even recovery. Of course I had to stay sober to paint. I could do that. I just couldn't do anything else. Not an unreasonable sacrifice, I thought. One must submit oneself to fate, to the dark perfection. Even the experience with Jack was worth it, I decided. I needed this suffering, it was a feast.

Yes, I thought all the way home, yes, yes, how exquisite, how ideal my life was; it was an ideal, shining and distant; I was, in myself, brilliant and immense and distant.

At home I squeezed pigment, picked up my brush. This was the moment, that familiar weight in my hand, the bright color awaiting the tune of my nerves, the precise, inspired stroke.

I was painting the young Doberman. I strengthened the line of his flank. Deepened the shadows. Deeper and darker. At first euphoric, soon I grew restless. The background wasn't right. It was muddy, I couldn't get rid of it. I put a smile on the dog's face. A wide yellow grin. I made his eyes as big as saucers. Like pinwheels, with sparks. There was a fire on the couch. Knots of flame, burning his body black. His black body, pink inside, like sirloin. Fire. Flames wreathing his head. Still that wide yellow grin. Devildog. I saw a movie by that name once. Hellhound.

I put down the brush and started to cry. My beautiful painting. My favorite. It had been the only one I was really proud of as a work of art; I was looking forward to unveiling it to Mrs. Fishbeck-Perry. She wasn't only a dear old lady, a bit nutty about her dog, she was a trustee of the Whitney. "Frankly, my dear," she told me, "I think there will be a return to the subtle portrait. All these painters with their symbolic objects floating in space—engaging, perhaps, but somewhat obvious. It can all be conveyed by a look in the eyes, even in the eyes of a dog. You have so much talent, I'm glad you've found your subject. And won't it be lovely, Alexi," she said to her pet, stroking him with her old, nearly transparent hand, "a portrait of you! Maybe in a museum someday!"

I looked back at the painting. Smeared clots of color, thick drips, a creature composing itself out of itself with no hope of a departure. That red and black was only the trail of the exertion, how to twist, how to squirm out. Can't be done, beast. This painting was no different from the other. That lovely airy interior, the young head like a wing in the air: exactly the same, I could see it now. All my paintings were the same. A stubborn, raw, unchanging piece of work, like a chewed-off leg in a trap over which enchantments sometimes played, directed by the perverse spirits.

Loathsome—

I ran out of the apartment.

And there was the city with its people and its cars, its noise and confusion, its business and its charms. Cluttered streets, lights, cops, couples, the homeless in the doorways, the warm dark bars. Nobody cared who went in and sat down and ordered. I had money in my pocket. I had a bank card that would get me more at midnight, at two, at a quarter to four. In New York they won't stop you at nine drinks or ten; they won't arrest you for stumbling drunk down the street, for forgetting your address or your name. The city was full of bartenders with other things on their mind. Some are drunks and addicts; some are sober and watch with pitying remote eyes. Once you order a drink from one of those, you're on your own. With your margarita, your gin and tonic, your English ale.

I was hurrying to Jack's. I wasn't sure I would make it. So many blocks, that glittering diagonal, so many sidewalk cafés with glasses of wine. I could lift one off a table, drink it as I walked. Toss the glass into traffic, do it again. Hardly a moment empty-handed from my place to his.

I felt so sorry. So apologetic. So sorry. He had confided in me, and look what I had done. I remembered the years of his marriage, the peculiar self-loathing paralysis which results when you embrace something you think is all you are good for. I remembered his timidity, his modesty, and his violence. The slow wearing down of his distrust that I could not take seriously. How could anyone distrust me? Wasn't I

helpless, invisible, hollow, the empty urchin waiting for the
new wine? (At a café table, a blond twenty-five-year-old.
She smoked a cigarette, drank, looked at her watch. I
wanted to join her—in through the nostrils like a demon.)

Poor Jack. Poor darling. I wanted to rock him in my
arms. I wanted to abase myself on the floor. Sweetheart. I
was trembling. I saw the light in his window. I would suck
at his lips. Darling. I put the key in the lock, climbed the
stairs. Precious. Nibble little portions of his cheek. I love
you. I would fall at his feet. Protect me. I opened his
apartment door—

And everything slowed down. Jack wasn't home. He had
gone out, perhaps twenty minutes ago. The ice in his glass
had not yet melted. It still held its form, it was waiting for
me.

I sat down at the table and took off my shoes. I took off
my socks, rubbed my feet, sat back up. I leaned my elbows
on the table. The bottle of rum he'd been drinking was dark
and high-shouldered, like a tower in the middle of a plain.
From its unstoppered neck the rum-breeze poured, welcoming the traveler, the lonely and weary.

Myers Dark—but the label was bright, the label was
golden yellow. I could imagine that label as a door thrown
open to the brightness inside, to an island all in sunshine on
a tropical sea. On the terrace of the decaying hotel exiles
and newspapermen drink rum in the shade while the sun
falls beautifully through bands of pale green, and the palm
fronds stir up a languorous breeze. The waiter comes, on
soundless feet, with new drinks and a white towel to wipe
clean the table. Seashell ashtrays, thin brown cigars. The
faint smell of men's sweat. A late dinner, a slow flirtation,

native dancing in the seedy lounge. The fierce sweet blue of a southern midnight. No morning until afternoon.

Perhaps there would be children there, lovely smooth-skinned girls to whom I could give something. The cool of my house or my fresh food, stories of America or birth-control pills. They would come walking in single file, with herbs they had gathered. The eldest would be my favorite, the one with high breasts. Eleven, or twelve, or thirteen. She would stand dreamily in front of my mirror, trying on my silk clothes. I would hang a piece of jade in the hollow of her throat. After a while I would realize she was coming too often, asking for too many gifts. I wouldn't mind. I would drink the local wine, and each day she would bring me more bottles gathered in her fist. I would drink and drink and drink as she watched me, her chin resting on her palm. She would become harder to see, doubled, transparent, yet I would notice her carrying things out of my house: my mirrors, my silks, my bed. I wouldn't mind. The floor of the shower would be so cool to sleep upon, and the spiders would walk across me with such delicate, ladylike steps.

I raised my head from where it had sunk toward the table and the bottle. This was my enemy, in its usual garb. What you do with bottles is to leave them alone. They can't touch you if you don't touch first; they can't tilt their own selves and trickle their stuff toward you; they can't creep it up your arm and your neck and your lips, or slide it down your throat by themselves. No, they can't do that. They sit, modestly waiting.

And I waited; I couldn't do anything else. I wanted a glass of water but I didn't dare get a glass. To hold a glass in my hands, to even move— I know how it happens. You get up, you're even planning to leave, you're going to an AA meeting, and your hand shoots out and wraps around the bottle. ~~You get the smell up your nose now and your lips right on it~~ where a few drops linger, tasting better than anything will ever taste. You've forgotten that: the shock and hunger of your rightful nourishment right there on your tongue, fanning out its incredibly beautiful and complicated flavor.

I sat there remembering how it tasted, blossoming down my throat like a great red flower. Remembering the old civilization. Vampire villas perched on the cliffs of my brain in the city of immortals where I used to live. Those bodiless ones were my companions, sipping with their old unreal tongues the real juice of my emotion, they imparted an ancient wisdom: Solitude is never final. The homeless will abide with you. Indeed, I was a refuge for thousands. Give me a tenth drink and out they will come, chattering, whispering, giggling. We're here! We're here! All the voices together, yet each one distinct, a company of revelers and seers. They carried me off piecemeal; how could I mind their industry? To be one among many, to be the most important one. To be the ground, the home, the language. Lolling back in my chair, delivered.

But after the voices, silence; after the silence, sleep. After drunken sleep I would wake up the next morning mechanical. Thought mechanical, emotions mechanical, even pain was mechanical. How else could I have endured so much of it? The headaches, the nausea, the anxiety twisting me apart like a paper napkin. It all happened to a creature that was not quite alive, that was put together funny and felt no surprise. I was like one of those machines of the nineteenth century, straps and pulleys and counterweights, vital parts sliding in their grooves with little shrieks.

Then all I wanted was death. Death close, dark, velvety, incurling and warm. It seemed so familiar to me, like that which has always been missing. The hole in my life where the joy seeped out. Oh, can't I join them, the absent ones, to the beginning of history, the dead? No differentiation between us: solid black, soul to soul.

Even now, how it beckoned. The eternal parent calling me to bed. You're tired, Gwen. All those hours of early drunkenness, the first passionate drink of the evening, the second drink that transformed, were only the merest sketch of what it's like in death. How could it be otherwise? What I loved was the dissolution. No separate Gwen. There is no separate Gwen. There is no separation.

The rum bottle waited, impersonating a grassy bank, a pile of gifts on Christmas morning, a soft mat of yellow leaves, a man's arm up near the shoulder.

Gwendolyn, said death, reminding me of that period of childhood when I fell in love with my name. I said it slowly, I said it syllable by syllable. I was proud of its length; it seemed to me like a train winding through a verdant countryside. To have been named this name that was of course my proper name made me feel as if my insides were being tickled with a feather. Gwendolyn, they said. They knew!

Why should I die? I felt an impulse of grief, and pushed my chair away from the table. In the immortal city where the alcohol vampires live, one brain is as good as the next. They leap from one to another, like socialites doing the clubs. Death hides in life because there's nowhere else, otherwise it would be there, wouldn't it? If there were an underworld guarded by a three-headed dog, if there were a palace for all the sacrificed maidens?

But I couldn't think about this. Death couldn't be understood. It wouldn't be death otherwise, it would be just a change, and change wouldn't be change without risk of death. Yet it seemed as if the only alternative to thinking about it in this agonizing way was to do it. To let go.

My hand snaked out for the bottle.

20

The morning before my father's funeral, Lucy and I went to view the corpse. We were driven there in a rented car by my father's aunts, three big, bluff, red-haired women in their sixties. I sat in the front seat, wedged between two of them, filled up with the strangeness of grief. It was a strangeness nobody else seemed to feel. Lucy was upset in a wholly ordinary way, as if his death were a piece of criminal negligence. "I bet it never occurred to him that somebody'd have to bury him," she said. My mother felt the same, although she was less upset about it. I don't think she was glad, but she felt the relief people feel when they get out before the crash. Only Roy, who had never known him, seemed genuinely sad. We little girls had lost our father. More than that, it was a mystery to him how a man could be self-destructive, and faced with that mystery, he expressed a certain awe. My great-aunts were sorry, of course, but far too knowing.

We would go in one at a time to see him. That was how it was done. My mother had prepared us, and said we didn't have to go. "It's only his body," she said. "You won't like it." She combed her blond hair into a twist.

"I'm going," I said passionately, as if defying her to stop me.

"Me too," said Lucy.

I didn't want Lucy to go. I didn't want anyone but me to go. What did they know about it? Falling downstairs drunk—I had done that on New Year's Eve when I was alone in the house getting over the flu. At midnight I was drinking brandy and milk in bed, dressed in my flannel nightgown and Christmas-tree patterned knee socks. I started downstairs for a refill and slid, rolled and bumped to the bottom. It didn't hurt. The glass didn't break. I filled it up in the kitchen, then sat on the bottom step drinking it, looking into the living room as I used to do when I watched my father. The room shone with ghostliness, the alcoholic spirits drifted like the guests in Bunuel's great film *The Exterminating Angel* who are mysteriously unable to leave the dinner party. It occurred to me that my father might call tonight. He had taken to the occasional drunken phone call, which I answered jealously and listened to, not for the rambling words but for the peculiar languor I felt at the sound of his voice. Sensuous, passive, and dumb, my body curled around the telephone while I said what I needed to to keep him going. "I don't know how you can listen to that," said Lucy. "He's paranoid and boring." My father was a textbook salesman now. He found conspiracies in the history books. He was always just about to be fired. It didn't matter. With the arrogance of a sixteen-year-old in 1972, I dismissed his job as of no importance; it was his essence that counted. His voice over the phone wire, fading in and out, crackling, dreamy, as if he were only a voice—

He didn't call and I went to bed. I walked upstairs slowly, as if wading through water, in a state of drunken terror. I had been afraid of falling again. It had seemed to me that I was wading out to sea, gradually deeper and deeper, out to the drop-off point.

And then he was dead. My mother walked in to where I was playing cards with Lucy on the floor of her bedroom one warm April morning, walked in with such a mouthful of news. She held it for a minute, her lips queerly stretched, as if it were a little live rat in there. "Your father is dead."

It seemed to take me a long time to hear this. What had she said? "Your father—" I had seen him four months ago. Months were shorter than they used to be, how interesting it was to get older, but still it was long enough. "Is dead." I couldn't look at her face so I glanced wildly around, my palms pressed against the floor. The objects in the room, the bed, the chair, the rug underneath me, seethed with a suppressed, alien life, their resemblance to their counterparts of a moment ago cunningly deceptive. They pressed close, probing my weak senses. I had no defense against them; I was not superior, I could not even remember the relationships of physical space. Everything was right on top of me, as if I were a blind woman suddenly able to see. So this is color, this harsh immediacy.

Lucy started crying and the spell was broken. The inanimate world retreated, I was part of a family.

We ate breakfast. That's what we did first, we went downstairs and my mother cooked eggs. There was something very warm and homey about it; she must have been being sweet to us, but I don't remember. I was thinking about the moment of death.

Did he feel it, did he know? He was drunk, of course, he fell down the stairs in his Brooklyn apartment, but there was plenty of potential for knowledge, for an instant which in my imagination stretched out forever. The snap of a neck, the realization (which I had just experienced) that neither your surroundings nor your self are fixed, there is neither hierarchy nor control.

Even so I, I could not believe it. It was chaos, and here was order. I was a daughter, I had a father. He was sly, wild, maudlin, funny and bitter. He had a good eye, a sharp mind, a cowardly heart. He was alive.

I was alive. I left my mother and Lucy, shut myself in my room and looked in the mirror. My skin was so smooth, my eyes fresh and warm, sparkling with mysterious luck. My heart was beating calmly, the sun pouring in the windows. Sunday morning. I could stand this way forever and not grow any older. How could the day pass, how could anything change, how could he be dead when I remembered him?

I hadn't seen him in four months. What was the difference? Yet as I began to lull myself with that thought, awaiting my store of memory, I discovered what I had only suspected before. Memory was not a record but a force. Not a refuge but a raging creation. He was built up, torn down, rearranged, his death a move to be integrated everywhere. Whatever I thought of—the last time I had seen him at the

Riviera Cafe, the nights I used to come downstairs and tune into his twilight zone, being lifted out of the car when he had driven at night, and slung over his shoulder as I pretended to still sleep—was either poignant or tragic or terrifying. It was obvious this end had been intended all along, or so my memory said, busily writing its story. I could feel the events shift. That's not how it happened, I thought, but how could I know? I was only given the revised version. It made me sob, as it was meant to. The sorrow, the misery. The inevitability. Who was watching me then? Who had my future in hand? I had not thought of myself as superstitious but it didn't matter, the structure of the myths were there, and maybe it was all the same. Daddy in heaven, Daddy in the underworld. Daddy with the devils, or Daddy alone. Shut up in a small room, still foggy from the booze. It didn't matter. He was caught somewhere I couldn't go. It was done that way on purpose. I wasn't allowed, I didn't deserve, I couldn't ever. The door shut. Shut—until my own death, and even then, even then, I knew better than to expect my devotion to be rewarded.

Yet I seemed to see my father as he had been when I was very young: tall and distant and infinitely desirable, coming nearer and nearer, lifting me up. Instantly setting me down again with an angry exclamation—I had a dirty diaper— but that second in his arms remained, and now I had it clearly in focus. Fire-red, ash-pale, the sweetness of evening in a house in the middle of nowhere. My house. My father transformed, a note of music resounding.

I drifted downstairs. I hugged my mother, talked to the people who had come over. Everybody admired my self-possession. So brave, they said. Such a brave girl. I took over the bar duties from Roy, who had to make calls about funeral arrangements. I mixed drinks for our guests, mixed them strong. He should have gone into a hospital, they said. Norah offered to pay, you know. Did they think he would have taken her money? I served the drinks, imagining my mother's friend Eileen having one too many, crashing her car on the Long Island Expressway.

We arrived at the funeral home and parked the car. It was a cool day without a breath of wind, the sky grey and faintly luminous. We were close to the East River and I had an impulse to go down to it, which I had never done in sixteen years in Manhattan.

We went inside. The foyer was overheated and weirdly lit, casting a greenish glare on the black-and-white checkerboard floor. I was to go in first. I knew what to do. I had to find the message. The meaning of death was written on a corpse, the writing hard to decipher, but I wasn't worried. There was nobody there to hide it. He couldn't distract me, nor scare me, nor confuse me, nor charm me. If there were such a thing as a third eye, mine was open. My whole body was an eye; I was shivering in the light.

The funeral director took my arm. I shook his hand off. Creepy corpsey hand, I thought, he plays with the dead bodies. With the dead girls. He takes their insides out.

I walked by myself into the viewing chamber, my foot-steps tapping loudly on the floor. The room was large and square with high ceilings and red drapes. His coffin was in the center, up on a pedestal. It seemed to take me a long time to reach it. His profile rising, that beaky nose. A lock of hair, his hands folded on his chest.

Eyes shut, mouth still. I could just make out the bruises beneath the powder, but there was no face there at all. Each feature swam in the blank like an object without analogue, like something never made. No message. This thing would not even decay, I thought, there was nothing in which the rot could take hold. Almost fainting with horror, I yet reached out a hand and touched. How cold it would be, how cold. But I felt warmth. A shock of heat up my finger like a tongue of flame. I snatched the finger back and put it in my mouth, sucking out the burn. The finger grew cold. I grew numb. I couldn't feel it at all. I buried it in my pocket and hurried out of the room.

I told Lucy not to look. "It's too awful, really." She listened to me, took my advice. Even knowing her, I was surprised. I felt both envious and scornful. As I convinced her, as we waited for our great-aunts to be done, I wanted to go back. I was sure I had missed something. I wanted to touch him again.

21

The building door slammed, there was a step on the stairs. Soft weary steps, a pause. I broke out in terror. Come back, come back, I used to say in my passionate teens, but I didn't really mean it. I never meant it. Didn't I?

Those last afternoons when we met our father in cafés, he would talk intensely about beauty and the secret meaning of history. He was full of references we couldn't possibly catch, but it didn't matter. All I had to do was pluck a phrase or two out of his discourse and say whatever came to mind; he would listen sagely, impatiently, then begin again. The high nonsense of an unedited mind.

Lucy would sit miserably, slouched and pale, while I conversed with our father, giddy at my own acrobatics. I delivered myself of all profound opinions as if tossing them into a dark wind. Most were lost. Some my father heard but heheard at a crazy angle: words bent like a coat hanger used to unlock a car. And he would respond to what he heard, and I would have to pay careful attention again to find a phrase I could manage. My father saw me as an equal because he saw himself oppressed; there was no helplessness to compare with his. Oh, Lucy, I didn't understand a word he said either. I felt so delicately put together: my brains, my prettiness, my poise, it could so easily disintegrate. In dreams I had no face, only an unformed lump; I looked in the mirror, there were no eyes.

Another step. How the heart beats when one is unaccustomed to using it, how the head spins. How long messages take when there's no blood to carry them.

I wanted the role of the loving daughter; I imagined I would have been good at it. That's all it was, imagination. And that's all that this is, too. In college I used to play records of wolves howling, open all my windows. Imagination.

But how far does imagination go? Does it go all the way, down to the sea where the children flourish? No, it can't go that far. It stops here, the step on the stairs, the body undone.

I was astonished by the purity of my fear, which was like a beam of light flooding the whole weird landscape. I was paralyzed in the middle of this terrible idea, that my father was coming back for me because I had called him, without having to strictly believe it. Although in fact I could believe anything. In this brain all thoughts were equal. Hadn't I worked at it? As a child, discovering the privacy of mind, I imagined fantastic things as an exercise. Day after day I did this. I was an artist, I had the power.

An artist. In adolescence how the myth took hold. It
~~explained everything. (This is my soul, in all her wild~~
abundance. Fecund and free, like the goddesses of old.) I
remember the exultance: rushing home after classes to be
alone and paint. Or sitting by the window in the late afternoon, with a drink or a joint, watching the world go by. I
knew what I knew.

Knew what? That one cannot put one's trust in mortal
things, so cling therefore to the phantasmal? Away at
school, the year after he died, I was distracted by the press of
social life, the boys in the dorm across the meadow, the late-
night comings and goings. My mother had thought boarding school would take our minds off the tragedy, and she
was right. But back in New York again, in the tutoring
school where I learned to paint one on one with the teacher,
where I studied symbolic logic and the history of revolution,
what else could I become but a slave to the imagination,
which I mistook for a country I could visit at my leisure? I
thought the dead lived there helplessly, like plants. I thought
the artist could pluck whatever flowers she chose. Thought
my suffering would all be grand and, anyway, was mostly
over.

It occurred to me that my idea of an artist, especially as I
grew older, was one who must forfeit for the joys of creation
the more ordinary joy of knowing oneself created. When I
cleaned my brushes at the end of a workday, I felt that
craving for memory we call nostalgia raised to such a pitch
of ferocity as to be unbearable. What I received as a gift I
tried to give back, but it stalled somehow, and that gap, that
halt in the return, ravaged me like a stoppage of blood or
breath.

"Your mother thinks I'm an alcoholic," my father said to me not long before his death, a year after my mother remarried. "She doesn't remember how she used to like a few drinks herself. We'd go out dancing. Once we drove all the way to Atlantic City, your mother wanted to stop for a hitchhiker—this evil-looking fellow—at three in the morning. Everything was fine then, you betcha."

"What happened, Daddy?"

"She lost her spontaneity. She forgot how to enjoy herself." He put a cigarette in his mouth, struck a match. The flame jumped around his face until finally he put his other hand on his wrist and the flame steadied enough for the goal to be reached. I wanted a cigarette too, but couldn't bear to show off my healthy hands. I watched him suck the smoke in hungrily.

"How do people enjoy themselves?" I asked.

"Oh, baby," he said. "You know."

I didn't know. I believed. Believed most earnestly in pleasure, in the enjoyment of all earthly things, from the feel of cool sand at the beach at night to the smell of a boy's neck to the taste of red wine. When I was a sophomore in college, my first love, Henry, would come to my room after classes. I would lock the door, put a blue tablecloth on my desk, and we would drink Portuguese wine out of ceramic wine cups. We ate smoked baby oysters and bottled artichoke hearts and, after two glasses of wine, made love. I was so young but felt much older than he, like an archaic woman capturing a downy twentieth-century boy. He had blond fuzz all over his body, as if he took extra vitamins for heat. After sex I would fall asleep and Henry would clear the dishes, then go to the library to study. How to keep

from remembering—the red wine like a red rose in the cup.
The days of sunlight on the vine, months of ripening in the
barrel, whole years within those drops on my tongue. The
result was to pluck me out of time altogether, or so I
imagined. I was too greedy, that's all; I used up my store of
eternity. Now I'm yoked to time, to the work of living, and
I'll never have a moment when the harness melts away.

Except, perhaps, this one.

This one? O sheer delight, absolute and sudden: I was
inhabiting the slow bloom of a second. The room grew big,
still and close, each object vibrant in its shadow. O beauty
as it had always been; of course there was company here.
The tables, the walls, the windows, looking at me like the
old women in English villages who lean on their fences at
dusk to watch the tourists go by. I was a tourist, lingering in
this strange, infinitely familiar place; I came with the news
of outside, the fear, the shame bred in the depths of the
body. It was not that I lost my fear though I felt as light as
air; it was not that I saw through shame, it remained solid
enough. But whoever might be coming up the stairs, the
living or the dead, was a part of me; I could feel him
growing out of my flesh; he was already present, I accepted
him; I could not be harmed.

I knew this to be true as I had always known it. One night
twenty years ago I stood by an open window in the summer,
the wind lifted my nightgown, ran round and round my
legs, then settled into the warm shimmer of August in the
country. That wind from across the ocean! A wildness rose
up in me, I would marry the wind. I could live on darkness.
On wind, on darkness, on anything, I could live forever.

I had known, but grew confused. Who was this important I? Is forever a part of time? And what are the rest of you doing here? I built up pride with it. Built up the winey girl who had secrets upon secrets, who wrote me notes for my sick and forgetful mornings. "It's worth it," inscribed in her dopey scrawl. "It's worth it." The mistake was to dream of being exempt from the return.

The room was like a face, watching. I felt that shiver of being looked at, not knowing by whom. Go ahead, look at me, I thought, and the message I got was, Beautiful, beautiful, beloved and beautiful fading as I heard the key in the lock. Oh, the return (such kindness how my life goes by, such kindness that I drank too much and now cannot at all), the return. The weight of it, the clutch of greed. I could still choose my direction. But was there really a choice? I was in time, I had that immense benefit; the hand on my back, gentling me forward.

The door opened and Jack came in. "Gwen!" he said. He smiled, he laughed to see me. He came right over and kissed me on the mouth. Then he saw the bottle on the edge of the table, the bottle I had held to my nose, had rubbed on my cheek and put down. He picked it up immediately, took it over to the sink, and emptied it. I watched as if he were saving my life, as if I had been just about to drink it. And maybe I had been. The grace of the moment was still here; he was as much a part of it as I was. "God, I'm sorry I left that there."

"It's your apartment. You had no reason to expect me."

"Oh, yes I did. You said you loved me more than anything on earth; I haven't forgotten." He gave me a huge grin, opening his face so wide, then added, "I should be angry at you now. I'd like to be." He took my hands, gripped them hard, then lifted them to his lips and kissed them. "You did come back because you loved me, didn't you, not to pick up your leather underwear?"

I bent my head, nuzzling against his chest. "I forgot about my leather underwear. I forgot about a lot of things."

"Well, that's okay. That's okay." He was looking at me with such exuberant doubtful affection; words came to his lips, were almost spoken, fell back again, he shook his head, he said nothing, I wanted to explain.

"I thought you were my father's corpse walking upstairs," I confided.

That hit him. He stopped smiling, I couldn't read his expression. Maybe I shouldn't have said it, I thought. But I had to speak. I described, haltingly, what I'd just been feeling, what I'd just been imagining, what had happened. The words were inadequate and the experience began to change. I felt such grief at that, but it would have changed anyway. I watched him as I spoke. I knew he got some of it, which parts I wasn't sure, how much I wasn't sure, and there was something else going on, of course, that I didn't understand either. I could feel: The poor thing, the poor thing, inflicted with my zombie fantasies, bearing up under what had no relation to him at all. Yet there was a relation. Jack wasn't my father, thank God, but the spark between us contained my whole past as well as his. I didn't understand but I believed. What he did with it was up to him.

There was a pause. He finally said, "I don't know what to say about that. I'll have to think about that. But you know, Gwen, any way you find to love me is okay with me. As long as you do."

"I do," I said. I looked at him, his soft grey eyes, his

coarse dark brows, his baffled intelligence, my own baffled
intelligence—like two rocks being ground together—and
reached up and kissed him. "I do."

"Well, I've got some news then. Ruth called. She wanted
me to meet her in London; some mutual friends of ours are
there. I almost went; I thought what a good opportunity to
get away from you. Of course you had kicked me out, and I
didn't want to be in the same city. I thought, I'll go to my
wife; her sterling virtues came to mind. But I couldn't
delude myself, the woman was still talking to me. I realized
I didn't want to hear anything she said. So I declined the
invitation and told her why. I couldn't help it, I couldn't
pretend, though I felt like a shit, telling her on the phone—"

I didn't want to hear this now. I wanted more kisses, I
wanted to luxuriate in our reunion. Surely he could have
given me an hour.

"So I told her I wanted a divorce. I decided that no matter
what happened with me and you—and last night was hell,
my darling, I hope yours was, too—anyway, I couldn't go
back to Ruth. I was feeling pretty sorry for myself but also,
you know, that I had no choice. Better an honest man—
anyhow. She was very cool about it. I have no idea how she
feels. I said, 'Is this something you want too?' and she
replied, 'What I want is no longer your concern.' You can't
help admiring somebody like that."

"Do you feel guilty?"

"Oddly, no. It seems like exactly what I should have done
years ago, and she knows that. I don't think Ruth wants a
husband anymore, particularly, but she's not one to cut ties.
It's funny. It was what I was attracted to in the first place, I

think: that sense that she was loyal. That's not exactly the word—you don't want to hear this."

"Did you tell her about me?"

"Yes. She said she thought you were very pretty."

"Oh, thanks, Ruth. I really appreciate it."

"I muttered something about how young you were and she said, 'But, Jack, you're so young yourself. It's your most endearing quality.'" He looked at me with a little smile on his lips: I thought it was remarkable that he could love me, that it no longer mattered what she said. (Or did it? Loyal— no, that wasn't the word for it.)

"Congratulations," I said.

"Yeah. Yeah, I guess that says it. You know, I'm a little drunk, I need something to eat. Will you come out to dinner with me?"

"Yes."

"I don't know, I might ask you to marry me over dessert."

"As a matter of fact, I believe you have already asked me to marry you." We were out the door, he turned and looked at me.

"No," he said, "that was canceled when you kicked me out." We walked down a flight of stairs. "I stopped here on my way up tonight," he said, as we passed the landing. "I sat down and cried. I haven't done that in twenty-five years. The thought of coming back to an empty apartment . . ."

"I'm sorry."

"I'm not asking for sympathy. I've already told you it was all right. I just wanted you to know."

"I know."

"Okay."

We ate dinner at the Astray Café, lingering at the table for hours. Jack told me outrageous stories about his friends' divorces, and I heard more about his life with Ruth than I strictly wanted to know. He became more and more manic, his face not still for an instant. He talked like a man let out of prison, as in fact, he kept saying, he felt. It was almost frightening, that energy; it poured out of him. I could even smell it—slightly bitter and acidic—and he broke three of the twelve cigarettes he attempted to light. It was the cigarettes that finally got to me.

"I won't kiss you if you smoke any more," I warned. He stopped talking and gave me a dirty, sexy look.

"Yes, you will. And if you won't kiss my lips you can kiss something else." I smiled, he was like a twelve-year-old.

"Perhaps," I said.

"I remember you," he said, "slouched over in that corner, laughing at me on our first date. I was trying to finish my dinner—"

"And I wanted you to hurry up."

"—and I could see down your shirt the way you were sitting. Your face was flushed as if you'd been fucking, and I had such a hard-on I was afraid I wouldn't be able to get up. I considered asking you to go under the table and give me a blow-job."

"I'm sure you considered that very carefully. Just the sort of thing you might have said that night."

He gave me a look. "I think I should keep you gagged when I'm not using you."

"You're so disgusting when you make the effort."
"I'm not the one who throws up in French banks."
"I should never have told you that."
"That's when I knew I could trust you."

22

Lucy wouldn't talk to me for a long time. I called her soon after my rapprochement with Jack and she said she wasn't ready to discuss it yet. I called her again a few weeks later, she was still cool. I was upset but it felt containable. Everything felt containable; whenever I grew anxious, something turned in my mind, like the turning of a bookcase, to reveal the secret chamber, and I found a fresh store of patience. I tried to explain this to Jack: "I always thought faith was believing in something that may or may not be there. You took a chance. I could see why people took the chance, but it wasn't enough for me. But it's not like that. It's more like what the body knows, if you let it. It's not an attitude but a suspension of attitude." He listened with a little smile. "You think I'm an idiot."

"Not at all."

"You want me to shut up."

"No, I love it, it's like being in bed with a nun."

I kissed him hard on the mouth, biting his lips. "I said a prayer the first time I went to bed with you."

"Oh, shit. Don't tell me."

"I prayed to be there. Completely present."

"I'm not sure that one's been answered yet."

"What do you mean?"

"Nothing. You just float off now and then. Actually I like it, that faraway gaze, but sometimes I feel lonely."

"Well, so do I."

"How can you feel lonely? You believe in a higher power." His tone was sarcastic but not too much so; he mostly sounded jealous.

"I'm just following the evidence. It's the scientific method, you know." He gave me a skeptical look. "It works," I said. "You've seen me get happier. Maybe that doesn't make you happy."

"It does. Believe me, it does. All this change, it's hard for an old guy to take . . . You're making a presumption that God exists. I simply don't happen to share it."

"I thought you believed in a wimp God."

He laughed, shaking his head. "Hey, I had to say something. There you were talking about God on our first date."

I was embarrassed. "You think I'm an idiot."

"No. But this is something you're doing by yourself. All I can do is watch."

I wasn't doing it by myself. I went to meetings every day and even managed to speak. The first time my panic was so severe I just made noises in my throat. My face was crimson but it didn't kill me. That simple and most obvious truth,

that it didn't and wouldn't kill me, was a revelation. I felt
that someone had forgotten to tell me that. Who? Well, I
would get to that later. For now it was enough to know that
I'd been wrong, and that nobody was making me stay that
way.

My progress was very slow. I hung back, took phone
numbers and never used them, talked to Jack about things I
should have said at meetings. But it didn't matter. I looked
at the newcomers in their sullen gloom, protective cigarettes held in disdainful fingers, and felt a relief and gratitude that grew stronger every day.

Still, I worried about Lucy. The anxiety was containable
but I had to contain it. Without panic, strangely enough,
fear became richer and more knowable; it kept pace with
me, meeting my insight with its sorrow, my laughter with
its tenacity. I began to feel responsible in a way I never had
before. "What if she never speaks to me again?" I asked
Jack.

"She will. She's your sister."

Yes, she was my sister, that was a comfort. She couldn't
really get away. There was a cord between us that would be
inexorably drawn in; it was being drawn in, I could feel it,
even in the silence.

Ruth came back and Jack talked to her. Only once did she
veer from her pose of cool nonconcern; Jack wouldn't tell
me what she said but he came back shaken. He watched TV
all night and drank beer; I watched with a strange mixture
of pity, jealousy, and excitement: there was so much yet to
find out about him, to experience. Maybe I wouldn't like
what I found. Maybe I would.

He moved in with me and worked every day at my

kitchen table. I went out apartment hunting, came back in the late afternoons. "You want me to get out of here during the day, just tell me," he'd say, glancing up from the type-writer; then a fresh burst of words would tap out like machine-gun fire. I kept thinking I would tell him next week. He had a deadline, he was paying the rent. And I was intrigued; I took every chance he was out of the apartment to read his novel, especially the crossed-out parts. (I would paint again soon, I could feel it building.) Then I would glance around at his shirts, his piles of books and mail, and feel schoolgirl infatuation, wifely possessiveness, and the life-long loner's terror of invasion—all at once. By the time he got back I'd be on the couch, bitching about how much room his stuff was taking up. He'd bitch right back. He'd found the coffee cups under the bed, the socks under the refrigerator. I liked things out of sight; he preferred them clean.

He started spending hours, or it seemed like hours, mak-ing dinner every night. I was expected to do the dishes. "Isn't it easier to make a phone call?" I said.

"You know how much that costs, night after night?"

"Maybe ten dollars extra for an hour of work saved. Our time is worth more than that."

"That's such a fucking yuppie thing to say."

"Listen, you thousand-year-old man, you pre-war ar-tifact. How can I be a yuppie? I haven't worked in ages."

"It's true, you're not a yuppie. You're an east-side princess."

"And you're an old fuck."

He grinned. "I know that's all you see in me, but should I complain?"

"You make such a mess," I said. It made me intensely nervous to see him in my kitchen.

"So *you* cook."

"No. I'll burn myself." He shrugged. "Frogface," I said. He didn't reply. "I'm talking to you." Sullen and hopeful.

"Yes, Gwendolyn?"

"Why do we fight so much now?"

"Fight? This isn't fighting, this is domestic life."

"I don't think I like it."

"You'll get used to it."

It was Malcolm who finally brought Lucy and me together. He suggested the four of us meet in Central Park; we agreed.

"He's never spent any time in the country, he thinks plants have a soothing influence," said Jack. He had seen Malcolm several times already. He told me it was the tiniest bit like talking to Ruth; Malcolm was so calm, so assured, that quiet, eager-to-please boy we knew had metamorphosed into a diplomatic, professional New Yorker.

"I felt like the kid, I'm telling you. His suit cost more than my whole wardrobe. Hell, I don't know, Gwen. I'm probably being wildly optimistic, but I don't think he minds that much. He said he knew his mother and I were unhappy together, that it used to bother him. I said, when did it bother you, and he said mostly in the last few years, before that we seemed okay. I mentioned that period I was so worried about, and you know what he told me? He said he admired how cool I was about it. As if a bunch of women plotting to castrate every construction worker who made a sexist comment was nothing to worry about. I could sort of see what he meant. Anyway, I know he likes you."

"Did he say I was pretty?"

"He said he thought you were a great person."

"Well, I think he's a great person, too."

"Your sister, on the other hand . . ."

"Don't start," I said.

Lucy and Malcolm were waiting for us at the entrance. They were standing close together, tall and dark and casual in their Reeboks and rolled socks, cotton painter's pants and oversize button-down shirts. "You guys look like an ad for something tasty," I said.

"Marriage," replied Malcolm, and I laughed. Lucy's face was unreadable. She had cut her hair short, it gave me a pang.

"I like your hair that way," I said, feeling gentlemanly, and she took the compliment like a boy, with a gruff shrug. "So, shall we stroll?"

Quite quickly Jack and Malcolm fell behind. I could barely hear them, they were discussing botany. Just as well, I thought; they would probably communicate better that way: by osmosis. Lucy and I walked past the zoo, which was closed for renovation.

"Remember Daddy sticking his arm in the tiger's cage?" I asked dreamily. "What if he had been dragged in and eaten?"

"You would have jumped in after him."

"You wouldn't have let me."

"Should I have?"

We walked on. We matched each other's pace instinctively, speeding up, idling, pausing to kick at stones or bottles. I told her I was marrying Jack. She countered with the news that she was having a baby.

"Well, well, well," I said. "I'll be its aunt and its grandma at the same time."

"That would appeal to you."

"Not to mention being your stepmother-in-law."

"Christ, Gwen, I thought you wanted to be rid of me. You sure picked a weird way to do it."

"I have an ambivalent nature. Why did you think I wanted to be rid of you?"

"Because you picked the one man to sleep with that you knew I would object to?"

"That's not why I picked him. Besides, I'm sure there are lots of others you would object to. I can think of five or six right off the bat."

"I'm sure you can. But isn't it true? I'm not saying you don't care for him now." She said this last a little distastefully.

"I loved him immediately."

There was a pause. I was remembering how much love I had felt for Lucy on the morning of my birthday: that pure uprush of feeling. Where had it gone? I felt defensive now, yet very much in need of her presence. "Thanks for the peaches," I said. "Thanks for coming over. Really."

She was looking straight ahead, her lips parted, as if she had forgotten her lines. I admired her profile. She has more strength in her jaw and the bridge of her nose than either of our parents; I envied, for a moment, the baby she was

carrying. "Jack told Malcolm you got together at our
wedding."

"He said that? We didn't 'get together,' we just, I guess,
flirted . . ."

"Did it ever occur to you that maybe I wanted to get away,
too? Have a family of my own, a different family?"

I was surprised at how much this hurt my feelings. No, it
had never occurred to me. Why should it? She was always
the one calling, writing me letters. Lucy's voice on the
phone wire, so warm, so urgent. But of course, I realized,
there had been weeks, sometimes months, between those
phone calls. It took me so long to recover from each one,
from her disapproval and liveliness, her peremptory ques-
tioning; I never thought maybe it took her time to recover,
too. "Well, you can have Ruth all to yourself," I said. "You
never did like Jack."

"I guess, with both you and Malcolm leaning on me, I'm
going to have to learn," she said sullenly.

I could have been insulted at this. I even tried to take
offense, it seemed the loyal thing to do, but I didn't feel it.
Let her be cranky, I thought. She's entitled. And there was
some pleasure, I had to admit, in knowing that she didn't
see what I saw in Jack. She was simply blind to his charm.
(My mother wasn't. She told me, "Of course I knew it as
soon as I saw you together at our dinner party." "You did
not, Ma." "Yes, I did, I told Roy. I said, 'I hope Lucy doesn't
mind, but I think Gwen's happy.' He's a dear, Jack is."
"Didn't you worry about Ruth?" "Oh, no, darling, you're
so much more attractive.")

By the time we turned around to rejoin the men, Lucy

had thawed a little. I had told her I was sorry and she agreed to accept my apology. "For the secrecy," I added.

"Well, that is pretty important, you know. You should realize that."

"I'm beginning to."

Jack took us all out to lunch at a sub place he knew on Amsterdam, a little joint with four tables and tomato-red walls. Lucy and Malcolm ordered beers, Jack and I drank Diet Coke, and we toasted their baby and our marriage. "At least I don't feel anymore like I'm betraying our bachelorette days," said Lucy.

"You were the rabid antimarriage one."

"I made a speech when I was fourteen, at my mother's wedding to a guy I was jealous of. That shouldn't brand me for life, Gwen. The way you kept sidling out of relationships—not that I blamed you, some of the guys you picked up"—Jack was grinning, was she saying this for his benefit?—"with no explanation, or at least none to me, I felt like you thought all men were beneath you and maybe all women, too."

"That's what you thought?" Malcolm was looking anxious; he cleared his throat and Jack nudged him to be quiet. Lucy and I were sitting side by side; two beers had flushed her cheeks and her voice was high.

"I thought you were a snob. Not socially but according to some private standards nobody would ever meet. God, I remember you in college. I'd ask why you didn't like someone, you'd say, 'She bores me,' and leave it at that, as if we were all put on earth for your amusement."

I was wounded but it was a clean wound, and I was

curious. There was so much I didn't know. "So why did you act like you thought I was so great?"

"I didn't 'act like.' I have an ambivalent nature." There was a pause while we all considered Lucy's ambivalent nature. "You know, this food's not bad," she said. "They use real mozzarella."

"I know," said Jack.

"And the bread's good, too. It's not that soft shit you usually get."

He nodded. "So," said my sister, getting up from the table, Malcolm following, but with a languor that made it seem like his idea. "I have to be somewhere at three." She gave me a kiss and shook Jack's hand. "Take care of my big sister, she needs it."

"Nah, she doesn't need it. She just likes it."

Lucy gave him a half smile. "You could be right."

"I am right."

She started to say something, then changed her mind. "See you at the hospital in seven and a half months."

"I'll call you tomorrow," I said.

———

"Do you think we'll ever have a child?" Jack asked me that night.

"I don't know. Do you want to?" The idea scared me more than anything had in months. I saw myself standing before my ruined painting, my hellhound. Loathsome.

"I'd like to do it right." His hands were on my breasts, stroking, pulling, a little too rough.

"I thought everything was fine with Malcolm now."

"It's fine because he's made it fine. Because he wants it to be. Why do you think he wants it so goddamned much? I'm glad he does, I guess I could have been worse, but—I don't know, Gwen—I feel like I missed something."

That last sentence pierced me; I missed something too. I miss something. I wanted him to be even rougher. I wanted him to maul me until there was nothing left. I turned toward him feeling ferocious. We would maul each other, but he looked so sad, so yearning and incomplete, that I kissed his mouth, I kissed his neck, I kissed his chest and his belly, pressing the soft folds of it around my face like a pillow.

His hands were stroking my hair, cupping my head. He had me in his grasp, his elbow on my neck. I smelled the dry clean odor of his genitals—he had just showered—and felt cheated by that cleanliness; I need to inhale him, the salty sour essence he could neither hide nor change. A minute, two minutes, it began to come out, his skin secreting himself, the beloved information. I took his penis in my mouth. His hands tightened on my head. How this suited my addict soul: the pleasure roundabout, unchanging, askew. Not even pleasure really but excitement, reassurance; his heavy life on my conscious tongue, in my brain's anteroom. He whispered my name. My head began to shiver.